Watch for the Entire
All My Tomorrows series
by Joan Byrd
From Indigo Sea Press

indigoseapress.com

A New Beginning

Book One of the
All My Tomorrows
Series

By

Joan Byrd

Star-Crossed Books
Published by Indigo Sea Press
Winston-Salem

Star-Crossed Books
Indigo Sea Press
PO Box 67201
Winston-Salem, NC 27114

First Star-Crossed Books edition published
July, 2017
Star-Crossed Books, Moon Sailor and all production design are trademarks of Indigo Sea Press, used under license.

For information regarding bulk purchases of this book, digital purchase and special discounts, please contact the publisher at indigoseapress@gmail.com

Cover design by Pan Morelli
Manufactured in the United States of America
ISBN 978-1-63066-461-9

I dedicate this book to:
My husband, Ray Byrd,
who gave me support and time to write;

My niece and little buddy, Dene Murrell,
who was my dearest friend when I wrote this book in the 70s;

And Patrick, my guardian angel.
Without him and his outstanding gifts of storytelling, there
would be no book.

I will love you throughout all my tomorrows.
—Joan Byrd

Chapter One

Wilmington, North Carolina, 1973

The rain beat heavily down on the windshield, as Reverend Gene Scott made his way slowly in the mid-day traffic.

At last he would find out if his request to be transferred to the mission field had been accepted. He had waited four long weeks for this day to arrive.

The car in front of him cut off at the stoplight.

"Oh shit!" he said to himself. "If I'm late for this appointment, I will never hear the end of it from Weber."

The car finally started up again and sped down the highway.

"Thank God."

He continued slowly until he came to a stop in front of the Weber's house. He sat gazing at it for a moment as he gathered himself.

Bishop Henry Weber and his family lived in a three-story early American dwelling that implied old money. The bishop, his wife Karolyn, and their lovely—completely spoiled—daughter Gloria Ann all loved the finer things in life. Reverend Scott nodded slightly as he looked at the shiny red sports car parked in front of his 1962 Chevy.

"I see sweet little Gloria got herself the car she wanted." He chuckled. "She thinks she can have everything her little heart desires. Well, there is one desire she'll never fulfill."

He climbed out of the Chevy and made his way quickly up the steps to the huge double door. There was a loud ringing noise within the house when he pulled on the gold rope. The door. opened revealing the heavy form of Earl Johnson, the rotund butler who had been with the Webers for many years.

"Oh. It's you." He extended his hand for Reverend Scott to hand him his raincoat. "Your coat, sir, if you please. It is dripping on the floor.

"Oh, gladly." Reverend Scott carefully took the raincoat off and handed it to Johnson. "Just drop it anywhere. I shouldn't be long."

1

Joan Byrd

"Hmm." The butler turned quickly and headed out of the room calling back to Scott, "Wait in the library please. The bishop will see you shortly.

Scott watched until the butler had vanished from his sight before he made his way into the Weber's well stocked library. He walked about the shelves looking through several interesting looking books. He picked up one entitled *The Captive Virgins.* He flipped through the pages, reading passages randomly. Bishop Henry Weber walked briskly into the room and glanced at the book in Scott 's hand.

"Little out of line for you, Scott." He laughed and retrieved the book and set it back on the shelf. "Gloria Ann. She has to buy those silly, trashy books." He laughed and shook his head. "She thinks they're romantic. The fancies of a young girl's heart."

"I didn't come here to discuss your daughter 's interest in books sir. I have been beside myself waiting for the results to my request."

Scott stood silently, waiting for a reply. His six-foot-seven body towered over Weber's chubby five-foot-eight.

"Oh sit yourself down, Scott, and relax." The bishop motioned toward a chair—as well appointed as he was—that faced his desk. Then he sat down in the dark leather captain's chair. "Now Scott, before we talk business, Gloria Ann wanted me to ask a favor of you. It's nothing big, just a small favor." He smiled genially. "You'd do that for her, wouldn't you?"

"That depends. What is it?" He found himself gazing warily, uncomfortably at his own hands.

"She just wants you to have your picture made with her. That's all."

He couldn't keep the incredulous tone out of his voice. "Why, for God sakes?"

"Look, Scott, I'm not asking you to jump off a twelve-story building, here. Just help us both out and have your picture made with her, Scott. It would make her so happy."

"Aren't I entitled to know the reason she wants this?" Scott shifted uncomfortably, moving his legs into a new position.

She just wants a picture of you two together. That's all, nothing any more nefarious than that, I assure you." The bishop laughed and took a box of chocolates from the top drawer of his

2

desk. He held them out to Scott. "Have one. They're delicious."
"No thanks." Scott tried to quiet the sound of his teeth gritting.
"Could we please talk about my transfer."

What about the picture?" Bishop Weber bit into a creamy
chocolate •

"Alright, alright, fine I'll take the picture. Now what about the
outcome on my request for the mission field?"

The bishop sighed. "Scott, my good man, I do wish you would
reconsider the matter. Look what all you're giving up. A big
church—which you yourself built up to what it is, one of the finest
in our state. And think of all the programs you've started here, and
ask yourself what will happen to them if you leave."

"Sir, I know what I am giving up. I also know I need a new
challenge. I need to get away and find myself again."

"Scott, missionary work is not for you. It's my business to
know these things and to make these judgments." He paused to let
his words hit home. "The people here love you. The wonderful job
you've done will go to pot if you leave now."

Weber stuck another other piece of candy in his mouth. He
reflected and then began again. "I'll tell you what your real trouble
is. . . Memories, bad memories of the past. Memories of losing
your family. That's the real problem. Isn't it, Scott?"

Gene Scott got up and walked to the window. The rain was
coming down in sheets. It had been on such a day that his wife
Faye and his two children, Tracy, thirteen, and Billy who had just
turned nine, had perished. They were on their way home from
school. Sliding out of control in the deluge, a milk truck ran in
them, head on.

He remembered how the police officer had called the
parsonage, telling him that he had some really bad news.

"Is that the real trouble," Scott asked himself. He shook his
head silently. No. He had only good memories here of his family.
How warm and gentle Faye was, how shy and sweet Tracy could
be when she wanted her old man to give her something . . . . Oh
Tracy. Sweet, beautiful Tracy. . . . And then there was Billy—
active in sports, just like his daddy. He could remember   Billy
bragging in front of other boys, "My dad could've been a pro, a
real pro if . . ."

No. No bad memories. Just memories.

Bishop Weber touched Scott lightly on the shoulder. "I'm sorry to bring all that business back up, Scott. But don't you see, you can't run away from memories. They're always inside you. And no excursion to the mission field can change that."

"I'm not running away from memories, sir. I just want to start a new life for myself. I want to help people where they need help, real help. "

"Scott, Scott, this is ridiculous. It's—"

"It's what I want. Now, did I get a transfer or not?"

"Scott, you are a stubborn-headed fellow if I ever met one."

Bishop Weber produced an expensive cigar—a Cuban if Scott didn't miss his guess—from a humidor that matched the wood on his bookshelf. He lit it gingerly and gave a little cough as he exhaled.

"Very well, yes, yes, you idiot. The commission endorsed this stupid notion of yours." He laughed forcefully. "They even think you will make a good missionary."

"So do I!" Scott laughed. Relieved, he fell back into his chair. "How soon will I know where I'm going—and when?"

"My, my. aren't we full of ambition. What do you hope to achieve by doing this? Now that the process is over, just tell me. What is your purpose?"

"I told you, sir. I want to give my life in helping others. Somebody has to do God's work. We all can't sit back in luxurious finery and expect it to get done by itself."

"Ha! You mean to criticize me?" Weber slapped his fist on the desktop. "Then by George, I'll see to it you will be stationed in the hardest mission field I can find, young man."

"That's fine with me, sir." Scott rose. "Is that all, sir?"

The bishop drew a deep breath, composing himself. "Sit down, please." He picked out another chocolate and stuck it into his mouth. "Scott, you asked why my Gloria Ann wanted that picture taken with you. Well, obviously, my daughter . . . she loves you."

"Yes, I know that, sir. But I don 't love her—well not that way. I love her in a Christian way. And that's certainly not enough of a reason to marry her."

"Since you mentioned it, she's got her mind set on marrying you, Scott. Talks about it all the time. What do I tell her? You had

4

a daughter, as I recall. She had you wrapped around her finger. So how can I break my little girl's heart?"

"Bishop Weber," he said deliberately, "I will tell her. Just as I've told her a hundred times. She has this bad habit of not hearing anything except what she wants to hear."

"Now Scott, that's a little harsh. You underestimate her and her willingness to persevere after what she truly wants. But she's not demanding or overbearing. My baby is as kind and understanding a person as anyone I've ever known."

"Sir, she is not a baby any more. That's the trouble with her now, if you'll excuse my being so blunt. You still treat her like a child when she's thirty-years-old, giving her everything she asks for."

"Well Scott, maybe you should give some thought to the reality that you're not getting any younger either. At thirty-six you need a wife, especially being a man of God."

"Missionaries don't need wives, not when they're in dangerous locations."

"Well, as Gloria Ann keeps reminding me, you wouldn't have to go on any stupid dangerous missions if you stayed here   and got married to someone who really loved you. . . . Now I'm asking you, one last time, to reconsider. You could have everything. And you know I would see to that."

"No, sir. When I finally get married, if I ever do, it will be for love, do you understand me, Bishop? Is that so hard to grasp?"

"I can't understand why you don't love Gloria. She's beautiful, smart. She's everything a man could possibly dream of in a woman."

Scott struggled not to raise his voice. "I don't love her, sir."

"'Love!' That word again huh. Look Scott, you will grow to love her. It's inevitable that a man would fall in love with someone as wonderful as she."

"Look, Weber." He stepped toward the bishop. "You can't turn love on or off. It's just not done like that. Besides Gloria and I have absolutely nothing, I repeat *nothing* in common."

"Oh, Scott, don't be so skittish. You would grow to love the things she loves."

He shook his head. "I don't think so. She's a party-goer. She likes fast times and a steady supply of new, beautiful things—rich, costly things I could never give her—things that have no appeal to me." Scott looked at his watch. It was half past four. "Time for me to get back to my church. I really must be shoving off, Bishop."

The door slung open and, swinging her long, red hair, Gloria Ann Weber came into the room. She wore a green silk pantsuit that clung to her shapely body perfectly.

"Gene, darling. You're just the one I wanted .to see."

Scott sank back into his chair, gripped with a sense of being captured. "There's that word 'want' again," he thought.

She threw her arms around his neck and kissed him and sat down on his knee in one smooth, uninterrupted motion.

"Darling, we have a dinner party tonight. It will be at Silvia's ." She giggled. "Just think—all for me! The party is all for me, and you of course, Gene darling."

"I can't go, Gloria, I have a guest sermon tonight at Saint Luther's."

"Oh daddy, I need some money to buy me a new dress. Oh yes, Gene, dear, please wear a suit and tie. Not you turtleneck sweater."

"Gloria Ann, I can't go and that's final!" Scott stood and set her on the floor. "I'm sorry to disappoint you, but I promised Ted Royal weeks ago I'd preach at his revival."

"Daddy! Dear Daddy, do something. This party means so much to me!"

"Scott, I'll get a stand in for you. It's no problem." He smiled at his daughter as she ran over and hugged him.

"Oh Daddy, what would I do without you?" She kissed him and dashed to the door, turned back coyly. "Oh Gene, darling, pick me up at seven sharp. I can't be late. And we'll drive my car instead of that monster you drive." She laughed and blew him a kiss as she hurried out the door.

"Sir, I think that was a mistake. I can't lead her on just to satisfy her fantasy."

"Don't be a jackass, Scott. Taking Gloria out is an honor not a chore. Live man, while you can." He motioned toward the door. "Go get cleaned up for your date. I'll take care of your guest speaking spot tonight."

"Well thanks for that." Scott walked quickly to the door. "However, sir, she'll have to realize sooner or later there will never be anything between us. She doesn't get everything she wants." He forced the door open with a powerful thrust and walked through it.

Scott found his regular end seat in *Joe's Bar*. He pulled at the knot in the tie that threatened to shut off the air in his throat.

"Damn thing," he mumbled.

"Why you wearing a tie there, Reverend?" It was Joe Turner, the owner of the bar and keeper of his own little place of business. He laughed at Scott's discomfort. "Wait. Don't tell me. Let me guess. Gloria Ann Weber. Could that be correct, sir? "

"Right on the nose, Joe. How'd you ever guess?" Scott took a big drink of the cold beer Joe set before him.

"Word gets around, Reverend. She's got her eye on becoming your Mrs." He shook his head. "I don't envy you, Reverend, not at all."

"Well, she might as well forget about me cause I'm moving on, Joe."

"You gonna give her the old slip, huh Rev. Pretty smart, pretty smart," he laughed conspiratorially. "So where 'bouts are you going?"

"I don't know yet, Joe. Some mission work." He looked at his watch—ten minutes faster than the clock above the bar. "Is your clock right?"

"Always Rev. Right on the button, so I don't miss 'last call.'" He picked up the empty beer can. "Got time for another one sir?"

"Better not, Joe, I'm already twenty minutes late." Scott shook his head and laughed to himself. "Poor little sweet Gloria will be pulling out her overly done hair do if I don 't split now." He tossed fifty cents onto the bar. "Last of the big spenders, huh Joe?"

He walked slowly out to his car, laughing to himself. "She'll probably feel like killing me, the darling little angel."

Scott stood on Weber's doorstep and started to ring the bell when the door flew open. Gloria stood staring up at him with her hands on her hips.

"You are late Gene, very, very late. Where the devil have you been?"

"Getting beautiful so I match you. Can't let you out shine me."

"Enough with the cute remarks, Gene Scott. We don't have the time nor do have I the patience to deal with them now!" She grabbed her mink drape and twirled past him.

"We're taking my car, Gloria." Gene walked straight to his Chevy and pulled opened the passenger door for her.

"No way darling. We are going in mine." She walked confidently to her red BMW.

"Then I guess we won't be going at all." Gene sat down on the curb. Casually he fished a cigarette from his pocket and lit it.

"Get up, you—you . . . ." She sighed and smoothed her hair gingerly. "Oh, very well, dear. We'll take your hideous monster."

He got up and opened the door again. She sat down facing outward, then slid her knees forward, showing the full length of a shapely leg. He chuckled as he walked around to driver's side.

"She's tries so hard to sell the merchandise."

Scott climbed in and drove in silence to Silvia Sander's home. It loomed before them like a beast rising up from the sea. The iron gate stood open, so they pulled right up the long drive to the house.

Gloria twisted in her seat, suddenly anxious. "Oh dear, what excuse can I give them for being late? A flat tire? No one would doubt that with us riding in this rattletrap," she laughed.

"Nothing doing, Gloria. I'll be glad tell them why we are late."

She gazed at his form, his strength so apparent as he helped her—elegant in her evening dress—from his antique Chevy.

"I hope no one saw me get out of here. Gene. This car—it's, it's, well it's just ugly." She patted his arm as if consoling him. "Daddy will buy you, new one. A wedding gift."

"There is not going to be a wedding, Gloria." Scott gripped her arm tightly. "Do you understand?"

"Gene, darling, you are wrinkling my sleeve, precious."

She pulled loose and walked quickly up the steps to the door. Scott followed her, trying not to show the disgust he felt.

"Why can't you ever listen to me, Gloria?"

"Gene, Gene darling, I do. You just say silly things."

The door opened and Gloria gave the butler a faux smile. She pulled Scott close, lifted her lips to his ear and whispered, "Be on your best behavior tonight darling. There are a lot of important people here tonight. Even someone from the newspaper as well."

She took his hand and pulled him into the large, living room, filled with well-dressed guests. "Hello, everyone! We finally made it."

A slender blonde—a bleached blonde—twisted over to them with, a drink in either hand. "Gloria, dear sweet Gloria." Silvia Sanders' eyes widened as she looked over Scott, as if marveling at his handsomeness. "Gene, so nice of you to come. What kept you, dear?"

Gloria cleared her throat. "You know that old car of Gene's, well—"

"I needed a drink," Gene blurted, "before I could take Gloria out. So I stopped by Joe 's for a brew." He smiled at the flustered expression on Gloria's face.

Silvia Sanders burst into laughter. "Oh Gene, darling, how sly you are." She handed him a drink "Here, have another. After all, you'll be spending the entire night with our charming Gloria."

"Thank you." He smiled at her as Sylvia walked away to smooze with other guests.

Gloria's voice was sober. "Gene Scott, if you can't say anything nice, please refrain from talking at all." She sipped her drink and faked another smile at a passing guest.

"Sorry, Gloria. I'm just being myself, that guy you adore."

"Try being a little more the way I need you to be tonight, will you?" She set her glass down heavily on an ornate table. "Let's dance."

"Gloria, I feel out of place at these kind of parties. I can't be who I really am, the person you'd like me to pretend I am. This kind of life may be something you're suited for yourself. I could never fit in."

"Yes you can and you will." She took his empty glass and set it beside hers. "Now be a good guy for once and dance with your sexy little date."

He gazed at her for a moment before taking her in his arms and beginning to dance to the slow music."

". . . Gloria, seriously, you must drop this talk about marring me . I'll be leaving soon."

"What? Don't joke like that, Gene." She smiled, disbelieving. "Daddy would never let do a stupid thing like that."

"Ask him, Gloria. Go on. Ask him. I'm resigning from my church. I'm going into missionary work. Right away."

9

"No. No, I won't believe this—this stupid thing you're saying." She laughed as if her laughter washed away all he had said. "I'm going to the lady's room. Be right back."

"Gloria, let's leave."

"Gene, darling, it's our party. We can't leave. Now be a good boy."

"Stay if you like. I'm going." Scott turned abruptly toward the door

"Gene! Please stay" She whined, sounding like a petulant child. She even began to cry.

"It's no good, Gloria. I'm totally uncomfortable here. You can stay. I'm sure one of these rich, young, single guys will be delighted to take you home." He frowned at her tear stained face. "Hey, stop that. You'll ruin all that makeup art work."

"What—what can I tell them? I have to give Silvia and the others a reason as to why you left 'our' party." She clung to his sleeve.

"Tell them whatever you like. I'm sure you can come up with something proper." He pulled loose from her grip and walked out the door.

Gloria made her way slowly back into the living room where Silvia Sanders met her in the doorway.

"Where is Gene darling?"

"He had an emergency call. Something very important. It simply could not wait one minute." She laughed. "I suppose I must get use to that sort of thing. A minister 's wife is always second in his life."

And to herself she said, "Father won't let you desert me, Scott. He will make everything right."

Taking Silvia's hand lightly in hers, she laughed softly and asked, "Where is Darby, that darling reporter from the *Times Daily*?"

Sylvia glanced over her shoulder and called, "Darby, you darling little reporter, would you come over here for a second!" She waved her hand gracefully, as if casting a spell.

The journalist answered immediately. "My dear Miss Sylvia, my services are always at your disposal."

"You know Gloria Ann Weber, don't you dear Darby?"

"Oh yes, yes indeed." He smiled from behind his wire rimmed

glasses. "We've had a few interesting conversations over the phone and in my office."

Gloria forced a smile. "Darby, love, did you get any pictures of Gene and myself tonight like I asked?"

"Oh yes, several very good ones." He winked at her smile.

"Excellent! You must take them right away and print them. Pick out the best one and blow as big as you can. I want to see it on the first page. If it's a matter of money, I'll pay anything. Tomorrow's edition is what I'm shooting for!" She laughed. "Then I want you to write up our wedding announcement under it, got it?"

"Oh yes, yes." Immediately Darby walked toward the door. "It shall be the first thing your eyes see when you look at your paper in the morning."

"Good!" Gloria waved him out the door. "Get to work."

She smiled at Sylvia. "Dear sweet Gene will see I mean business when he reads about our wedding plans tomorrow. Bright and early."

Chapter Two

Reverend Gene Scott tossed about in his bed. It had been one of those nights he could scarcely sleep for brooding about his situation. He wanted nothing more than to get his mission orders so he could get far away from the delightful aggravating Gloria Weber. His restlessness kept him in bed later than his usual six a.m. rising, the hour he typically got up and started his get-ready-for-work routine.

Pogo, short for Polard Goings, carried the morning edition of *The Times Daily* into the parsonage, laughing to himself. He had been with the Scotts for about ten years when they took him into their home and their hearts. He did small jobs around the church and helped the Reverend in anything he wanted him to do. He tiptoed into where Scott lay restively and held the paper over the bed.

"Wake up to the news.," he laughed. "May I be the first to congratulate you."

"What the hell are you talking about?"

Scott slowly opened his tired eyes. His first sight was of that photo of Gloria and himself from the party, framed with a large headline: "Scott and Weber to Wed."

"Oh my God!" He sat straight up in bed and grabbed the paper from Pogo. "That little smart ass has really out done herself this time!"

"Now, now, Gene, don't take it so hard," Pogo laughed. "Things could be worse."

"How?" Scott mumbled.

"We could have an earthquake. The world could come to an end. Something terrible like that could happen." Pogo ambled lazily toward the kitchen.

"Do you think there's a chance something like that might happen? At least it would keep you from getting married."

Scott rolled out of bed and yanked off his pajama bottoms. "Anything's better than marrying that little spoiled brat." He pulled the White turtleneck sweater over his head.

12

A New Beginning

"Coffee?" Pogo called from the kitchen.

"Right! Good and black." Scott made a face in the bathroom mirror. "I could use all the help I can get this morning."

Pogo handed Scott the steaming cup of coffee as he sat down at the kitchen table. He lifted it to his lips and the first big sip burned his tongue.

"Shit! The trouble with Gloria is she never listens to a word you say."

"She thinks she's the only one who knows what should be done, Gene." Pogo bit into his doughnut. "Might as well face it. You're doomed to marry a redheaded know-it-all."

"Pogo, just shut up if that's all you can say." Scott reached in the box of fresh doughnuts and pulled out two. "Where did you get these?"

"Scouts came by bright and early this morning." Pogo smiled to himself "Boy, what a scout."

"Patti Jane Martin, I bet."

Pogo's face turned red. "Reverend Scott, it's not wise for a preacher man to make bets."

"Now Pogo, you've had a thing for Patti Jane a long time. Why not just admit it." Scott rubbed the top of Pogo's head playfully. "At least she's shy and quiet."

"Yeh." Pogo leaned on his elbow. "She's something else."

"Why don 't you quit being stupid and ask her for a date?" Scott glanced out the window to see a warm, sunny day, a break from the clouds and rain.

"Do you suppose she would date me?" Pogo straightened up in his chair.

"You never know, not until you ask." Scott walked to the door. "Just watch out for the holes. They can be tricky."

"Holes?" Pogo swallowed. "What holes?"

"The ones in her doughnuts. Obviously." Scott laughed and walked out into the sunshine. "Pogo!" he hollered.

Pogo appeared at the kitchen door. "Yes sir."

"If this grass dries out enough in the sun later on today, I'd like you to start mowing it. Got it?"

"Oh, yes sir, Scott. Anything you say." Pogo laughed and hopped down the steps two at a time. "Where are you off to?"

"The bishop better have my orders today. That's where I'm

13

going. So don't expect me back until I get things straightened out."

"Yes sir." Pogo stared into the car. "Good luck with all that."

"Thanks, Pogo. I think I'm going to need it." Scott started the Chevy.

He drove straight to the Weber's house. When he reached their home, he ran up the steps and yanked the doorbell rope. A minute later Earl Johnson opened the door slowly. Scott pushed passed him unceremoniously. And stood in the entry.

"Alright Johnson, go tell Bishop Weber I'm here to see him, right now."

"My dear Reverend Scott, you don't seem to realize that it's just past nine a.m. The bishop is having his breakfast in bed. He does not wish to be disturbed." Johnson raised one eyebrow."

"Oh really! Well like it or not he will see me!" Scott walked over to the stairs. "Which room?"

Earl Johnson raced over and stood between Scott and the staircase. "Sir, this is an outrage. I tell you, you cannot go up there!"

"Out of my way, Johnson." Scott pushed past the shaken butler. "I am going up and I'll find him if I have to look in every room up there."

Taking two steps at a time, Scott made his way quickly up the fancy staircase. Johnson tried to keep up, but Scott's quickness made it impossible for the aging butler to stay with him.

Scott slung open the first door he came to. Gloria Weber sat up in her bed, sipping from a coffee cup. Her red locks protruded from great rollers and cold cream hid her face. Frozen in shock for an instant when she saw Scott staring in the door at her, she jumped, turning over her breakfast tray onto the floor. She grabbed at her hair frantically before her fingers found the sheet, which she pulled completely over her head.

"Gene! Good Lord! What are you doing here?" she screamed. "I—I—"

"I never believed that aliens actually came to earth," he laughed, "but right there, hidden under that sheet, is the proof that Martians are among us."

"Ohhh! Shut up and get out!" she whined. "Please! Johnson, you useless turncoat, get him out of here!"

Johnson tugged Scott's arm. "Please, Reverend Scott, please, come with me to Bishop Weber's room."

Scott walked out in the hall. "Which one, Johnson?"

Johnson shoulders slumped, a look of defeat on his face. "This way sir, but he's not going to like it. "

"You think I like having to do this?" Scott moved past him. "Just spare the sorrow and show me the way."

"Alright! Alright." Johnson moved quickly down the hall to Henry Weber 's bedroom. He tapped on the door and opened it slowly. "Excuse me, sir."

"Johnson, what was Gloria screaming about so early in the morning?" He stuffed a piece of toast in his mouth.

Scott pushed past Johnson into the bedroom.

"Scott! What in the meaning of this?"

"Have you seen the front page of the Times this morning, Bishop?"

"Oh yes, yes I have. Marvelous picture it was of you two. Of course Gloria was the outstanding one in the picture, but yours wasn't too bad either considering."

"Look, you had better straighten out that thick-headed daughter of yours pretty soon, or I'll do it. I can guarantee you, my way will stay with her much longer."

"Calm down, Scott. Calm down." Weber motioned for Johnson to hand him his robe. "This little matter can be taken care of peacefully. Wait downstairs for me in the library. I'll get Gloria Ann and be right down."

"Yes you will, or I'll be right back up here."

Scott stormed out the bishop's bedroom.

He paced the library floor for what seemed hours—though it was only about fifteen minutes. At last Weber and his headstrong daughter came into the room.

"Alright, Gene, sit down." The bishop took his seat behind the desk. "So you still insist on going on this missionary kick?"

"I never once thought otherwise." Scott struggle with the urge to shout. "Now, when do I go?"

"Alright, Scott, if you 're in such an all-fired hurry. The end of this week soon enough?"

"Suits me fine. Where am I going, by the way?"

"Daddy, you can't do this! Make him stay." Gloria whined.

"Gloria, please stay quiet!"

15

It was odd to Scott to hear Gloria's father speak to her harshly. He turned to Scott, his face full of anger.

"Scott, I'm sending you on the BaKuba mission. I was going to send Martin, but I'm taking him off the assignment and sending you instead. He's probably a better man for the job, but if you want something rough to prove yourself, then this is definitely it."

"The tougher the better." Scott relaxed and leaned back in his chair "Anything to get my mind off of everything that's been happening around here."

"Gene, darling, do you realize what you are doing?" Gloria took his hand gently. "You might get killed in that terrible jungle!"

"Baby, I'm sending him on this mission just so he can get a taste of the dangers and the ugly stinking world of a missionary." Bishop Weber took his daughter's hand and guided her to sit on his knee. "He won't have to spend an entire four-year assignment over there if he gets his job done right."

"I'll stay as long as necessary." Gene Scott stood up. "Who fills me in on the details?"

"Dying to get started, huh Scott?" The bishop opened his candy box and selected a big piece. "Very well. I'll get in touch with Martin. He 'will fill you in on everything there is to know. I'll have him come over to your church. Good enough for you Scott?"

He nodded. "Good enough." He started toward the library door, then stopped. "One more thing before I leave. Better get busy Gloria explaining to the press and your public why the groom is skipping town."

Scott laughed aloud and hurried out the door, listening to Gloria break into a temper tantrum.

Pogo was mowing the church lawn when Scott returned to the parsonage. He stopped when he saw Scott pull up and walked over to meet him.

"Well, when's the wedding, the. big event of your life?"

"The only big event of my life is going to be knocking you on your ass if you don't shape up." Scott put an arm around Pogo's shoulder. "Any calls?"

"Just Hazel Purit. She's called three times already."

"My, my, persistent isn't she." Scott envisioned the obese

A New Beginning

leader of the Women's Christian Club. An active church member for many years, she never hesitated to share with the community her ideas for improvements needed to be made. "Did she say what she wanted?"

"Nope. Said she had to talk to you." Pogo took a soda from the refrigerator. "Probably some social project she's working on."

"That's all I need right now. To get tied up on the line with her." He grabbed his last beer from the refrigerator. "Make a note to get beer."

The phone rung just as Scott took a big sip.

"Yum. That hits the spot." He winked at Pogo. "Get that, will you? If it's Hazel Purit, I'm not here."

Pogo answered the phone. An instantaneous smiled flashed across his face. "Oh yes, he's here. One second."

Scott checked the time: 11a.m. "Who is it, Pogo? Weber?"

"Nope! Purit." He couldn't restrain a laugh.

"Pogo, you little rat, you know I don't have time to chatter about flowers and such." Scott groaned as he took the phone. Hand over the mouthpiece, he said, "Go mow the lawn, you boob." He held the receiver to his ear. "Hello, Scott here."

"Reverend Scott, I've been trying to get in touch with you all morning."

"I'm terribly sorry, Hazel, but we've been tied up with the bishop."

"It's quite understandable Reverend. I just want to inform you about the woman circle's new project. I'm sure it will be of some interest to you. Now—"

"Mrs. Purit, I'd like nothing more than to discuss this project with you, but I'm completely tied up today. It can wait, can't it?" Scott thought to himself, "I hope."

"Oh, Reverend, it's of the up most importance. It's a must that I talk with you, now!" As she spoke, Mrs. Purit's voice became more high-pitched.

". . . Very well, but make it as brief as possible." Scott thoughts were not so generous: "Shit, woman, this is a total waste of time."

"Well, Reverend, we thought—seeing as how there is going to be a new Mrs. at the parsonage—

Scott buried his face in his hand, shaking his head.

17

"—that the place could use a little fixing up. Now the flowerbed for instant. Why Reverend Scott most of the flowers are dying. Not saying anything against Miss Weber, God forgive me if I judge a soul, but the poor dear doesn't know much about gardening."

"My dear Mrs. Purit, I can assure you all these ideas, thoughtful as they are, are totally unnecessary. Gloria. Weber and I—"

"Reverend Scott, men know nothing about such things." She cleared her throat. "Now we thought tulips would be nice around the parsonage."

"Mrs. Purit, I don't think I'll be tip toeing through any tulips this year or anytime soon."

"But, Reverend, we thought taking on a new wife—"

"There is not going to be a new wife, not now and not for the foreseeable future." Scott gritted his teeth. "That's what I've been trying to tell you. I'm going away to do mission work in Africa." He listened for a few seconds to the woman's stunned silence. "Perhaps your new minister's wife will be a good garden keeper."

"Oh, no! Reverend Scott, you can't leave us. We need you."

"Mrs. Purit, I really have to be going. Good luck on your projects in the future."

He dropped the receiver onto its cradle before she could think of anything else to say. He took a long sip of his beer, raced to the door and spat the warm beer into the yard. He grabbed the can and poured the remaining contents into the sink. "Damn, my last beer too. That busy-body Purit, I wish she had a tulip up her sweet— Oh shit, why do I let everything get beside me. Devil, leave this place."

The phone rang out loudly and Scott grabbed it. "Yes, Scott, here."

"Scott, this is Martin. Is it okay if I come over now?"

"Sure, come on. I've been waiting to hear from you."

"Yeah? Is that why your phone is busy every time I've tried to call you?" Martin asked sarcastically.

"Church business." Scott grinned. "Come on over. I'll be waiting."

He set the receiver on the hook and walked over to the opened window. He had to yell loud enough that Pogo could hear him over the lawnmower.

"Hey Pogo, come here. I need you!"

Pogo came running all the way into the house.

"What up?"

"Rev. Martin is on his way over. You'll have to fix supper. I may be eating late. Put it in the oven if you finish."

"Wait a minute, Scott. I cooked for you the past three days. What happened to our taking turns?"

"Let's face it, Pogo, you're a better housewife than me." Scott laughed and went to his study to get ready for Martin.

"Thanks a million, honey." Pogo made a face. "Housewife. I'd rather be called a homemaker. At least I can out cook you."

"Amen, brother!" Scott shouted from his study.

At four o 'clock, Reverend George Martin pulled up in front of the parsonage. He walked swiftly up the walk and knocked heavily on the door. Pogo opened it and stood smiling at the dour face of the minister.

"Good evening, Reverend Martin. Please come in."

"Afternoon, Goings. Where is Scott? I·want to get this meeting over with as soon as possible." Martin handed Pogo his hat.

"Did I hear my name?" Scott appeared from the kitchen door.

"Well, if it isn't Brother Martin. Good to see you again, George"

"Yes, of course. Where can we talk?" He glanced around the untidy room.

"In the study. This way." Scott nodded toward a door. He turned back and called back to Pogo. "The potatoes could stand a little salt."

"Thanks." Pogo nodded. "Just go about your business and leave the cooking to me."

As he closed the study door, Scott smiled at Pogo broadly. "Well Martin, have a seat and we can get to work."

"Before I begin, Scott, I would like to say one thing."

"Shoot." He produced a cigarette and lit it.

"Do you mind? I'm allergic!" Martin pretended to cough.

Scott snuffed out his cigarette.

"Thank you. This is a church manse, isn't it? I'm a little surprised you're using tobacco inside the church's parsonage. You think your congregation would approve?"

19

Scott slid into his worn captain's chair and motioned the other minister toward the chair on the other side of his desk. "Smoking is the least bad thing that happens in this house of God, George."

"Hmm. Well frankly, Scott, I feel you are making a big mistake by going on this mission."

"Oh? What makes you think that, Brother Martin."

Clearly prepared with a mental list of objections, the minister launched into a sermonette. "There are numerous reasons this is a bad idea for you. For one thing you do not have the experience required for this kind of assignment, and for another you are not trained at all to do this sort of thing." Martin feigned a smile. "You have to admit that I have all the qualifications and could do the job perfectly."

"Sorry to disagree with you, George, but I feel perfectly capable of handling this job."

"And, while I'm at it, I don't appreciate you coming in from the blue and stealing it away from me. I detest being replaced by a 'pulpit preacher.'"

Scott stared at his lumpy colleague, trying to choose his words carefully. "My dear Brother Martin, I had absolutely no say in choosing this posting. The bishop assigned me to this mission, and I never—"

"And he shall regret it later when you fail!" Martin's face flamed red and his left eyebrow arched.

". . . How unchristian to wish failure on another minister, George. For me, I intend to serve faithfully and victorious to the glory of God." He held his voice in check. "And now, Mr. Martin, I insist that you tell me about the place called BaKuba."

Martin seemed to remember himself and his calling then. "Very well, Scott." He crossed his legs. "BaKuba is a small valley surrounded by mountains. There are two tribes in the valley of BaKuba, The Lavites and the Karubi Tribe. Both tribes are constantly at war with one another. The Lavites will be the first tribe to concur. They are more easy-going and have permitted at times outsiders to come in. Many of them even speak English fairly well. However they are a proud race of people. Your job is to win their confidence. The idea is to show them simple improvements and new ideas intended to give them new ways of helping their people."

A New Beginning

"And bring them the word of God," Scott added. "Have you a map of BaKuba with you?"

"Yes, and it is intentionally drawn for outsiders, so you should be able to find your way. Of course you will have a guide, at least to get you there." Martin's voice dropped to a cynical mumble. "Since you have never been in the jungles, you are likely to get lost."

"I've been lost before, George. That holds no fear for me." Scott studied the map before him carefully "What about the other tribe, the Karubis?"

"The Karubis are a nasty bunch of wild natives. They retain certain cannibalistic traits. On occasion they are still known to indulge in a little human flesh." He shivered involuntarily. "If you're not careful, Scott, you could end up as their main course."

"Well, if the way I cook is any indication of the way I taste, I'm sure they would regret having eating me." He could not resist a chuckle.

"Jest now, suffer later," Martin said with a grunt. "The Karubis are quite loyal to their own tribesmen, but they hate—and I mean hate—outsiders."

A grin crept across Scott's face. "Do they eat anyone besides outsiders? I mean, they could starve to death waiting for a visitor stranger to pop into their camp."

And somehow he managed to not laugh as Martin choked and gave a real cough.

After a moment, he cleared his throat and continued. "Of course they worship false gods. The Karubis have a. huge statue of their god. They call it *Maka*. They offer sacrifices before this statue and hold special celebrations in which they dance and carry on 'til all hours of the nights. Usually they hold such a feast if they have captured a victim for their pot."

At length Scott nodded. "I can see I have my work cut out for me." He stared into Martin's eyes, contemplating. "So I suppose ultimately my job is to see that these two tribes learn to live together in peace."

"Correct. That's the bottom line." Martin stood up. "Are there any more questions on your mind? Go ahead and ask them now, for I am a very busy man."

"Yes, actually. There is one question I would like to ask before you depart, Martin." Scott stood as well and led Martin to the·front door. "Just how many missionary journeys have you been on?"

"Well . . . a . . ." Once again Martin's face grew a bit crimson. "Actually just one, but I was under one of the best missionary doctors of our time."

"Oh really? Who?" Scott resisted the urge to smile as he watched Martin's mouth twitch."

"Doctor Rolland T. Tanriff. It was almost five years ago, in an African jungle."

"Was that by any chance for the construction of that children's hospital in Taroo. I remember reading about that."

"Ah, yes, that's the one." Martin wiped the sweat from his brow.

"My, I heard your group was in great danger." Scott couldn't resist the ironic smiled creeping across his face. "I'm so glad you survived to tell the story. Did all those little children threaten you continually, Brother Martin?"

"Jest all you want, Scott. You will find life in the jungle is not nearly as comfortable as your parsonage here."

Martin stepped out the front door and Scott stood in the threshold behind him.

"I suspect I shall think about you very little in BaKuba, Brother Martin." Scott patted him on the shoulder. "I expect I'll be far too busy staying out of stewpots and battling false idols to think much about the comforts of home."

". . . Good luck, Scott. God knows you'll need it." Martin shielded his eyes against the late afternoon sun. "Well, at least you will have one thing going for you. God will be working for you."

"Martin, I'm going to work for God and we can't be expecting anything of him." Scott's eyebrows went up arched. "You shouldn't expect God to do man's work for him. He depends on us to get it done."

"So do you expect to do it without God?" Martin's voice was haughty, indignant.

Scott's voices was calm, measured. "No, damn it. I expect to do what I've been called to do for God, for his name and his glory. " He motioned to his heart. "Here is where he will be, with me always."

"Yes, yes of course, Scott." Martin turned away

unceremoniously and walked toward his car. "I for one pray to God to help me out of all my problems and worries."

"Don't you think it time men got off their knees and starting working out their problems for themselves?" Scott said, casually following him. "God is pretty busy, you know, and he needs all the help he can get." He shut the car door for Martin.

"Do it your way, pastor." Martin started the motor. "I won't be surprised to read about your misfortune in the near future."

"Once again, you wish ill on a Christian brother? Thanks for your confidence Martin. It is what I expected from you."

The self-righteous look colored Martin's face again as he lifted his chin and backed a little too swiftly from the driveway. Gene Scott stood watching as he sped down the street, then turned and walked slowly into the kitchen and sat down beside Pogo who, unconcerned, was busy feeding his face.

"Well, Gene, why the long expression? Is this mission work going to be harder than you thought?"

"No. It's that George Martin. He's a pain in the ass." Scott took a sip of the iced tea in front of him. "This is pretty good, Pogo."

"Whatcha mean, 'pretty good'? It's great tea." Pogo laughed as he passed Scott the potatoes. "So when are you leaving?"

"Friday morning, bright and early." Scott stretched his arm across the table for a piece of bread. "I'll probably pack most of my gear tonight."

"I am going with you, right?" Pogo propped his elbow on the table, his demeanor serious for the first time.

Gene smiled, rueful at the idea of leaving his friend behind. "No. I want you to stay here, Pogo. The church is going to do fine without me, but it couldn't get along with you."

Pogo's disappointment was apparent and abundant. "Ah, come on, Gene. That's a lot of bull." Disconsolate, his gaze dropped to his hands.

"I want you to keep flowers on the graves for me. Would you do that for me?"

"Sure, Gene, you bet." Pogo ran his fingers through his hair. It's yellow roses for the missus and red roses for the kids' graves, right?"

"Right. Once a week Pogo. Don't forget." Scott leaned back

in his chair and rubbed his stomach. "Boy, Pogo, you sure know how to cook."

"Think so?" He laughed "If I get fired from the handyman's job at the church, I could always get a job as a cook."

"Yeh, then you might could afford to take Patti Jane out." Scott patted Pogo on the head. "I'll help with the dishes and then you can help me pack."

"Whenever you offer to help, I always know there has to be a catch," Pogo teased.

"Let's get a move on." Scott got up and tied an apron around Pogo's waist. "You know, you're sure to make Pattie a great wife."

"Thanks, dear." Pogo punched Scott's arm.

"Oh, and Pogo, always remember what I told you about the holes." Scott hit him with the dishtowel. "And in the doughnuts too."

Pogo s face instantly become crimson. Scott picked up a dish and whistled.

Chapter Three

Gene Scott received his final instructions in person from the bishop before loading his gear into his Chevy. Bishop Weber stood comforting his weeping daughter and she watched Scott climb in behind the wheel. She grabbed his arm and began pleading with him.

"Oh Gene, darling. Please you can't leave me, please!"

Bishop Weber pulled his daughter away from the car and frowned down at the driver.

"Scott, I just want you to know, that I'm against this stupid thing you're doing. Besides hurting my baby, you will probably get your fool self killed!"

"Bishop Weber, I'm sorry if your 'precious' darling daughter has been hurt, even though I tried repeatedly to tell her that I had no serious interest in her. She refused to listen, so I can feel no guilt on my part." He looked about for his passenger. "Pogo!" he shouted. "Come on, or I'll be late."

Pogo ran from the Weber's house, a half-eaten apple in his hand, and jumped into the passenger's seat. Scott started the motor and looked up at Weber.

"As for getting myself killed, I wouldn't worry too much about that, Bishop. You've always got Martin if I get eaten."

He laughed as he pulled away. He felt a real sense of fulfillment and joy as he reflected on departing from the place he had called home for the previous thirteen years. He slowed down, nearly to a stop when he reached the graveyard. His eyes fastened on three graves laid out neatly in a row.

". . . Pogo," he said in a soft voice, "don't forget the flowers."

"Don't worry, Gene, they were like my family too." His voice was filled with emotion.

Scott sped down the road, closing everything out of his mind that he left behind, except for those good memories that he knew he could never forget.

Susan Andrews grabbed her brother's arm as he started to run towards the ship.

"Jobi, can't you ever stay put? Wait for Mom and Dad, will you?"

"They're so slow, and I want to see that ship close up." Jobi Andrews stretched his twelve-year-old body to its full length. "I'm not trying to go on it. Just let me go up closer."

"No way, you're staying right here until Mom and Dad get here."

Susan held on tight to her little brother's hand. She looked around sadly at the place she was leaving. All the friends she had made over the past four years would be far away from her new home. Though, she realized, it was really nothing new to her. At seventeen she was growing weary of moving all over the country. Owen Andrews, her father, was the chief builder for the Eli-Royal Food Company. His job sent him from one place to another building new plants. She watched as her father and mother made their way through the crowded shipping dock.

"Children, are you in that big of a hurry to get away from us for a few weeks?"

Owen Andrews smiled at his daughter and son. He and his wife Shirley had tried to figure out a way that they could make this move without it being so difficult for their children. Susan and Jobi where going to spend a few weeks with their granddad, Dr. William T. Rogers, while Owen and Shirley Andrews made ready their new home on the small island of TarSa, near Hawaii".

Dr. Rogers, Shirley's father, was always the ambitious, outgoing one in the family. "Anything goes" was his favorite saying. He had made Africa his home ever since his wife had passed away.

"Mom, don't you think we should have told Granddad we are coming?" Susan let go of her tight grip on Jobi's arm. "He might be too busy."

"Your grandfather will love having you two around. You know how he loves you and makes over you when he comes for a visit. And he was insistent that we have an open invitation to come whenever we want." Shirley kissed her daughter's cheek. "Now, stop worrying about it. He loves surprises."

"Your mother's right, Susan." He laughed and rubbed Jobi's head. "Besides, you 'll have your hands full taking care of hot stuff here."

A New Beginning

"I'm old enough to take care of myself, Dad." Jobi picked up his suitcase. "Sis is the one you had better worry about, stealing all those boat officers' hearts." He made a face mocking a lovesick fool. "Poor, unfortunate sailors!"

"Jobi! I'm going to murder you!" Susan punched her brother's arm. "That's not funny."

"Alright you two, behave." Shirley Andrews brushed Jobi's hair out of his eyes. "Now remember what I told you Jobi and listen to your sister.

"And don 't you forget that!" Susan smiled down at her brother. We shall be friends on this vacation, since we have to be together for about a month. Is it a deal?"

"You bet, sis." Jobi hugged her. He was secretly proud to have such a beautiful, shapely girl for a sister. Even though she was just seventeen, he thought she was as glamorous as any movie star. At school he had bragged over her with some of his fellow classmates. After all she had been voted Homecoming Queen, and that proved to him that he was right.

"I'll watch out for Susan, too, Dad. I won't let any guy near her. You can count on me."

Mr. Andrews laughed. I don't doubt that son." He gazed at his daughter. "Although I can't blame the boys for trying."

"Oh Dad!" Susan put her arm around her father's waist. "I will miss you both. I only wish we didn't have to leave here—move away, I mean."

"This will be the last move, baby, if everything works out the way I'm hoping it will." He kissed her. "Now better run along before I decide to take you with us to help with the move."

"Be careful Susan and Jobi. And please eat properly." Shirley Andrews took a tissue from her pocketbook to wipe her eyes. "Susan, see that Jobi gets his bath and eats everything on his plate."

"Don't worry, Mom. Jobi and I will be fine." Susan kissed her mother's tear stained cheek. "We'll write as soon as you send an address."

"Be sure to call us when you arrive in Africa, Susan. We won't leave here until we hear from you. I should have my loose ends tied up around here by then." Mr. Andrews handed the heavy luggage to a steward and waved at his children as they made their way onto the ship.

27

"Goodbye Mom, Dad!" Susan shouted from the deck.

Jobi was so busy looking at the huge vessel that Susan had to turn him around to wave at his parents.

"Jobi, you can look the ship over later. Tell them goodbye."

Jobi waved wildly and shouted to the top of his lungs, "So long, Mom! Bye, Dad! See ya!"

"You don't have to scream, Jobi. They can hear you. "Susan looked around to see if anyone was staring at them. A tall, strongly built man—very masculine, she thought—was smiling over at her. Her heart did a flip as they stared at one another.

Then suddenly she realized she was staring at him and he might think her some kind of flirt. Quickly she turned to face her brother—and caught her breath. Jobi had disappeared somewhere on the deck.

"Jobi!" she called, but her voice was lost in the noisy throng milling on the deck. "Oh Jobi, if I get my hands on you, you're a dead boy!"

She glanced around to see if the man was still standing nearby. To her delight, he was. Only now he was busy talking with a young man and seemed to have lost interest in Susan.

"I hope he's sailing with us on this voyage," she thought.

Then came the sound of Jobi's voice calling her from somewhere down deck. "Hey, sis, come see this. Come on!"

"Oh Jobi!" she thought. "If I have to come down there I won't know if this man is going to stay on the ship or not."

With one last glance at the stranger, she made her way through the crowd to where her brother stood. The man did look in her direction, then turned quickly when she looked his way. She hurried on through the crowd.

Gene Scott had not noticed the girl standing near the rail until the boy beside her starting yelling to someone on the dock below them. When he did see her, his eyes fastened on her and he could not pull them away. It made him jerk inside involuntarily when their eyes met and held each other for a brief minute.

She was beautiful, yes, he told himself, but he had known many beautiful women. Even Gloria was beautiful. Still, the mere sight of a lovely girl had never caused this feeling that suddenly burst upon him. Come to think of it, he had never experienced this

A New Beginning

feeling before, not even with Faye. His eyes followed the young woman as she disappeared into the crowd.

Pogo pulled at his arm. "Hey Gene, can't you hear me?"

"What? Did you say something?" Scott looked at Pogo's smiling face.

"Something over that way interest you?" Pogo teased.

"Ah, no. No, I thought I saw someone I knew." Why, he wondered, was he lying to Pogo. Maybe because he wasn't sure what had just happened to him.

"I'm sorry for letting my mind wonder. What was it you wanted?"

"I just asked you if there was anything else you wanted me to do before I get off the boat. They said five more minutes."

"Oh. No." Scott reached in his pocket, pulled out his car keys and handed them to Pogo. "Here. It's yours now. It's not much, the old monster, but she still has a lot of miles left in her. Something to remember me by."

"Oh, Gene, I could never forget you, not ever." He felt a lump growing in his throat. "Don't worry about anything back at the parsonage. I'll keep it clean like always, unless the new minister's wife doesn't want me."

"You don't have to worry about that, Pogo. Reverend Steele and his wife are a beautiful couple and they are looking forward to having you around." Scott patted his friend on the shoulder. "Take good care of yourself, Pogo. That's one more thing you can do for me."

"You're the one I'm worried about. Going into the heart of Africa, knowing you're headed to what might be terrible danger." Pogo stared down at his feet. "Suppose we will ever see one another again?"

"You bet, Pogo, you bet!"

Scott and Pogo stood smiling at each other and that was the moment a voice came over the loud speaker.

"All persons besides passengers, please leave the ship at this time. Repeat, all persons besides passengers, please depart."

"Well, I guess this is good bye, Gene." Pogo stretched out his hand.

"Just for a while. We will see each other again." Scott shook his young friend's hand.

29

As much to hide his emotions as to obey the loudspeaker, Pogo turned quickly and hurried from the ship. Scott watched him disappear into the crowd below.

Late in the afternoon Scott strolled along the top deck looking out into the vast ocean surrounding the ship. From nowhere, a boy ran right into him a full speed.

Jobi Andrews felt a little dizzy after running into the big man who helped him off the deck to his feet.

"Hey, kid, what's the big hurry?" Scott laughed. "Are you hurt?"

"No. No, sir." Jobi looked around to see if anyone had followed him. "Must have given him the slip," he muttered and he laughed."

"Gave who the slip?" Scott smiled down at the grinning boy.

Jobi stopped laughing when he saw Scott looking at him. "Oh, nobody, sir. It's nothing really." He forced a scared laugh. "Who are you? I don't think we've met, sir."

"No, we haven't. I'm Scott, Reverend Gene Scott. What's your name?"

"Andrews, Jobi Andrews." He swallowed. "Did you say 'Reverend'?"

"That's right." Scott laughed and rested his hand lightly on Jobi's head. "How about a soda, to celebrate our new friendship? The ship's canteen is right over here."

"Sure! That's sounds way cool." Jobi walked along quickly, trying to keep up with Scott's long strides. "Boy, Reverend Scott, you sure have got the muscles. Do you work out in the gym a lot?"

"Occasionally." Scott grinned as he took a stool in front of the soda fountain. "So, are you traveling alone?" Scott asked, knowing that the girl he had seen had been with the same little boy. This might be his chance at least to find out who she was.

"Oh no, sir. My folks would never let me do that."

They were interrupted by a waiter asking them what they wanted to drink.

"Oh a chocolate milkshake for me, thank you."

"Aren't you afraid it will spoil supper for you?" Scott winked at the waiter secretly.

"No way. I have them all the time."

"Okay, a chocolate for my friend Jobi. I'll have a cherry shake."

"Yes, sir," the waiter replied dutifully.

Jobi's eyes seemed to swell to twice their size as the waiter sat the large shake in front of him. "Oh man! That looks delicious!"

"Dig in," Scott said, chuckling. He stirred his shake for a minute, watching the boy devour his drink. "Now, Jobi, what did you say was the name of that girl who's traveling with you?"

"I never said there was a girl traveling with me, did I?" Jobi looked up at Scott.

"Well yes, I'm sure you did." Scott focused on his shake, drinking it quickly.

"Not so fast, Mr. Scott, or you 'll get one doozy of a headache." Jobi laughed.

"Yes, yes, thanks for reminding me. Long time since I drank a milkshake. Now what did you say her name was? Who is she?"

"My sister? Her name is Susan. We're on our way to Africa to visit our granddad. He's a doctor—and a great one at that. Sis didn't want to come. She's afraid some animal will attack her." The boy laughed loudly. "They would turn her loose when they had a better look at her."

"You mean she's homely?"

Jobi nodded. "Ugly as can be."

"Now Jobi, I bet you 're stretching things a little bit. I didn't get much of a look at her, but I bet she's really sort of pretty." Scott emptied his glass. "She is pretty, isn't she?"

"Yeh, I reckon. . . . For a sister, she's okay." He stood quickly. "Which reminds me, I was supposed to have my bath an hour ago. She's probably waiting for me with a belt."

"What kind of belt does your sister wear?"

"Oh. It would be my dad's. She probably brought one though, just to keep me in line."

"Maybe hopefully she won't hurt you too bad." He smiled at his new little friend. "Just tell her we men got to talking and the time got away from us."

"Right! That's pretty clever for a preacher."

"You ought to hear me in the pulpit. See you, Jobi."

The boy turned to leave and saw a man staring at him from the doorway. "Oops. I think I've been discovered."

Scott turned to look at the stranger who was staring at Jobi. A heavy set, middle aged man stood before him, glaring, hands on his hips. There was something vaguely familiar about him.

"What did you do, Jobi?" Scott asked softly, grasping the boy's arm gently. "Tell me, and maybe I can help you."

"I don't think so, but I'll tell you any way. I won't be any worse off." Jobi jumped behind Scott as the rotund man came towards them.

"You're Reverend Scott, are you not?" The man tried to reach around him and grab Jobi.

Scott blocked the fellow's hand. "Yes, that is correct. What is it you want with this boy?"

"He ran off with my toupee." His fat cheeks turned a slight red, though his scalp, glistening with sweat and completely bald, remained quite pink. "I demand that he give it back."

"Oh yes!" Scott snapped his finger. "I knew I recognized you. You're Mr. Copper, aren't you, of Copper Enterprises?"

Marvin Copper glanced around to see who was watching them.

"Yes, that also is correct. Now, if you don't make that young lad hand over my toupee I shall have him reported to the captain!"

Scott looked down at Jobi. "Well? Give the man back his hair."

"I don't have it sir." Jobi revealed his empty hands.

"Then what the devil did you do with my toupee, you little brat?" Copper face grew even redder.

"I didn't mean to let it happen, Reverend Scott, but the wind took it right out of my hand." He looked down at his feet.

"Where is it now, Jobi?" Scott waited patiently for the boy to answer while Copper angrily shifted from foot to foot.

"In the sea, sir, it flew over the side of the ship." Jobi grabbed Scott's arm tightly as Copper came toward him again.

"Why you little brat! My toupee, overboard?" He seemed ready to start crying.

"Calm yourself down, Mr. Copper. You and I both know Jobi never meant for your hair to blow away." Scott struggled to keep a straight face. "I happen to know that this ship has a wig shop, and I'm sure it's open right now. Why don't you go get fitted for a new toupee and have the bill sent to my cabin, 136-C."

"But Reverend Scott, I did it. I should pay for it."

"You've said enough, Jobi. It's time for you to be quiet." His gaze shifted from the boy to the grown man. "Fair enough, Mr. Copper?"

The large man took a deep breath. "Very well, Reverend, but somebody needs to keep that kid on a chain!"

Mr. Copper turned and walked swiftly from the ship's canteen. "Thanks Reverend Scott, you saved my life."

"Well, then this trip hasn't been a complete failure yet, has it?" He laughed and slapped Jobi on the shoulder. "Run along now, before you start to worry that pretty sister of yours."

Jobi gave Scott a puzzled look. He waved goodbye as he hurried from the soda shop. Scott turned to the waiter, who had taken in the little scene.

"So, how about if I put this on my room tab? And put a buck on there for yourself."

"Two shakes and a tip for room 136-C."

"Oh, you remembered."

"I never forget a suite number, Reverend." He wrote down the charge and shook his head. "You know, you really helped that kid out of a fix."

Scott laughed. "Well, maybe it will be worth it in the long run." He walked back to his cabin, remembering the girl's expression when their eyes met.

Chapter Four

Susan Andrews got up the next morning and showered. She selected a matching shorts outfit with a little halter top. She slapped her sleeping brother on the bottom. He sat up in bed rubbing his eyes.

"Hey, can't a fellow get some sleep around here?"

"Okay, lazy, up." She looked through the small window that faced the ocean. "The sun is out and the sea is calm. It's a beautiful day."

"Great!" Jobi jumped out of bed and pulled his clothes on. "What about a swim this morning?"

"We're going to eat breakfast first." Susan got her bag and hung it over her slender shoulder.

"Breakfast? Are you kidding?" Jobi turned up his nose. I'd much rather go swimming."

"You can swim later. Right now you're having breakfast and that's that!" She opened their cabin door and walked out into hallway. "Now, come on."

"Alright, I'm coming."

He followed his sister through the hallways and up the stairs to the dining room. A server showed them a vacant table and they ordered their breakfast.

Susan's eyes wondered around the room, coming to a standstill abruptly when they focused on a man seated on the far side of the room. The same man, she realized instantly, she had seen on the deck the previous afternoon. Jobi saw his sister staring at someone and followed the direction of her gaze.

"Who's over there that's so interesting sis?"

"Huh? Oh, nothing, no one?" She took a sip of her orange juice.

Jobi noticed Reverend Scott was sitting where Susan had been looking. Excitedly he said, "Hey sis, see that man over there with the black pants and white turtleneck?"

Her face lit up. "Yes, what about him?"

"He's my friend." Jobi took a big bite of toast.

A New Beginning

"Your friend," she replied, full of curiosity. "Ah . . .I mean how is he your friend? How do you know him?"

"I met him yesterday. We had a long friendly talk—over a shake in the soda fountain shop." He took a bite of bacon "Real cool guy, that Scott."

"Scott? Scott who?" She moved closer to her brother.

"It's not Scott who, it's who Scott." Jobi laughed.

"Oh. Oh, alright, alright! What' s his name?"

"Gene Scott, Reverend Gene Scott." He looked up at his sister with a broad smile. "And he's my friend."

"A minister." She sighed, considering this new revelation. "I might have known he would be something good and important like that." She gazed across the room, a dreamy expression on her face as she looked at Scott. "Why is he on the ship? Where is he going, do you know?"

"Come to think of it, no. I guess I forgot to ask." Jobi pushed aside his half empty milk glass away. "Would you like me to ask him?"

"Oh, would you—I mean, it .a would be the polite thing to do, wouldn't it?" She looked down at her filled plate of bacon and eggs.

"Eat up sis, remember what Mom said," he smiled triumphantly.

"Okay, okay. But you drink all your milk." She slid his glass back in front of him.

"Make a deal with you, sis" He turned his nose up at the milk. "You don't have to eat and I don't have to drink that icky, half-warm milk, deal?"

Laughing, she shook his hand. "Okay, it's a deal,

"What-sa matter, sis? Too in love to eat'?" He picked up the bill for their breakfast and handed it to his sister.

"Oh Jobi, don't be so silly. She feigned a laugh. "I just . . . well, he's your friend. So I thought it would be the polite thing to do for you to introduce us."

When her brother didn't respond, she stared deeply into his eyes. "Jobi, introduce me to your friend."

"Sure, sis. I guess that would be 'polite,' huh." He smiled and hopped up. "Come on."

"Oh, not here, Jobi! Later. Outside." She took her brother's hand and walked out of the restaurant toward their cabin.

Scott had watched Susan and Jobi walk into the dining room and once again was struck with the recognition of the girl's beauty and his strange reaction to her. He couldn't understand the funny butterfly feeling he had when he saw her. What was happening to him? Why was he having these odd feelings over a young girl who couldn't be more than sixteen or seventeen.

"Perhaps," he told himself, "she reminds me of my daughter Tracy. She would be about her age if she were still alive. But if that were the reason, then why didn't Jobi have the same effect on me, since he would be Billy's age, or close to it?"

Scott felt a tug on his sleeve.

"Hey, Gene, can't you hear me?" Dr. William L. Danfield asked as he sipped on his coffee.

"Oh, I'm sorry doctor, did you say something?" Scott motioned for the waitress to bring him a refill for his own coffee mug.

"Yes. I spoke to you several times. Seems as if you were focused on those two kids that who just left. Do you know them?"

"Well, sort of. I met the little boy, Jobi, yesterday." Scott blew across the top of the steaming coffee before taking a sip. "I'm gonna drink all the good coffee I can before I end up in the jungle with a bunch of guys who can't brew a good pot of joe."

Danfield laughed. "Yes, I know what you mean. There will be five of us all together, Gene: you, Michael Sorensen, James Tabor, Raven Jones—our guide, and myself. Five men facing well over 300 natives."

"Well, doctor, let's not forget we're on God's team. So there is our advantage. That puts us in the lead already." Scott rose and stretched. "What say we put all this mission talk aside for now, and go play some deck shuffleboard."

"Sounds great, only I must warn you, I'm hard to beat at this game."

"Good I like real competition in all my sports!" Scott laughed.

"Even when it comes to your women, Gene?" Danfield asked with a grin.

"Especially my women, Danfield. It helps me know if I'm the kind of man I'm supposed to be."

Scott led the way to the top deck and an open shuffleboard court. "Grab a cue."

"You want to make a little wager on the side, Gene?" Danfield picked out a cue with an air of absolute confidence.

"Name it." Scott laid the wooden discs down in their proper places.

"The loser has to ask Anna Polk for a date." Danfield sized up the marked divisions painted on the deck.

"Who the hell is Anna Polk?" Scott looked at Danfield curiously.

"See that woman sitting over there with her back to us." Danfield pointed quickly at the heavy-set woman doing needlepoint. "She's on this cruise to snatch on to a husband, or so I've been told."

"Oh! Well, just to stay on the safe side, we had better leave Anna Polk alone. Think of another wager." Scott drew a deep, big breath of the briny air.

"What's the matter, Gene. Afraid? Think you might lose?" Danfield laughed aloud.

"Look, I was thinking of both of us when I suggested we leave Miss Polk alone."

"Well, seriously, that's the wager I want to make."

When Scott glanced up at him, Danfield's face darkened suddenly.

"Why, what's the point? . . . Unless I'm missing something." He stared at the doctor "Unless there's something you're not telling me."

Danfield grinned sheepishly. "I guess I can't fool you Scott. I am sorta trapped into a date, a dinner date, with her tonight."

Scott couldn't hold back his laughter. "And you're using this game to try and get out of it?"

"Well, is it a bet?" Now his expression was one of helplessness.

Whether it was sympathy or mischief he was feeling, Scott nodded his head. "You're on." He motioned for Danfield to go first.

As they approached the swimming pool, Susan and Jobi realized they had it pretty much just to themselves. Jobi climbed up the ladder to the diving board.

"Come on, sis!" he yelled from the top.

"I think I'll just get in the shallow end, Jobi. I don't want to get my hair wet." She climbed slowly into the water. "Hey, it feels great Jobi."

"That's good 'cause here I come." He soared into the air and disappeared beneath the water with an amazingly large splash. Instantly he was back on the surface, swimming toward his sister. He stood up beside her, shaking his head vigorously as she leaned away from him.

"Hey, Sis, it's no fun if you don't get wet all over."

She wasn't really listening to her brother. Instead she had discovered Gene Scott playing shuffleboard a few feet away from them. Her eyes melded to the muscular body that was so evident, despite his long-sleeved shirt. She watched silently as he slid the discs down the deck.

"Hey, earth calling Susan. What's up, sis? Has the sun got to your brain?" He glanced over to see what had her undivided attention. "Hey, I see my friend Reverend Scott playing shuffle board."

Scott sent another disc flying down the deck.

"Hey," Jobi said quietly, he's pretty good too."

"Yeh!" Her voice, unabashed, was full of infatuation. "He looks really good."

"Would you like to get introduced now?" Jobi asked his sister innocently.

She turned to him quickly, wondering if he had been aware of her dreamy obsessing about Gene. "Ah, not right now Jobi. We wouldn't want to interrupt their game." She forced a smile "Would we?"

"Whatever you say, sis." Jobi dipped beneath the water and popped back up. "I'll introduce you when their game is over."

". . . Okay. But don't tell him how old I am. Hear?" She pulled herself up on the side of the pool and sat kicking her feet in the delightful water.

"Don't tell him how old you are? Why not, for gosh sakes?" Jobi slashed water up on her, trying to get her hair wet.

"Jobi, stop that!" she laughed. "I just don't want him to know how young I am."

"Wh—Oh, I see!" Jobi laughed aloud.

"No you don't see, little brother." She rubbed some suntan lotion onto her legs. "I just, well . . ."

"Want him to like you as a 'woman'? Am I not right?" Jobi pulled himself up next to his sister. "Well sis, why don't you admit it, you're really stoned over him."

"Okay, okay, so I think he's good looking. That's not a big deal. Well, is it?"

"For you, I guess not." Jobi grinned broadly and then looked around when he heard the sound of Scott's laughter.

"Well, Danfield, looks as if I win the game, but you win an evening with the fair Miss Polk."

"Very funny, Gene, very funny." Danfield set his cue down and unceremoniously started to walk away.

"Oh come on. Don't you want to play another game Danfield? No need to be a sore loser." Scott tried to stifle another chuckle.

"I'm not a sore loser, Gene. I just have to find someone else I can round up to fall for the same bet, someone not as good as you are." He waved and walked down the deck out of sight.

Scott lay down his cue, then turned toward the pool when he heard a whistle.

"Hey Reverend Scott, could you come here a minute?" Jobi motioned for him. "I want you to meet my 'older' sister."

"Oh! Glad to!" He smiled at the beautiful young woman who had so intrigued him. "You must be Susan. Jobi said that you were traveling to Africa to stay with your grandfather."

"Yes, we are." Her smile was shy, but lovely. "It's a pleasure meeting you, Reverend Scott."

"The pleasure is mine, I assure you." He sat down next to her and pulled off his tennis shoes, dipping his feet into the cool water. "Oh, isn't that refreshing. It does the trick."

"Yes, refreshing. It is. Very." She swallowed. "Tell me, if I may ask, Reverend Scott, where are you heading?"

"Well I'm headed to Africa as well. Only I have a missionary post there. Is this your first time going to the 'dark continent'?"

"No, it isn't. Is it for you?"

"Yes, but I've read so much about it I feel as though I've already been there." He shrugged. "Does your grandfather work in a hospital?"

"Sometimes he does. It's a small hospital out in the jungle. He does a lot of house visits too. My granddad, Reverend Scott, is a very active man. You would never believe he is as old as he really is."

Susan gazed up into his eyes, and found that his were transfixed by her. For a long moment nothing was said. Finally it was Jobi who broke the silence.

"Is this mission post going to be dangerous, Reverend Scott? I mean, I've heard about all the dangerous things missionaries do. Some of them even get killed."

Susan heard herself gasp. "Jobi! Don't say things like that!"

"Actually he's right, Susan. Some of us do get killed. But then people get killed every day in lots of other ways, don't they?"

Scott patted her shoulder, surprised to feel it tremble beneath his touch.

"Yes, they do." She turned her eyes to the pool to avoid Gene's eyes. "Is there danger where you're going, Reverend Scott?"

"Well, if you consider that there are two tribes that are continually at war with one another and one of them is cannibalistic, I guess you could say there is some danger involved."

"Oh!" She lifted her eyes, filled suddenly with tears, toward him, then looked away.

A pensive feeling came over Scott. He wondered if it was pity he saw in her expression. Or was she aware of the attraction he felt toward her. He was filled with uncertainty.

"Of course I won't be alone. I'll be with four other fellows. But more important, God will be with us all the way."

"Was God not with those other missionaries who got killed?" Susan felt her voice quiver as she tried to talk. "I—I mean, what if something happens? You can't just rely on God to intervene, can you?"

Gene found himself smiling. What a clever, bold, articulate girl—and it made her all the more attractive. "Seriously, it's not all that bad. Just look how your grandfather has lived among the natives and he loves it, from the way you describe him."

"Friendly natives yes, but not cannibals." Susan tried to compose herself and reign in the multitude of emotions she was feeling. "I mean, why would anyone send you to do such a dangerous job?"

"Somebody has to do it, Susan." Gene pulled his feet out of the water.

"Why you? Couldn't they have picked someone who knew more about the natives' customs?"

"Look Susan, I'm no better than any other man. I ask for a mission, and I got this one. You seem to have a really big heart, Susan. I mean, you don't really even know me. I'm pretty much a stranger and yet here you are, worried about the danger I might be facing."

"Sis really can be pretty considerate at times, Reverend Scott," Jobi said.

"I—I only want people to be happy and spend their lives in a peaceful way. One that's full of love, not hate." She pulled her bathrobe around her shoulders.

The movement caused Scott's eyes to fall inadvertently to her shapely body. He looked away to Jobi.

"Say, what are you kids doing tonight? How would you like to have dinner with an old man?" Scott patted his chest. "My treat."

"We would love to do that. Wouldn't we, sis?" Jobi bumped Susan's arm.

Despite herself, she broke into a smile. "That sounds . . . very generous of you, Reverend Scott."

Scott's eyebrows rose in approval. "Great. It's a date, then. I'll meet you in the dining room around seven. Is that early enough?"

"You bet, Reverend. Seven o'clock. We'll see you then." Jobi draped a fluffy towel around his head and began to dry himself.

"Well, good. See you then." Despite himself, he glanced once more at Susan before rising and heading down the steps toward his cabin.

Chapter Five

Susan had carefully picked out the yellow low cut dress to make herself look as grown up as possible. She put the finishing touch on by adding some Hands Off perfume. Then she stood back to see her reflection in the mirror. The new push up bra she had bought to complement the dress, did wonders, she thought.

"Oh, if this dress doesn't weaken him, nothing will." She giggled aloud.

"Did you say something, sis?" Jobi came out from the bathroom in his underwear.

"No, Jobi. I was singing to myself." She twirled around the room and fell across her bed. Sitting up, she slipped her feet into her yellow heels. "How do I look?"

Jobi stood staring down at his sister, his mouth open.

"Well, what do you think?" She stared at her brother impatiently.

"Sexy! Scott will get a jolt out of you tonight." He smiled and shook his head as he slipped on his blue slacks and matching sweater. "Poor Gene Scott. He doesn't even realize he's being baited for the Andrew's catch."

"Oh, Jobi, don't be so childish. I put this dress on because it happens to be the nicest dinner dress I brought with me." Susan combed through her shoulder length black hair. "There. All ready."

"I'm ready—ready to eat! I'm starving to death." He put his hand on the cabin door. "I could eat a horse."

"Well, they serve just about everything, but I doubt if horse is on the menu." Susan grew serious for an instant. "Now, remember. Reverend Scott is paying for our meals. So don't overdo it. Understand?"

"Gotcha. Let's go, it's ten till, seven."

Together they walked out of their cabin and headed for the dining room.

Gene Scott stood right outside the dining room waiting for his invited guests to arrive. William Danfield turned the corner with

Miss Anna Polk gripping his arm tightly. Scott smiled genially as his colleague passed in front of him.

Well, good evening, William. I see you have a dinner date tonight."

"Yes, Gene, indeed I do." Danfield forced a smile. "Would you care to join us. We'd be delighted to have you as our guest." A desperate, pleading look came to his face.

"I really would love to William, but I have guests myself." Scott smiled at the helpless doctor.

"How nice for you." His eyebrows arched. Without looking at the woman on his arm, he said, "Miss Polk, after you."

"Thank you, you darling man," she replied, and then smiled at Scott. "Where have you been hiding?" She gave him a subtle wink.

"Come along, Miss Polk. Allow me to tell you everything about the very eligible Reverend Gene Scott."

Danfield grinned at the sudden panic on Scott's face and walked into the crowded dining room.

Scott mumbled to himself, "Sorry, Miss Polk, I'd much rather be devoured by cannibals."

It was at that moment he saw Susan and Jobi walking toward him. Irresistibly, a smile spread across his face.

"I see you made it." He glanced at his watch. "And right on time."

As he lifted his eyes, they fell on Susan's breasts in the gown. He blinked and looked toward the dining room.

"Well let's be going."

He led them through the door to the maître de stand, from which a waiter showed them to a table. Scott helped Susan with her seat, inadvertently giving him one more terrific view. Once again he forced himself to look away and sat down between the brother and sister. He lifted a menu and focused on it, avoiding another look at the beautiful young woman.

"I hope they have something good to eat, I'm starved."

"Me too!" Jobi's exclamation was louder than he had intended and elicited a frowned from Susan.

Scott, on the other hand, smiled. "Well, let's see if we can get them moving around here." He motioned to a waitress. She came to them quickly, smiling a little too much at Gene Scott.

"Yes, may I help you?"

43

Joan Byrd

"Yes, we would like to order now." He returned her smile, though without any passion behind it. "And if you don't mind, tell them to hurry it up in the kitchen, would you? This young man and I are about to starve."

"Anything you want, sweetheart." This time she winked at Scott "Really—anything."

Susan cleared her throat. "Well, I'll take the meatloaf with cream potatoes and green peas, if you please." She handed the menu back to the server, slapping it into her hand.

The young woman glared at Susan momentarily and turned to Jobi. "And what do you want, kid?"

"I'll take the same as my sister," he responded, looking over at Susan, who was gritting her teeth. "And Pepsi to drink, please."

"I don't recall what you wanted to drink, sweetie." She feigned a smile.

"I am not 'sweetie,' miss. And my brother is not 'kid.'" From the corner of her eyes she saw Scott smiling at her. "To drink, I'll take coffee, thank you."

Shaking her bleached blonde tresses, as if to discard Susan's comments, the server smiled down at Scott. "And what for you, honey?"

"I think I'll take what the kids—oops, I mean 'young people'—are having."

He couldn't resist smiling at Susan, who pretended to smile in return."

"And I'll have coffee to drink, like the lovely lady."

"Alright doll, I'll try to rush them up—just for you." She flounced toward the kitchen, shaking her behind with each exaggerated step.

Susan mumbled, "I sure wish she would swing herself right off the side of the ship."

"Did you say something, Susan." Scott leaned back in his chair, suppressing a smile.

"No, I was just thinking out loud. Lovely night, isn't it?"

"Yes, exquisitely beautiful," he said, making certain not to look at the front of her dress. He sipped from the water glass before him. "What grade will you be in when you start back to school after the summer vacation?"

"I'll be in the seventh." Jobi smiled triumphantly.

"How about you, Susan? What grade will you be in?"

"Actually I've graduated from public school Reverend Scott." She looked down at the napkin in her lap. "I finished . . . several years ago."

"Oh. You must be one of those students with a genius IQ.". He moved his arm so the server, who smiled coyly at him, could set down his food. "I thought you seemed very bright."

"If there's anything else you need," the server interrupted, her face very close to Gene's, "don't hesitate to call me. My name is Cathy." She turned and shimmied across the room.

"Nope, she's no genius, Reverend Scott. My sis is just older than she looks," Jobi said, taking a big bite of meatloaf. "Some people just can't believe it."

Susan frowned over at her brother. "Yes, they just can't believe I'm as old as I am." She swallowed, desperately thinking of how to change the subject.

"You don't say." Gene tried not to smile as he blew across his coffee cup. "So just how old are you, or is it not my business?"

"Well . . . I . . . ah . . ."

"Just take a guess Reverend." Jobi picked up his Pepsi and took a drink. "Go ahead. Guess."

"Gee, I can't imagine." Scott rubbed his forehead, contemplating. "I was assuming she was around sixteen, seventeen."

Susan's eyes widened.

"Oh, wow!" Jobi laughed. "You're way off. She's almost thirty."

Instantly Susan choked on the bite of meatloaf she had just taken. Gene patted her on the back.

When she had composed herself and taken a drink, he spoke up quietly. "My, my. Almost thirty." He gazed at her. "Honestly, that's kind of hard to believe."

She smiled sheepishly, looking back into Gene's eyes, before turning toward her brother. "Jobi, why don't you eat more and talk less."

"He can eat more than that?" Scott reached for a piece of bread and tore it apart. "So thirty, you say? Hard to believe. But I know you would never deceive a friend, so I believe you. Just think, Susan, I'm only six years older than you." "

"Thirty-six? Oh that's not too bad." Quickly she looked down at her plate. "This is very good meatloaf, isn't it?"

"Oh, yes. Very good." Scott watched Jobi, who seemed to be adding something in his head.

"Hey, sis, that's almost twice your—" He stopped instantly at the sight of Susan's glare. "Twice as good as your meatloaf." He smiled—or tried to.

"Yes, it is, isn't it." She looked back to Gene, who was amazingly focused on his supper. "I can fix excellent strawberry short cake though. "

"How are your cherry pies? And cakes? And other sweets?"

"Oh, I make them out of this world, don't I Jobi?"

"Huh? Oh sure. Yeh. They sure are. Just great." His mouth was jammed with bread.

"Well, that's great. It's sure something to think about."

He smiled, exchanging glances with her. His eyes fell slowly to her low cut dress and well-rounded bosom. He drew in a deep breath and looked back into her staring eyes.

". . . Susan, did you leave off part of your dress in your cabin?"

Jobi laughed and Susan cleared her throat. Quickly he looked back to his plate.

"Oh Reverend Scott, that's cute." She tried a natural laugh, but it came out a little shaky. "Don't you like my dress?"

"Well, yes but . . ." He looked over at Jobi, who smiled at him, waiting to hear what was coming next. "Well, it seems to me that the rest of the men around here are really enjoying it too."

Susan straightened. She looked around to see several men staring at her. She smiled with a sense of delight and accomplishment.

"Well, if I can brighten up their day, what could it hurt?"

"What could it hurt? Seriously? Well it could hurt plenty if they got the wrong idea about what sort of person you are. I mean, do you really want to play the temptress?"

"Is that what you think, Gene?" She gave him an altogether seductive smile.

He felt his jaw drop and, to his surprise, his stomach fluttered. All he could do was laugh and make light of the moment.

"So you're a little Delilah, an intentional temptress?"

She smiled and looked down at her lap, trying to decide how

to respond. "Does that make you Sampson, who provoked temptation in the first place?"

He smiled at her clever retort and motioned for the server, who came to the table immediately.

"Where is our bill, Cathy?"

"Here you are darling." She kissed it and handed it to him. "So let me ask, what are you doing tonight, doll?"

"He's taking me for a moonlight stroll around the deck, aren't you?"

He looked at Susan, first in amazement, then admiration.

She moved closer to him. "Aren't you?"

Gene shrugged and looked up at the server. "You heard the young lady, I'm taking her for a moonlight stroll."

The server paused, sizing up the girl. "Well then, sugar, what are you doing later tonight? Much later, after the 'young lady's' bedtime?" The waitress gave Susan an icy smile.

"He'll be in bed, too," Susan offered quickly. "He has to get up bright and early for church services. Don't you, Reverend Scott?"

Instantly the color drained from the server's face.

"The lady's right again, Cathy. It looks as though I'm all tied up." He glanced at Susan with a conspiratorial grin.

The server gathered herself, apparently deciding not to give up. "Well, what about tomorrow after church? I could use a little spiritual uplift and I don't go to work until after six."

"Oh no, Gene." Susan put her hand on his. "Don't you remember promising to show me how to play shuffleboard?"

"Shuffleboard? Well there are certain subtle aspects to the game that you could use some help with." Scott turned to the puzzled server. "Well Susan is right again. I guess when you get to a certain age, you need to avoid too much excitement, Cathy. Susan and I—us older people—have to stick together."

Susan forced a laugh. The server gazed at them, shaking her head in bewilderment.

Jobi tapped her on the arm. "They sure act strange sometimes, don't they?"

Cathy nodded in resignation. "Yeh, kid, they do. Oh well, handsome," she said to Scott, "maybe sometime when you stop playing with Alice in Wonderland, you might want to date a real woman. So just let me know."

Susan gritted her teeth. "Oh, that bleached—" When she heard Gene laugh, she rose quickly. "Shall we a go?"

"Sure. I think the moon is high in the sky already."

He signed for the meal as Susan and Jobi stood waiting. They walked onto the deck into the gathering twilight, Scott draping his arms around their shoulders.

"How's that for a moon?"

"It's just beautiful." Susan stared at her brother, twisting her head and moving her eyes in an exaggerated motion toward their cabin.

"Something wrong with your neck sis?" Jobi averted his gaze to keep from laughing, causing Scott to look at Susan.

She feigned a wide smile. "The sea is so peaceful at sunset. Don 't you think it's peaceful?"

"I think it looks a little rough." Jobi peered over the side.

Susan jerked him back from the rail instantly. "Stop that Jobi. Now! Mom told you to get to bed early every night. So you'd better go get ready." Susan pointed toward the stairway leading to the deck below. "Go on. I'll be down later."

"Now, Susan?" He gave his sister a pleading look.

"Jobi, please."

The little brother followed Susan's eyes toward Gene. "Oh. Sure sis. Now that you mention it, I am getting a little bit sleepy now come to think of it." He stretched and yawned. Turning to Gene, he said, "Don't keep my sister up to late, huh, Reverend Scott."

"Not to worry, Jobi. We all have to get to bed early so we can be up for worship services in the morning." He smiled at Susan. "Isn't that what you said, Alice?"

"Very funny." She nodded to her brother. "Go on down, Jobi. I'll be down soon."

After he disappeared down the stairs, she turned toward Scott. "Do you think of me as a child, Reverend Scott?"

"What happen to 'Gene'?" He grinned when her face grew red.

"Well do you ?"

"Susan, I can't believe you are as old as you say." He leaned against the rail, gazing at the twilight settling over the sea. "Why

48

is it so important for you to be thirty? I think being in your teens is terrific. It was for me. Believe me when I tell you there's no need to rush into being a grown up."

She grasped his arm and pulled him away from the rail, startling him.

"You still haven 't answered me, Gene. Do I not appeal to you at all?"

He laughed. "Do you think I'm going overboard."

He stared at her and, after a minute, she turned to look at the ocean.

"Susan, in some ways you're very much a woman." His eyes fell to her bosom again and moved across her form. "But lying about your age is a way of showing that you're still a girl in ways too."

"I never said I was thirty," she said. "That was Jobi."

"Yes, but you didn't correct him, did you?" he retorted. "You are what you are and you can't change that just because you want to be different—want to be older." He turned toward the water standing next to her and taking one hand in his. "Maybe we had better go down now. I wouldn't want you falling asleep during my sermon."

She sighed and spoke without looking at him. "Yes,   I suppose you 're right." She looked up into his eyes. "I wouldn't like the preacher pointing me out."

He laughed and put his arm around her shoulder. They walked slowly down the steps. She stopped when she reached 136-D.

She grasped the door handle. "Well, this is it."

"I see we're almost neighbors. I'm right down the hall in 136-C. "

"Imagine that." She smiled. "If I need some help in the night, I'll know where to come."

"Yes, actually. I am always available for someone in need of help." He stood looking at her for an instant, not quite ready for their encounter to be over. "Sleep well, Susan." He started toward his cabin, then glanced back over his shoulder. "And don't forget your prayers."

"Oh, I won't. You don't have to worry about that. Don't forget to say yours."

As she opened her door and entered the cabin, it occurred to her what a stupid thing it was to remind a minister to say his prayers.

Jobi must have been tired, she realized, because he was already sound asleep.

Susan pulled the yellow dress over her head. She hung it up carefully and reached for her night gown. Getting into bed, she stretched out under the cool sheet.

Her thoughts remained focused on Gene Scott. Why had she fallen in love with a man old enough to be her father? Nevertheless she was undeniably in love with him, she told herself. She had never felt this way before in her life. How could she ever have thought she loved Peter Simus? Everything she felt before, she realized now, was puppy love. Yes, she thought Peter was the one and only—but no more. Peter might be a friend, but that was all. Gene Scott, on the other hand, was already more—much more—to her. And this realization scared her, mainly because she knew that her loving him did not mean he would return her affection. Gene might not love her in return. Clearly he thought she was too young for him, just a child. It was time to ask for help from a higher source.

She folded her hands in a prayerful position, closed her eyes and whispered, "Gene ask me to not forget my prayers, Lord. So here I am, saying them. Dear God, help Gene Scott to fall in love with me like I do him. Amen." She took a breath and smiled. "I feel better already."

"I sure hope God heard you, sis. You're going to need all the help you can get to catch Reverend Scott."

She caught her breath. "Jobi! I thought you were asleep." She bit her lip. "Jobi, please, let 's let this be our little secret, okay?"

"You bet, sis, you bet. I wouldn't mind having Reverend Scott for a brother-in-law." He laughed. "That would be radical."

Susan got up and kissed her brother. "Thanks, Jobi. You can be a doll when you want to be."

"Yeh, I know. Now you better get your beauty sleep, so you can be a knock out tomorrow at church and then on the deck, you know, doing the old shuffle: one, two, three—hook a Gene."

She laughed out loud. "I agree."

Susan jumped back into her bed, thinking about the coming day and the time she wanted to spend with Gene. Finally she drifted away to joyous sleep.

Chapter Six

Reverend Gene Scott watched the people as they took their seats for morning worship service, all the while—despite himself—wondering if Susan would show up. It was a beautiful morning, the sun shining warmly on the deck and the sea a gentle calm. Just before the service was to begin, his eyes found Susan and Jobi making their way through the rows of folding chairs. They found places to sit near the front. When Susan glanced up at Gene, their eyes held fast, as if there were not another soul around them.

The ship's chaplain, Reverend Tom Rutherford, rose at the appointed hour and asked the gathering of worshippers to stand and sing two verse of "Holy Holy Holy." Gene Scott's voice, pleasant and powerful, ran through the clear, crisp air above every other singer. Gazing steadily at her hymnbook, Susan found herself smiling at the sound of it. At the conclusion of the hymn, Rutherford gave a brief invocation, then with a smile he began to introduce the guest speaker.

"Reverend Gene Scott has not only been the presiding minister at the Saint Peters Holy Church for eight years, but he has constantly reached outside the parish into the community through many programs to assist those less fortunate. I have known of Reverend Scott by reputation for years and it's an honor now not only to meet him in person, but also to welcome to our open sea service this man who is on his way to Africa to further the work of God. Gene is a very bright fellow, and he goes to the mission field knowing that he will encounter great difficulty, and perhaps even grave dangers. Nevertheless he goes to answer the call that has been placed upon his heart. Ladies and gentlemen it is my pleasure to introduce Reverend Gene Scott."

Susan 's heart fluttered when Gene stood up. She felt an overwhelming desire to clap, but her better instinct told her to remain still

Confident and peaceful, the minister exuded spiritual power from the moment he stood. He looked across the little congregation, smiling genially and patted the iron deck rail as he began to speak.

"Isn't it a beautiful day? And it's made all the more lovely by so many bright faces who have risen early to praise God this morning. When most people go on vacations, they don't seem to want to get out of bed for worship services. I was thinking it's a good thing God doesn't take a vacation when it dawned on me that a great many people don't seem to attend church at all. And I'm not talking about non-believers. I mean our brothers and sisters in the faith.

"How do people decide that it's okay not to come to worship? That belies the underlying belief so many have that we are attending services—coming to church—for ourselves. It's okay, we assume, to skip worship when the main reason we go is for our own needs. Yet isn't it true that, while we come together to be inspired and strengthened, the main reason we attend worship is to listen for God's call, to discover how God may lay claim to our abilities and use us to build the Kingdom of Heaven here on earth. Being lazy when it comes to our own gratification is one thing. But do we really want to cheat God of our presence, of our listening hearts, of our willingness to serve? Can you imagine our God not being there for us?

"Well enough about God's lazy children. Instead let's talk about God's hardworking, helpful, loving, generous children. You know—the good Christians gathered here on this perfect morning." As he looked across the gathered believers, his gaze rested momentarily on Susan and he smiled. "Now sometimes we find ourselves depending entirely on God to solve all our problems. We feel as though we can't cope with our troubles. So what do we do? We fall down on our knees and beg God to work things out for us. Well that's exactly the wrong thing to do. God wants servants with strong spirits. He wants us to fight the battle for ourselves, to learn, to grow, to become more self-reliant, and therefore more useful to the Lord. It serves God's purposes to strengthen us through the challenges we face in life. If God were to do all the work for us—and He could—then what use would we be to the Lord?

"Friends, if we, as children of God work for God together, listening to the calling God places upon our hearts and helping each other, then we are indeed going down that narrow path to salvation that our Savior speaks of in the Gospel. Why should God be expected to do the job He has given us to do? Yes, it's true that God never calls us to something without giving us the strength, guidance and resources necessary to accomplish the work He sets before us. Therefore it is up to you, it is up to me, it is up to all of us to work together for and with God."

Gene paused, extending his hands out over the rail. "Now I know the tasks God has for us may seem daunting. And we feel small and insignificant—all of us. Yet we must remember that God has made no mistake in whom He calls. We can do, each of us, what we are called. Only we must work together. We are like a big ball team, every player is essential if we are going to win. And it is our teammates that make the struggles we face endurable and even enjoyable. What an advantage, friends, for while we are on God's team, if we don't stick together to win together, then we might lose even though we are serving God and true cause. So, for God's sake, get off the side lines, jump in the game, fight for God!"

He stopped again, drawing in a deep breath as he gazed at the faces of those who sat silently listening, caught up in his words.

"So I encourage you never to forget that what we do is for the glory of God. Christ died for us. Isn't it time we really started living for him? . . . Let us pray." He lowered his head. ". . . Our most gracious heavenly Father, thank you for every blessing you have given to each of us. Give us the strength to fight for your cause. In the name of your son, Jesus Christ, we ask this and every prayer, Amen."

A relieved smile crossed his face as he lifted his eyes to those before him. He raised his hands to lift the congregants to their feet. "Would you please stand and sing one of my favorite hymns, 'Oh God Our Help In Ages Past.'"

He began singing, his strong voice echoing over the happy, energized worshippers. Susan and Jobi sang out as loud as they could. Gene smiled at them as they finished the hymn. Then he motioned for the crowd to remain standing for the benediction.

"I would like to say one thing before I pronounce the benediction. Brother Tom told you a while ago that I was the pastor at the Saint Peter 's Holy Church. I thought I would mention for those who are interested, the complete title of my church is Saint Peter's Holy United Methodist Church." He smiled at Reverend Rutherford. "I need to say as well that it's very gracious of Brother Tom, who is not of the Methodist denomination to allow me to preach this morning at the seaside chapel. Thank you, Brother Tom."

"Why thank you, Brother Gene. And what a wonderful message you brought this morning. So if you change your mind about doing mission work in the heart of Africa, you can come back here and preach for me every Sunday if you want."

Everyone gathered before them laughed.

"And while I'm not a Methodist," Rutherford continued, "I think they're a pretty fair lot. Why, I think they'd make good Baptists, don't you?"

Gene smiled broadly. "I would like to explain something to everyone, Brother Tom and I have a deep respect for one another. The first afternoon I was onboard, we sat and shared our faith with one another. And I was so grateful when he offered to let me speak this morning. True, he's a died-in-the-wool Baptist and I'm a unconvertible Methodist, but you can see how we have worked together to serve the Lord, which illustrates the very truth I was trying to express this morning. And in our brief friendship, Brother Tom and I have become very comfortable with one another—so much so that we can tease and joke with one another. Sort of like Bob Hope and Bing Crosby." He glanced at the chaplain. "Thanks again, brother. . . . And I pray all of you enjoy this day and your voyage, wherever the Spirit takes you. Now may the grace of the Father, the Son and the Holy Spirit rest and abide with you, both this day and forever more. Amen."

Gene stepped toward Rutherford and shook his hand. A number of people came forward to speak to him, thanking him for his words and the inspiration they had experienced. Susan and Jobi, he noticed, were not in the group that approached him.

As the crowd began to disperse, Rutherford shook Scott's hand and asked him to walk with him to his cabin. They laughed as they strolled along the deck.

"Well you certainly have the gift of preaching, Gene. I thought people were going to leap up off their chairs and volunteer to come with you on the mission."

"I hope it wasn't too much, Brother Tom. I mean, I know this wasn't a revival. Hope I didn't embarrass you." He put his hand on the shoulder of his new colleague.

"Not at all. Everyone was uplifted, including me. What are you doing today, Gene?" Rutherford unlocked his cabin door.

"Teaching someone the game of deck shuffleboard. Care to assist?"

"No thanks. That sun gets too hot for me during the day. Hot places are for the devil's children." He chuckled.

"And God created two great lights, the greater one to rule the day. I know you're a Baptist and all, but you need to get that Bible out and dust the cobwebs off." Gene laughed. "Thanks again for the privilege of preaching, brother."

They shook hands again and Gene walked down the hallway to his own cabin, whistling the melody of the last hymn.

He had just changed his clothes when he heard a knock on his door. Jobi stood smiling up at him when he opened it.

"Hi, Reverend Scott. You gave a totally cool sermon this morning. It was the best one I ever heard."

"Thank you very much, Jobi. Coming from a guy like you who never misses a Sunday in church, I take that as a great compliment." He held the door open to let Jobi into the room. "Where did you and Susan disappear to after worship?"

"Oh, I had to go to the john. And sis wanted to get ready for you"

"What?"

Jobi smiled at him. "Are you about ready?"

"Uh, yeh. All ready."

The two of them walked down the hall to 136-D and knocked on the door.

"Hey, sis, come out!" Jobi shouted through the door.

Gene straightened, startled by the volume of the yell. The cabin door flew open.

"Jobi, stop yelling! Are you trying to wake up the sea ghost?" Susan stop talking the instant she realized Gene was standing beside her brother.

"I decided I would go round up Reverend Scott since you were taking so long in the bathroom." He smiled up at his blushing sister.

"Well, you certainly look cool enough," Gene said, gazing leisurely at Susan in her yellow shorts and halter set. "I hope you don't sunburned easily."

"Oh, I'm used to being in the sun, Reverend Scott." She closed and locked their cabin.

"Yes," Jobi piped in, "we had a real groovy pool back home." He clapped his hands at the memory of it. "But Dad says our new house has a pool almost twice the size of our old one."

"Imagine that. Nothing to do all day but lie in the sun around a big swimming pool."

Susan wondered if she heard disapproval or even disgust in his tone. She frowned. For an instant she slowed, letting Gene, with his long strides, get ahead of them and catching her brother's arm.

"Jobi, Reverend Scott is not interested in what we have or don't," she whispered. "You don't have to tell him everything about our family. Understand?"

"Sorry sis." He gave his sister a puzzled look. "I only thought—"

"It's alright, Jobi. I don't quite understand him either."

She practically had to run to catch up with him. "Hey, Gene, what's the rush?"

He turned to her, surprised. "Oh, so we're on first name basis again?" He raised his hand as if to touch her face, then stopped himself. "Ready to learn the game?"

"Of course. Are you a good teacher?" She smiled at him.

"Am I good? Oh, listen to that, Jobi. She asks for free lessons and then wants to know if I'm a good teacher." Again he started to reach for her, this time following through with it and taking her hand. "You will never know until you give me a try." They stopped at the shuffleboard court.

"Alright. I'll take you up on that and give you a try." She could not hold back her coy grin. "At anything you want to teach me."

And again he stopped in surprise. His eyebrows arched as he tried to decide how to respond. Quickly he reached for shuffleboard cues, handing one to Susan. He lined up several of the colored discs.

Completely ignoring her flirtatious remark, he said, "As you see, there are divisions marked on the deck. Now you use these cues

56

A New Beginning

to pushed the wooden discs down the deck, like this." He drove the disc, which slid and stopped perfectly over the number 10.

"I can see it's going to be very difficult to beat the teacher," she said.

With a smooth motion Susan launched her disc across the deck. It smacked into Gene's, pushing it off the 10.

"Hey!" he exclaimed. "Not bad. Not bad at all for a beginner." Jobi patted his sister on the back. "Wow, sis. I bet you already feel like an old pro, huh?"

"Well, I don't think I 'm ready for the shuffleboard Olympics yet, but I might be ready for my teacher." Her head tilted to one side as she gave him a teasing smiled. "How 'bout it, teacher, are you game?"

"Well, I was taught never to turn a lady down when she asks you nicely." Gene extended his hand toward the deck. "You first, Susan."

They played eight consecutive games, Scott winning seven and Susan winning the last one. She smiled at her opponent.

"I have a sneaking suspicion you let me win that last game teacher."

"Don 't you believe that for one minute. I always play to win. At everything." He laughed and grasped her hand and Jobi 's. "Now let me treat you to lunch."

"No!" Susan pulled away. "Nothing doing."

Jobi looked at her in stunned surprise.

Gene as well had a look of shock. "Why? Did I say something wrong? Did I offend you?" he asked.

She broke into giddy laughter. "No, Gene. Let me treat you to lunch. It's only fair." She reached out and grasped the hand she had spurned. "And I won 't take no for an answer, so don't even think about refusing me."

Gene looked at Jobi and asked conspiratorially, "Is she always unpredictable and demanding like this?"

"Well, to tell you the truth, Reverend Scott, this is the way she always is. Only I just call her 'weird.'"

Jobi laughed as Susan smacked him on his arm.

"Oh, you two cut out the smart remarks," she said. "Otherwise I eat alone."

57

"We had better shut up, Jobi. We wouldn't want her eating alone. There's a definite danger of some stranger getting fresh with her.

As he trailed behind Susan with Jobi, Scott's eyes drifted to the rhythmic movement of her steps as she made her way down the deck that led to the dining room. Silently he thought, "And that is something to get fresh over."

Jobi, watching Gene staring at Susan's form, smiled up at him. "Is that what you're talking about?" he said in tone far too sly for his age. "I guess what you see is what you get."

Gene cleared his throat. "Just keep walking, kid, and leave the jokes to Bob Hope."

"Now that's what you call a great cheeseburger." Gene gently pushed his chair from the table and smiled at Jobi and Susan. "Thank you both for the treat. Now I'm off to jump into my swim trunks and hit the pool, just as soon as my food has had time to digest."

"Would you like some company at the pool?" Susan looked hopefully into his blue eyes. "Jobi and I had plans to go swimming later anyway."

"Company sounds wonderful! Never did like to swim alone." He helped her out of her chair and patted Jobi's head. "Besides, I feel like I've taken on the role of looking after you two on this fine ship."

"Well Jobi can be a handful at times, Reverend Scott." She smiled happily. "I'll welcome any help you can give me."

"Hey, sis, there's times you can use a guardian too!" Jobi frowned. "Wouldn't you agree, Reverend Scott?"

"Well I'll tell you, buddy, if Susan's bathing suit looks anything like the dress she wore last night," Gene's eyes were full of mischief, "I might have to protect her from all the hungry wolves lurking around the pool."

"I'll bet there are times when you could use someone to look after you, Gene Scott!" Susan turned and started walking along the deck toward their cabins.

"You have stoked my interest, young lady." Gene's quick steps caught up with her. "Why would I need a chaperone?"

She laughed. "Oh, as if I hadn't noticed how women are drawn to you, like that big flirt waitress!" She was glad to finally reach her room. "I think if we stick together we can ward off any unwanted attention, male or female."

Gene couldn't resist chuckling as he opened the door for her. "Sounds like a safe plan." He winked at Jobi. "Maybe they'll think we are a father and his children, having a fun family get away."

"Cute, Gene Scott." Susan grimaced, somewhat annoyed at his referring to her as his daughter. "Just for that, DAD, I might let my eye wander around the pool for an available man."

Despite himself, Gene felt an odd, fleeting moment of panicked jealousy. "Well there will be no flirting at the pool, young lady. So put on something that doesn't look so grown up."

He turned, confused about the jealousy that spontaneously seized him, and made his way quickly to his cabin. Gene stepped into his bathroom and splashed cold water onto his face. He stared at his reflection in the mirror.

"Get a grip, man!"

He pulled the turtleneck over his dark hair and flopped down in the chair by the dresser. He took his worn, well-used Bible off the dresser, opened it to Psalm 25 and started reading:

Mine eyes are ever toward the Lord; for he shall pluck my feet out of the net. Turn thee unto me, and have mercy upon me; for I am desolate and afflicted. The troubles of my heart ar enlarged; O bring me out of my distresses. Look upon mine affliction and my pain; and forgive my sins.

He closed the old Bible slowly, then shut his eyes in a prayer-like state. "My Father, this thing I feel for Susan grows stronger and I'm confused as to what it really is."

He opened his eyes and gently placed the book back in its resting place. As he unpacked his swim trunks and stepped into them, his eyes focused on the calm sea outside his small window.

"If this thing I'm feeling for her is what I think . . ." He closed his eyes. "Dear God, please help me stay strong and make the choice I know I must."

Chapter Seven

Susan and Jobi had gotten to the pool area first and found three vacant lounge chairs together. They threw their towels on the outside two and Susan sat down on the one in the middle. She was putting on suntan lotion when Jobi punched her arm gently.

"Hey sis, Reverend Scott is headed this way and boy do his muscles show now!"

Susan looked at the handsome figure walking toward her smiling brightly.

"Looks like you kids beat me here." He stretched his arms out to loosen them up and threw his towel on Susan "Ready to swim?"

She laughed as she stood up and put his towel down on the middle seat. Then she removed her cover-up revealing her red bikini. Despite himself, Gene's jaw dropped. He could not help staring.

"You look good in your swim trunks too, Gene," she teased and started toward the diving board. "Ready to make a splash?"

"Sounds refreshing, Susan." He thought to himself "I could use cooling down."

Just as she did a graceful swan off the board, Gene dove in from the side and met her on the bottom of the pool. They both came up laughing.

"Gene Scott, you startled me!"

As she continued to laugh, he realized she was even prettier when she smiled.

"Bet you thought a giant sea monster was about to get you."

They looked up in time to see Jobi on the diving board.

"Move out of my way, you two, I'm about to jump!"

Gene moved Susan to a safe distance as Jobi dove in like a pro and floated up to join them.

"How 'bout a race to the end of the pool, Reverend Scott?"

"Sure thing, kid!" He looked back at Susan's radiant smile. "Care to make it a three-way race Susan?"

"You're on, Gene." She focused on the far end of the pool. "Better get ready to lose, mister."

A New Beginning

"Ha! Daredevil Gene plays to win pretty girl." He laughed confidently. "Try not to get swamped by my wake."

"You're both wrong," Jobi laughed. "I haven't had a good race since we left home and I'm well rested and ready to go."

"He's right Gene, next to me, he's the best," Susan teased.

"That was before you met the champ of every race he ever entered." He smiled proudly "In swimming, biking, walking, running, rowing, skating—both ice and roller skates. On a horse, on a cow, or on a pig."

Susan couldn't control her laughter. "A pig? Seriously, Gene Scott? Let's make a bet. Winner gets to pick where we eat supper."

Without giving any thought to whether or not he had an evening conflict, Gene said, "Deal!" He rubbed his hands together as he kicked his feet to stay afloat. "And I know where I want to go!"

"Too bad you won't be choosing." Susan winked at her brother "Ready speed?"

"Ready jet woman!" Jobi's eyes twinkled with mischief.

"Speed? Jet woman?" He chuckled incredulously. He squared his shoulders to the far end. "Old lighting flash Scott will be waiting for you at the finish."

"On your mark!" Jobi called. "Get set! GO!"

The swimmers raced across the pool at top speed. To their word, they all were fast, but Gene Scott reached the end three lengths ahead and hopped up on the side to wait. Susan and Jobi reached the end at almost the same instant.

"What kept you turtles?" Scott laughed and offered his hand to Susan.

She feigned a smile and accepted his hand. "Well, I guess nothing is faster than old lighting flash daredevil Gene."

Susan heard a loud whistle close by and immediately looked up to see Gene's reaction.

A male voice rang out. "Hey beautiful, tell daddy to get lost so we can have a little pool fun!"

An unmistakable dark cloud draped across Gene's face and felt him tense. He squeezed her hand tightly and lifted her from the pool, then turned to the brazen young man who had spoken. His muscles glistening in the afternoon sun, Gene towered above the youth,

61

"Look, buddy, I'd appreciate it if you'd keep your rude remarks to yourself. After all, it's hard to make passes at beautiful women when you have a fat lip!" His eyes blazed.

The young man stepped back, obviously shaken. "I was just admiring your daughter's beauty, sir. I didn't mean anything by it. I mean, as pretty as she is, can you blame me?" His voice trembled.

"Her beauty?" Gene drew close enough that only the frightened boy could hear him. "Are you sure it wasn't her body that drew out the devil in you, son?"

"Well, I just thought . . ." He swallowed anxiously. "If she wasn't spoken for, I'd like to ask her out."

"Sorry, but she has a guy. Why don't you move along?"

Gene took Susan's hand. "He won't be bothering you anymore, Susan. Are we ready to go?" He finally smiled, shaking his head and reaching down to pull Jobi out of the water.

After riding on the lazy river floats, they walked around the ship, talking and gazing out at the water. Then they made their way back to the pool area.

"By the time we shower and rest up, it'll be time to go to my victory dinner."

They retrieved their towels and headed down to their cabins. Gene waved to them as they opened their cabin door.

"Dress casual, I hate dress up!"

Susan and Jobi looked at one another and laughed.

"I wonder what he has in store for us this evening?" Susan asked as she opened her closet to pick out something casual.

"Don't know sis, but you can bet it's gonna be neat!" Jobi raced off to the bathroom to beat Susan to the shower.

Susan and Jobi smiled at one another when a soft knock came at their door. Susan opened it quickly, revealing a smiling Gene Scott.

"Well great, you both look perfect for tonight's surprise."

Despite the night chill that blew across the vastness of the ocean, the three of them shared a genial happiness. It seemed they could not resist smiling. They made their way down the deck in jeans and light sweaters. Susan noticed that Scott, as always, was wearing his signature white turtleneck, this time with khaki pants.

"Remember, Gene, you won, so dinner is on us."

He shook his head, but said nothing.

Susan and Jobi followed the tall man up the stairwell and down the deck. They passed the dining room where the flirtatious Cathy worked. Susan couldn't resist a private little smirk, feeling relieved.

To their amazement, they past every eating spot on the cruise liner, including the canteen which would be closing in an hour.

"Gene Scott, just where are we eating tonight?" Susan's curiosity got the best of her "I'm totally perplexed!"

Gene stopped at the elevator and pressed the button for the second floor.

"The shopping floor?" Jobi looked at his sister in confusion. "I don't remember any restaurants on that floor, Reverend Scott?"

"That's because there aren't any." Gene's eyes twinkled with mischief. "How would you kids like to junk it tonight? Popcorn, drinks, that special piece of candy!"

"The movies?" Susan broke into laughter. "Sounds heavy Gene!"

"Groovy! What's playing, Reverend Scott, a Bible movie?" Jobi gazed into the many shops as they passed by them.

"I'd like nothing better, son, but *The Ten Commandments* isn't playing. I have a list right here telling what the three movie theaters are showing on this passage."

Gene pulled a folded brochure from his pocket. "We have the choice of this year's biggest hits: *Paper Moon* with Ryan O'Neal and his daughter Tatum; *American Graffiti* with Richard Dreyfuss, Ronny Howard, and Cindy Williams; or the latest James Bond movie, *Live And Let Live* with Roger Moore and Jane Seymour."

"Wow! James Bond, that's my choice!" Jobi pulled at Gene's arm "Adventure, fighting, beautiful women!"

"Jobi? Beautiful woman, really? Remember you're twelve." Susan punched his arm. "I hear *American Graffiti* is really good, Gene."

"Well I don't know, kids, James Bond is a little too violent, not to mention the half-dressed women won't be suitable for children." Scott smiled at Susan's angry glare. "And really, Susan, *American Graffiti*? A lot of young kids drag racing and loud music."

"It's a lovely love story, Gene Scott!" Susan pouted for a

moment then smiled at him "But it's your prize, Reverend Scott, you choose."

"Why thank you, Miss Andrews." He could tell by her expression she didn't care for his remark "This is the deal," he continued as if nothing had been said to change the mood "The bet states you buy the meal, the junk, popcorn, etc. I insist on getting the movie tickets and I won't take no for an answer."

"Then we accept your kind offer." Susan laughed and pointed to the bright blinking neon lights. "*Paper Moon* next showing 7 p.m., and we're just in time. Grab those tickets, handsome, and we're off to the refreshment stand and our junky dinner!"

"My favorite kind!" Jobi stared at the wide selection of candy "I'm just not sure."

"Jobi, just get the M&Ms. That's what you always end up with anyway." Susan reached over and got a chocolate bar "I hope it doesn't drop on my sweater."

Gene watched her as she laid the wrapped candy on the checkout counter.

"What are you waiting for Gene, pick out your favorite."

"Well, I was thinking, Susan, if you drop your chocolate on yourself, you'll be a sweet little chocolate drop." He teased and reached over for a Babe Ruth. "God, I love these things!"

"I'll remember that Gene," she smiled up coyly, "and chocolate drops."

Gene cleared his throat and pointed to the popcorn. "May I have the tub and a large Coke, kids?"

"Make mine a large box," Susan said to the cashier, "and a large Coke. My brother will have the same as well."

"Hey, maybe I wanted a tub too, Susan!" Jobi set his M&Ms down on the counter.

"Well, do you?" she asked impatiently. "Don't take all day. The show starts soon and I hate walking in after the lights drop."

"Not really, sis. Just fooling. The large is fine with me; just make my drink extra-large." He smiled and slipped the candy into his pocket so he could carry his popcorn and big drink.

Susan placed her candy bar in her shoulder bag and held her hand out to Scott. "Give me that Babe Ruth. I'll put it in my bag. How you're going to manage that tub and drink is beyond me."

"Experience sweetheart." He placed the tub of popcorn in his arm and grabbed the drink "Not too close to the front, kids, the view is better further back."

"It's darker too." Susan smiled up with mischief. "Jobi, you go in first. Let Gene sit between us."

"You got it, sis." Jobi made his way down the row of seats and finally sat down. "Perfect!" He pulled down his drink tray and placed his big cup in the slot. "Boy, just did fit."

"I hope that drink doesn't go straight through you, Jobi." Susan turned to Gene "He always insist on the extra-large and halfway through the movie he has to excuse himself."

"Maybe we'll go together" Scott patted Jobi's leg. "Coke can run right through a big guy too."

"Great, Reverend Scott!" Jobi looked over at Susan and laughed "That will make two of us moving over Susan during the movie."

"Next time, I go in first!" Susan frowned at Jobi. The lights dimmed and the movie started.

"Cool. No previews." Jobi chomped down on his popcorn.

"No need for them here sport." Gene filled his mouth with a large handful of popcorn.

Susan didn't notice the young man sitting down next to her and was surprised when a hand reached over and touched her knee. She glanced quickly over at Scott. He was lost in the opening scene of the movie, so she pushed the fresh man's hand away and whispered, "Kindly keep your hands to yourself!"

The motion and her quiet words didn't go unnoticed.

Gene's powerful voice resonated in the darkness. "If you know what's good for you, pal, you'll stop your indecent advances and move to another seat in the farthest part of this theater."

Even in the dim light, Gene's eyes burned into the strangers. The man moved nervously out of his seat and disappeared.

Susan observed Gene closely as he spoke to the man. "Could he be jealous?" she wondered silently, "or was he just protecting me from that fresh guy?"

Gene's gaze turned to Susan's eyes after the man scooted away.

She forced a shaky smile and whispered, "Thank you Gene."

He chuckled. "You bet Susan. Seems like you need a lot of protection from fellows like that these days." He winked and turned his attention back to the movie.

Susan was finishing her candy bar when she noticed Gene throw his wrapper in the empty tub, then took his last sip of drink and toss the can inside. She smiled to herself and turned to watch the movie as she thought, "Oh, can't Gene see this movie is how a father and daughter respond to one another? What I feel is not the way I love my father." She glanced back at him. "I truly am in love with him."

Near the end of the picture, she felt Gene's arm gently drop over her shoulder. She closed her eyes dreamily for a second, then she glanced carefully behind him to see if his other arm rest on her brother, it did not. Susan had never known a feeling of happiness like this before.

The lights came on, the movie was over. Gene stretched up his long arms and yawned "Alright kids, grab your trash, it's time for bed."

"It was a fun day, Gene." Susan smiled at him as they made their way to their cabins. "Got any plans tomorrow?"

"I do as a matter of fact." He retrieved her key from her outstretched hand and chivalrously unlocked their door. "How would you kids like to spend the day with me tomorrow?"

"That sounds heavy, Reverend Scott!" Jobi's eyes grew wide with excitement "Don't you think so sis?"

"I can't think of a better way to spend a Monday, Mr. Scott." She opened the door "Thank you for asking us. What time does the fun begin?"

"All good days begin with a hearty breakfast." Gene checked his watch.

"Breakfast?" Susan and Jobi said in unison, making identical faces as well.

"Not your favorite meal, huh?" Gene laughed "Relax, I'll be having breakfast at 8:00 with my friend, Dr. Danfield while you sleepy heads are getting out of bed."

"Very funny, Rev. Scott!" Susan said, narrowing her eyes with a determined expression. "I can get up as early as you if I need to."

"Cool down your pretty feathers sweetheart," Scott chuckled softly. "You two breakfast lovers can come up sometime between 8:30 and 9:00. I'll bring my coffee over and join you while you have your cereal."

"And a bowl of fresh fruit," Susan added. "We look forward to meeting you in the morning. Try not to let Cathy take advantage of you while I'm not there to protect you

Gene laughed aloud. He patted the top of her head and walked to his cabin whistling.

"Rats!" Susan muttered, shutting and locking the door. "If that big flirt waitress tries to horn in on our fun day with Gene I'll—"

"Relax, sis." Jobi pulled out his pajamas "I don't think you have anything to worry about. I believe good old Reverend Scott is falling into the Andrews Trap."

"Do you really think so, Jobi?" Susan looked dreamily at the door. "After all, I have all day tomorrow to convince Gene that I'm what he needs."

Chapter Eight

"There you are, Gene. What kept you? Too much fun with those kids yesterday?" William Danfield teased. "The young can make us older fellows feel young again."

"Uh huh. And how is the lovely Anna Polk making you feel, brother William?" Scott smiled at the dark hair waitress who set a steaming cup of coffee down before him. "So that other waitress, Cathy, I believe, is not working this morning?"

"No sir, Cathy has the afternoon shift today. I'll tell her you asked." She smiled and held up her order pad.

"Oh no. I'd just as soon you didn't." He read her name tag. "I wouldn't want her to get the wrong impression, Wanda."

"Then she certainly won't hear it from me, sir." She smiled at the handsome man. "What can I get you?"

"Can't make it too heavy." He studied the menu "Those kids won't eat much which means an early lunch. Make it two eggs scrambled, bacon, grits and biscuits please."

The two missionaries watched her walk away before Danfield laughed out. "Those kids again, Scott? I'd think you'd want to spend your time with one of these single women on the ship."

"I choose my friends carefully, William." Scott took a sip of coffee. "And considering that, you ought to feel really grateful I consider you a friend."

"Suit yourself, Gene, stick to playing it safe, hanging out with children." He moved his hands so the waitress could set down his plate of food. "Seriously, Scott, time is running short. We've got to get together to go over this mission. Tomorrow is our last full day at sea before we depart Wednesday morning."

"I am aware of that, William." Scott took a big bite. "I've been preparing for this for years. For me all that's left is the details. I'll meet you tomorrow, right after lunch. That will give us all afternoon and night to complete our planning and coordination."

Danfield shrugged. "Very well, Scott." He seemed to relax. "So how much training have you had for the mission, by the way?"

"For the specific duties, I had a week crash course. I have

studied a lot of books, mission reports, backgrounds and the journals of previous missionaries. So I have a pretty detailed background." Scott laid his fork down and looked over at his companion. "I'd say my best training, however, came from my two years in the Marines. I anticipate that all those skills will come in handy."

"Sounds like you're ready alright." Dr. Danfield wore a thoughtful expression. "As for me, I had a month's worth of training. No service duty." He looked at Scott. "Two years in the Marines? How old were you?"

"Trying to figure the math, pal?" Gene smiled. "Just trying to add up how I served two years, graduated high school, went to college, then seminary for three years and served at two churches?" Gene leaned on his elbows, returning the doctor's questioning gaze. "I was fifteen-years-old when I joined the Marines. I was a big fellow, so I fudged my age and got in. Caught up my two grades I missed after quitting high school, graduated at eighteen, got into college, went to Duke Divinity School for three years when I was almost twenty-two, got my first church at twenty-five years of age, served four years then moved to my last congregational charge, where I served until now, about eight years."

". . . And after all that you decided to become a missionary." William Danfield admired the big man sitting across from him. "Gene, I read the report about you, about the loss of your family. I'm truly sorry."

The kindness in his new partner's eyes was obvious to Gene. "Thank you, William. They're in my past, and I'll always have good memories of them."

Gene felt a twinge of guilt that ever since meeting Susan, he hadn't thought about much else. He hadn't thought even once about the family he lost. And he wondered why Susan popped into his consciousness at that moment.

"I got married while I was in college, around the first of March. Tracy was born nine months later." He stared at his coffee cup. "I guess I was a lonely, virile ex-Marine."

"Though you did love your wife, right, Gene?"

Now Danfield's conversation was getting too personal for Scott. He decided to change the subject.

"Why don't we get back to the mission, William. That's my priority"

No sooner had he spoken than he noticed Susan and Jobi entering the dining room. It was almost as if some spiritual power was questioning the truth of his statement. His stomach filled with butterflies just seeing her. They spotted him and waved. He returned it smiling, then turned back to the doctor.

"Those two men helping us, Sorensen and Tabor, just what are their qualifications?" Gene's eyes wandered to the table were Susan was ordering.

"James Tabor and Michael Sorensen are good friends who grew up together, went to the same high school, were only separated when James joined the Army and Michael joined the Air Force, where he learned to fly. They are highly skilled in many areas. They follow orders well, are both great sharp shooters and are not afraid to tackle any job thrown at them." The doctor watched Gene as he spoke, aware that his attention was focused on the children across the room. "They'll be good men to watch our backs, Scott."

"They will be if they're as good as they sound, William." Gene stood and motioned for the waitress. "I think we've got ourselves a winning team." He told the waitress to put the tab on his cabin number. "I'm going over to where those kids are sitting, Wanda. When you got time, you can top off my cup at that table."

"Yes sir, I'll bring you a refill with their order." She gave him a smile that was uncannily like Cathy's and walked away.

"Spending the day with those kids again, huh?" the doctor's eyes fell on Susan "I must admit, she is one shapely little lady Scott."

Gene Scott stared down the doctor. "That poor girl has been harassed by every skirt-chaser on this boat. I hate to think that you see Susan in that light too, William. Anyway, I'm pretty sure plump Miss Polk, William, is about all you can handle."

"'Susan' is it?" Danfield smiled slyly "And she's only a kid to you?"

"That's exactly all she is and that's why your remark rubbed me the wrong way." Gene dropped a tip on the table. "See you tomorrow afternoon. I'll come to your cabin so we won't be disturbed."

A New Beginning

Danfield's eyes fell on the kids, both looking in their direction. "Sure, I understand." He laughed and stood up "Don't want your fan club interrupting our meeting."

"Have a good day, doctor." Gene caught the sight of Anna Polk headed their way. "Oh. Looks like you won't be spending the day alone either, my friend." he laughed at Danfield's fallen expression and walked across the dining room to join the Andrews.

"I see you finally broke away from your friend." Susan smiled relaxed, realizing Cathy had not been his waitress." Did you have a hearty breakfast?"

Gene stood back as the waitress set down the fruit and cereal. He pulled a seat out next to Susan and let the waitress fill his coffee cup. He nodded a thank you and turned to Susan.

"Looks like your breakfast is a lot smaller than mine." His eyes drifted to her short sundress. "But then I'm a much bigger person to fill up."

"What are our plans for today?" Jobi tried to speak with his mouth full "Besides having a hearty breakfast."

"Well, how 'bout we start out with a game of shuffleboard." Gene winked at Jobi "I can teach you and you can join me and my fine student here."

Susan smiled up slyly and looked at her brother "What do you say Jobi, want to give it a try, it's really neat?"

"If you don't mind, Reverend Scott, I'll just keep score." Jobi laughed as he finished his orange juice "I like watching you two go at each other!"

Gene paused momentarily as he reflected on what the boy meant, then spoke, "Okay, four rounds of shuffleboard, followed by a go at table tennis." He took another sip of coffee "Any takers?"

"Are you kidding, Reverend Scott?" Susan sat up straight. "Ping pong is one of my favorite games and I always win."

"She does. I play 'cause it's fun, but I've never won one game when she plays with me." Jobi smiled at his sister "She's the best."

"She was the best, buddy." Gene smiled when Susan's eyes grew dark and determined. "I'd think both of you would know by now, this big guy plays to win."

"We'll see, Reverend Scott." Susan forced a smile "This is one

71

game I know I can beat you at, daredevil Gene." She reached inside her purse and pulled out her new camera. "Before we play, do you mind if I take your picture?"

"What could it hurt—except your camera? Go ahead and shoot."

He leaned against the rail as she focused and snapped the picture.

"That was a great shot. Jobi, why don't you take your picture with Reverend Scott, then you can take one of me with him." She focused on the two of them.

"Susan, wait." Gene called to a passing woman. "Miss, could you take a picture of the three of us?"

The woman smiled. "Love to."

She took the camera from Susan and waited for the three of them to arrange themselves. Scott put his arm around Susan's shoulder.

"What a lovely family," the stranger said as she snapped the picture.

As she took the photo, Scott laughed and Susan looked up at him.

Susan retrieved her camera and thanked the woman. After putting it away, she smiled slyly up at Gene.

"It's not so funny, Gene Scott. We just might be family one day. You never know." Before he could reply, she started walking toward the shuffleboard court. "Let's play. I'm ready to beat my teacher."

"Keep dreaming sweetie. You already have a father." He handed her a cue. "And get ready to lose, at all these games!"

Susan frowned. "I'm not the only one dreaming, Gene Scott."

"I can't believe it, beaten in ping pong! Darn!" She dropped her paddle, shaking her head "I can understand how you could beat me in shuffle board but ping pong?"

"I did try to warn you." He patted her head in consolation when she finally smiled at him. "I admit, you are a very strong competitor."

"There's got to be something I'm better than you at." She shrugged her shoulders.

"I've got it—just the ticket!" Gene laughed and grasped Jobi and Susan by their hands. As he led them down the deck, he said, "We just have time to play before lunch break."

"What? Tell me?" Susan asked excitedly. "Think I can win this time for a change?"

"With the odds of this game, sweetheart, anyone can be a winner."

He stopped in front of the bingo room.

"Bingo?" Susan laughed "Let's hope I get the winning card. What's the deal? How do we play against one another?"

"We play several one line games, but bet on the full card." He looked at the ten people already seated, ready to play "If one of us gets bingo we can choose where we dine tonight."

"Gosh, I've got to win then." Susan laughed "I know exactly what I want."

"Yeah? Well remember, should you luck up and win, I hate dress up." He looked down at Jobi whose attention was on something down the hall "See something that interest you buddy?"

"Yeah! A Pac Man game!" Jobi's eyes grew big "Sis, can I skip the old bingo game and have a few quarters?"

"If you promise you won't wonder off." Susan pulled several quarters from her change purse. "When you run out of coins, come back in here. Got it?"

"Sure sis, no sweat!" he smiled at Gene. "Have fun losing, Reverend Scott!"

"Right. Just get your butt down to that machine before another funny guy decides to play." He rubbed his head as he watched Jobi dash away.

Gene and Susan sat down at a bingo table. A tall game steward came over with a handful of cards.

"How many?" He spoke with a nasal voice. "You may have up to four cards."

"We'll have one each." Gene smiled at Susan. "One card is all I need to be lucky."

"Yes, be sure mine says 'the luckiest'." Susan returned Gene's smile.

"*Madamoiselle*?" The steward shook his head and handed them a card and some chips to cover the numbers, then walked to the mike "We will start with one row winners. When bingo is called and the numbers checked for a winning card, please empty your cards for the next game. The prize is ten dollars for single line wins."

"Isn't that your friend over there, Gene?" Susan nodded toward William Danfield sitting next to Anna Poke.

"Why, yes it is."

He got the doctor's attention and waved. Danfield turned up his nose, feigning disgust at being caught with the chubby man chaser.

Before Gene or Susan could put down half a dozen chips on their cards, however, Anna Poke would yell out "Bingo!" It happened several times in a row.

Susan shook her head "Don't that woman ever lose?" She began to get nervous about not winning, worrying that her hopes for what she had planned would be ruined.

"Can't give up, Susan." Gene bumped his shoulder against hers. "Charming Miss Poke's luck will run out sooner or later."

"Well, I hope it's sooner because our sweet-talking bingo caller is pulling out his big board."

"Yeah, this is the big one alright. Winner takes all." Gene rubbed his hands together. "Come on lucky numbers!"

"Your numbers might be lucky, Reverend Scott, but mine are winners," Susan laughed softly.

Gene gazed at her, suddenly aware his heart was beating rapidly just from being close to her. The happiness she was feeling made her all the more beautiful. He knew he would have to pull himself away from her tomorrow and try to forget her and the feelings he couldn't shake when she was near him, or in his thoughts.

As Susan looked back into his eyes, the seriousness—and was that longing—in them took her breath away. She felt the cascade of butterflies in her stomach take all at once.

She forced out the words. "Are you ready? To play, I mean?"

"As ready as I'll ever be. Good luck, Susan." He winked, trying to release the intimacy and tension of the moment. He glanced down at his card hoping the game would soon start.

"Alright, the big game where you try to get your card full first." Without a smile he continued, "The winner of the full card will receive $100. We begin now."

Susan stared nervously down at her card as the steward called the numbers. It was all she could do to concentrate on the game. The vision of Gene's eyes locked to hers overwhelmed her.

On her card there were only two spaces left to cover. She glanced at Gene's card. He had three empty spaces left—or did until the caller said "B 6" and Gene smiled and covered up the number.

"Looks like we're even," Susan whispered.

Then she heard Anna Poke say a little too loudly, "Only two left!"

Susan glanced her way and saw her holding two chips over her card, ready to win.

"Darn, this is nerve racking!"

Gene laughed.

All three of them had the next number when the caller announced it. Now each of them had only one empty space left to fill.

"I hope it's time for miss charming Poke's luck to run out!" Susan said to herself.

She held tight to her last chip and crossed her fingers in her lap as the caller plucked the white ball from the cage, examined it and called, "I-15."

Susan jumped straight up "BINGO!" She laughed and clapped her hands.

Gene smiled broadly as he reached out for her hand and helped her back down "It's good you didn't knock your card off. Congratulations, Susan. You finally beat me."

"I don't know which feels better, beating you or that overbearing woman with Dr. Danfield."

Susan watching calmly as the caller's assistant checked her card and declared her the winner. The steward presented her with a new one hundred dollar bill. They came out of the bingo parlor laughing.

"Well, my game came with two prizes, Reverend Scott." Susan held up the bill. "Cash and my choice for dinner and it won't be where Miss Cathy works!"

Gene laughed. He waved at Jobi as he ran toward them his mouth open in amazement at the big prize Susan waved before him.

"Gosh, sis, you won!" he beamed "Where are we eating at?"

"I'll tell you later, Jobi, after we've done a little shopping." She slipped the bill inside her purse. "How 'bout it, Gene, we're right here on the shopping floor and Jobi wants to buy a souvenir from the ship."

He looked at his watch. "How about a quick lunch? You two can shop after that. I need to do a few things to get ready for a meeting with Dr. Danfield tomorrow anyway."

As they left the canteen, Gene said, "I'll meet you at the waterslide in about one hour. Jobi, remember you got to pack whatever you buy. It's got to fit in your luggage."

He waved as he walked toward his cabin and the Andrews siblings made their way quickly to the shops.

Jobi picked out a small replica of their cruise ship. Susan also found exactly what she was looking for: the perfect outfit for her surprise dinner with Gene.

They made their way back to their cabin, changed into swimsuits and got to the pool right on time. Jobi and Susan waved at their big friend when they spotted him on the slide. He returned it, laughing as he made his way to the bottom. They raced up to the top and slid down next to him. His eyes were on Susan's one piece black swimsuit. He thought it made her even prettier as it showed off her perfect curves. He dipped his head down in the water to keep from staring.

"And here I thought you two decided to skip the slide and let me make an idiot out of myself alone." He reached over and touched Susan's cheek "Race you to the top!"

He swam to the edge of the pool and made a dash for the steps, Susan and Jobi right behind him.

They came back down to their cabins laughing at all the fun things they had done, and the funny things that happened.

"You know you looked like a frog when you were swimming." Susan tried to catch her breath "That little girl was screaming so loud. I thought her mother was going to dive in and smack you!"

"How about when you were floating with your eyes shut and that chubby kid jumped in the pool and flipped you over?" Gene laughed loudly. "You thought the whole ship was turning over!"

As he watched Susan unlock the door, he asked, "So what's the plans tonight? How do I dress?" He ran his hand through his wet hair.

"Your famous turtleneck sweater with black pants and a jacket, if you have one." Susan smiled at him. "Nothing too dressy. Just nice. I'll be ready at seven. That's when you show up at our door."

She nodded as she closed the door, then immediately grabbed her brother's arm. "Are you ready to have the time of your life?"

"Sure, sis. What's the big secret? There's not that many places we can eat on this ship. And I think we tried them all."

"That's where you're wrong, little brother." Susan took out her new black jumpsuit. "You've been wanting to check out the Captain's quarters, right, to see how they drive this big ship and the boiler room where all the action takes place?"

"Oh, wow! Sis, are you saying you got us a dinner invitation from the ship's Captain?" Jobi's eyes grew big.

"I'm saying, I got you a special invitation to dine with our Captain." She smiled at her brother, who danced in delight. "It's 'boys' night' and I got you in at the last minute. The girls got to have lunch with the Captain today, now it's your time."

"Yea! Now I remember!" Jobi clapped his hands and pulled out his brown slacks and blue sweater "'Kids' day' with the Captain! I hope he shows us all the neat stuff."

"So," her voice was coy, "you don't mind me spending the night alone with Reverend Scott then?"

"Heck no!" He snapped his fingers. "Hey, I get it now. You got something real romantic planned for you and Reverend Scott. That's why you bought that jumpsuit and matching jacket!"

She nodded. "And the black stack heels and new gold cross neckless." She motioned to the bathroom "I feel generous this evening. You may take your shower first."

"Right. Then you can spend all the time you need without driving me crazy waiting on you to finish." He grinned and grabbed his clothes as he closed the door. She could hear him chattering happily. "Golly. A night with the ship's Captain!"

Gene Scott wasn't prepared for the vision that stood before him when Susan opened her cabin door. The perfect fitting jumpsuit accentuated the curves of her shapely body. Her hair was done in a long braid. Her high heel shoes made her that much taller.

As he slowly—with great appreciation—took in the sight of mature young woman standing before him, he thought to himself, "I'm so glad Jobi is going with us."

"Hi Reverend Scott," Jobi said as he walked past him into the hallway. "Cat got your tongue?" He smiled as he watched the steward coming his way "Mr. Cummings?"

"Yes, you must be Jobi Andrews." The short steward smiled at Gene. Then he noticed Susan and his eyes widened. "Are you . . . Miss Andrews, Jobi's sister?"

"Yes, I am and I appreciate your looking after my brother while he visits with the Captain." She smiled at the steward, purposely avoiding Gene, whom she could feel staring at her. She could feel his uncertainty and anxiety. "Jobi, behave and enjoy your evening."

"You too, sis!" he punched Gene's shoulder, causing him to jump. "You're in for a treat yourself, Reverend Scott. Susan filled me in on your special night. Have fun!"

Before Gene could stop him, Jobi walked away with the steward, happily chatting about the night events. Scott watched Jobi until he was out of sight. He felt Susan touch his arm and turned to face her.

"Reverend Scott, are you afraid to be alone with me? I'll not bite."

He tried to prevent his face from revealing just how reluctant he felt. "Don't be silly, Alice. Show me what you got planned."

He laughed and held her hand as they walked onto the deck. He slowed and started to enter the dining room.

"Nothing doing, Gene Scott," she said with authority. She pulled him forward, passing all the eating places until they reached the elevator.

"Now I know we're not going to see *American Graffiti* with you dressed like that," he teased.

"Nowhere close, mister. We are going much higher." Her chest was full of fearful, joyous anticipation as she led him upward. She wondered how he would like her surprise.

"The top deck?" He stepped outside. "There's no dining up here, young lady."

"No, but there is up there." she pointed to the small overhead lookout room. "A few steps up and we'll be at our dining spot."

"What's up there, Susan?"

Wearing a curious expression, he followed her up the winding steps to the small room where a table had been set up with two chairs. Candles were aglow and soft music played.

"How on earth did you manage this, young lady?"

"It appears my entry into the 'Dining with the Stars' contest paid off, Gene."

She smiled up at him when he pulled the chair out for her then walked across to his and sat down, amazed at her cunning and charm.

"The Captain of this fine ocean liner chose mine, so here we are: dinner for two, compliments of the Captain."

"Good heavens, Susan, what did you say to win this?" Gene watched as a waiter entered their little stateroom and placed two wine glasses down, then walked behind a portable bar. He turned back to Susan "I'm waiting, what did your brilliant mind come up with?"

"I just wrote how a certain Reverend Gene Scott was on his way to Africa to complete dangerous mission work and I thought he deserved to win this prize for devoting his life to God."

She looked into his eyes. They were lost for a moment as each gazed deeply into the other. Finally the waiter cleared his throat to get their attention.

"I will take the order now for your drink of choice. What would like, Reverend Scott, and you, Miss Andrews."

His eyes fell to her low neckline. Gene noticed and drew his attention.

"I'll take a beer." He glanced at Susan and held up his hand. "Wait. This is a special, once-in-a-lifetime night. I'll have a glass of red wine." He smiled at Susan. "What can he get you Susan?"

"I'll have sherry, please." She noticed Gene's eyebrow go up "It's quite alright, Reverend Scott. My dad let me have my first glass on my sixteenth birthday." She glanced away. "Some years ago."

"My, that was at least fourteen years ago, right Susan?" Gene laughed when the waiter got choked.

"Very good sir, sherry for the lady and for you the very best merlot this ship has to offer."

He left to get their wine. Gene and Susan sat across the table from each other, their eyes linked. Neither spoke until the waiter filled their glasses and excused himself to get their dinner.

Gene took a sip. "Mmm. That really is a good wine." He smiled as he watched Susan closely as she drank. "How's your sherry?"

"Excellent, Gene." She set down her glass. "Hope you like steak. They gave me a choice of steak, chicken or fish."

"I love steak, Susan." His eyes irresistibly fell down on her low top, then moved back up into her eyes "Did I tell you how beautiful you look tonight?"

"No you didn't, but thank you." She looked down to avoid his intense gaze. "I wasn't too sure you liked my new outfit."

"So this is what you bought today." He knew he was falling fast and he feared he could not resist the feelings flowing within him. "I guess you spent all your bingo prize on this?"

"I just wanted to look good for you tonight. You look very handsome to me, Gene."

Her eyes were so serious, he had to look out at the growing darkness. "Boy, it gets dark quick out here. Do you think Jobi is about finished?"

He turned to see tears glimmering in her perfect blue eyes, then he heard the waiter coming back. Nothing was said as their plates were set before them.

They ate quietly, saying little. After dinner they walked slowly down the deck toward their cabins. Susan stopped and looked up at the sky, filled with stars. She had not realized it was a full moon.

"Oh Gene, it's as if you could just reach up and touch those stars. They seem so close." Her eyes glistened in the moonlight as she looked at the heavenly vista.

Gene Scott's eyes could look nowhere but upon Susan. He was consumed by the fineness of face, her exquisite form and the feeling welling up inside him.

"Isn't it beautiful, Gene?" Susan ask quietly.

"The most beautiful thing I have ever seen."

He spoke so softly she turned, only to see he was looking at her, not the heavens. Wordlessly his hand cupped her face gently as his eyes focused on her soft lips, then his head began to move down toward her—when the moment was interrupted abruptly by Jobi's call.

"Hey, Reverend Scott, Susan! Boy, did I have a swell night!" He noticed instantly how quiet they were. "Hey, did I come at a bad moment and interrupt something?"

"Why no, sport." Gene drew a deep breath, realizing just how close he had come to kissing Susan. "You're right on time. We were headed down to the cabins. I was just wondering if you had gotten back yet."

For her part, Susan had never felt more frustrated than at that second. She thought, "Gene Scott, you never one time thought of Jobi. If he hadn't interrupted us, you would have kissed me."

"Hey sis, snap out of it! Reverend Scott asked us if we wanted to meet him at ten to play a few games then have lunch tomorrow." Jobi grabbed his sister's hand and broke her reverie. "I think that's neat."

"Sure, Jobi. That sounds wonderful. Thank you, Gene, we would love to join you, but I insist that we buy your lunch for all the time you've shared with us."

She turned away to hide her tears as she unlocked their door. Without looking back, she called "Goodnight," and walked quickly inside, shutting the door behind her.

Gene's head drooped. He closed his eyes, knowing he had disappointed her. He whispered softly, "Goodnight Susan," and walked slowly to his cabin

Chapter Nine

Susan and Jobi had decided to have a small breakfast brought to their room so they could plan their last day with Gene.

"Why didn't Reverend Scott ask us to come up for breakfast like he did yesterday?" Jobi bit down into his Danish. "Think he's tired of us?"

"I think Reverend Scott had a meeting this morning with Dr. Danfield to go over their mission." Susan took a sip of orange juice.

"Yeh. Yesterday when he told us to go shopping, he did say he needed to work on it." Jobi wiped off his sticky lips and said thoughtfully, "Susan when we arrive at Taboo, do you think Reverend Scott will get off at that port too or further up the coast?"

"I'm going to ask him today at lunch." She checked her watch: 8:30. "He told us to meet him at ten to play some games, then have lunch. By the time we get dressed, our fun day will start."

"Sis, I was looking on my map and I can't find Taboo." Jobi spread it out in front of Susan "Where 'bouts is our stop?"

Susan looked down at the atlas showing America and Africa, with the vast ocean in between. "We left from the North Carolina coast and we will arrive somewhere between Senegal and Gambia." She pointed at the location. "Granddad lives several miles outside of Taboo."

"I hope granddad's happy to see us." Jobi folded the map. "I guess we will call him when we arrive, right?"

"I'm not sure, Jobi." Susan picked out a short set to wear. "It all depends on where Reverend Scott gets off."

"Huh? I don't get you sis." Jobi pulled on his shorts. "Our ticket is for Taboo. We gotta get off there."

"Oh yes. I know." Susan went inside the bathroom to finish getting ready.

Gene Scott stood waiting on the deck when Susan and Jobi walked up smiling. He checked his watch, ten sharp.

"Right on time. Let's grab a cue and get to playing."

82

After playing shuffle board and ping pong, Gene led the Andrew siblings to the canteen for lunch. He opened the door for Susan, took her hand and walked over to a back table, Jobi following close behind.

"It's turned out to be another beautiful day." Susan smiled as she sat down "I can't believe we'll be docking tomorrow." she glanced over at her brother "In Taboo."

"Taboo?" Gene picked up his menu. "That's my stop too." He smiled at the Andrews. "Well, for me, I have to leave all the fun and games behind and get serious about this mission in front of me."

"Did your meeting go well with Dr. Danfield this morning?" The waiter came over to take their order. After he walked away, Susan continued, "And how was your breakfast?"

Gene gazed down at his hands, knowing Susan was trying to figure out if his meeting had been that morning. If so, it meant he was free for the day.

"My breakfast was hearty, as was Danfield's. We haven't had our official meeting yet." He took a sip of coffee and rose. "If you two will excuse me for a few minutes, I need to go to the men's room. Too much coffee this morning."

Susan watched until Gene was out of sight before whispering to Jobi, "Do you remember mom and dad said they would send us the new address so we could write them?"

"Yeah, so?"

"Well, I've been thinking about that." She glanced toward the bathroom. "They'll have to send it to the town, because there is no outside delivery in Taboo. When I call them after we arrive, I'll say granddad was in town getting his month's supplies and spotted us."

"Huh?" Jobi stared at his sister. "I don't understand."

"I'll tell them granddad said he had lots of things to keep us busy and we probably wouldn't get back in town for a while so we might not find time to write."

"Why would you tell them that, sis?" His face was full of confusion.

"I'm not entirely sure yet, Jobi, but I'm coming up with something. I've got some ideas." She spotted her handsome preacher headed back toward them.

Gene sat down just as the waiter set down their lunch. He offered a blessing and then smiled at the siblings.

"I didn't see you this morning at breakfast. Was it too early? Did you decide to skip it?"

"Nope, we had it delivered Reverend Scott." Jobi smiled at the cheeseburger in his hand "I'm glad I ate a light breakfast."

"Do you have any more fun things lined up for us today Gene?" Susan asked. "Swimming? Another movie night?" She took a bite of her BLT.

"Eating this fine lunch together is great." He winked at Susan and decided it was best to change the subject and keep things very casual as long as they were together. "You missed our favorite waitress this morning."

Susan straightened and stared at Scott. "I guess she was happy to have you all to herself!"

Gene laughed and patted her on top of her head. "She did ask me where the kids were and if I finally got tired of playing with Alice."

"And did you tell her 'yes'?" Susan looked at him warily. "Well, did you, Reverend Scott? Are you tired of playing with me?"

"Not on your life, beautiful." Immediately he saw the smile form on her lips. "Being with you two kids has really made this trip special. It has taken my mind off the troubles I might be facing when I reach Africa. You were the bright spot on this voyage."

"As you are to us, Reverend Scott."

Susan hated the thought of him going one way and her another once they reached Africa. She just had to think of something. Could she follow him, not with that trunk filled with her and Jobi's clothes? She would pick out a few things to pack in their two smaller suitcases, then maybe it would be possible. She could store the trunk in Taboo or at the dock and get it later when they flew to TarSa.

"Susan, are you going to finish your lunch before your toast gets cold?" Gene looked down at her half-eaten sandwich "Not hungry?"

"I—I was just thinking about all the fun time we shared and how tomorrow we would reach our port." She pushed her sandwich over in front of Gene. "I guess I just loss my apatite thinking this voyage would soon be over."

Gene Scott picked up the half sandwich and took a bite. "When your vacation with your grandfather is over, I guess you two will be headed home."

"To our new home we've never seen. Hopefully this will be our last move. At least that is what dad says." Susan took a sip of water. "We're moving to TarSa, a small island near Hawaii. I've seen pictures, a small charming town with neighborhoods, one church, one school, one hospital with good doctors. There are lots of cute shops."

"I know a little bit about TarSa." Gene nodded. "I've got good friends there. Small world."

He checked his watch and motioned for the waitress. It was time for his meeting with William Danfield. He knew telling Susan and Jobi goodbye was not going to be easy, but he had no choice. Whatever he was feeling for Susan had only grown with the past few days. Goodbye wouldn't be any easier for him either.

After they had finished eating, Scott stood.

"Thanks so much for lunch, Susan. It was kind of you to treat me." He stretched. "Well kids, I had a lovely morning, but now I must get to business." He thumped Jobi lightly on the head. "If I don't see you anymore before we arrive in Africa, please take good care of that pretty 'older' sister of yours, Jobi. She's way too pretty to be running around without a chaperone."

Susan got to her feet quickly, trying to conceal her anxiety. "So where are you going now?"

"I have a meeting with Dr. Danfield later this afternoon. We have to make last minute arrangements before we reach our destination."

"Aren't we going to see you again before we dock in the morning?"

Susan crossed her fingers behind her back.

"I kind of doubt it, Susan. I've been neglecting my last-minute preparation. If I don't get everything done tonight, I'm afraid I'll be putting the whole mission team in a tight squeeze when we reach Africa."

"Maybe I can help you." Her voice rose in excitement despite her effort to seem calm. "I'm actually a very good typist. And I have nice handwriting too, if you need it."

"Susan, sweet Susan, you are so thoughtful and kind to offer. Thank you."

Impulsively, he started to kiss her on the cheek. He glanced at the nearest tables and saw several people staring at them. And at one table a group of middle aged women began to whisper, their eyes fixed on Susan and him, holding her hand. Gene straightened.

"This is something I have to take on, just the doctor and myself. It's mostly planning and discussing things we will be doing. Thank you, though. You are sweet to want to help." He squeezed her hand, turned and walked quickly from the dining room.

When he had disappeared, she looked down at Jobi, staring at her sadly. "Will we ever see Reverend Scott again, sis?"

"Sure we will Jobi," she said firmly and she sat back down next to him. "I have no intention of letting Gene Scott just pop in and out of my life. I won't let him. . . . Delilah didn't give up. Neither will I!"

"Delilah?" Jobi stared at his sister. "What does that mean? I don't get it."

"Never mind Jobi, just trust me. We're going to see lots of Gene Scott." She signed for the bill for lunch and they walked back to their cabin.

The sky grew dark as the evening sun vanished from the sky. The moon was swallowed up by low hanging clouds. The sea whipped against the sides of the ship. Susan lay awake, feeling the rocking of the ship beneath her. A loud rumble of thunder sat her up straight in bed. She glanced over at Jobi, sleeping peacefully.

"Jobi," she called softly. She could tell by his steady breathing that he was sleeping soundly. "What good would it do wake him anyway?" she asked herself.

Even though he was much younger, he always delighted in making fun of her fear of thunder. Why, she wondered, was she still so affected by that terrible night. It was almost seven years ago. At times she believed she had gotten over the fear, only to be terrified when a thunderstorm rolled in. Perhaps this time it was the strange, unfamiliar surroundings that put her so on the edge of panic. And, as always, the memories began to flood her mind.

She had been staying with her grandmother, who was so desperately ill, alone in that huge, strange house—a house that seemed so vast and spooky to a ten-year-old. Though she was alone, she remembered being awakened by the touch of something cold, something she came to perceive as the touch of death. It was, she recognized, the wind blowing on her through the window that her grandmother insisted on keeping open. She rose to lower the window and as she reached the sill, shocking, brilliant light flashed across the black sky. The loud clap of thunder that followed immediately sent her racing down the hallway to her grandmother's bedroom. She tried to turn on the lights, but the storm had knocked out the power. Hands extended before her, she made her way haltingly to where her grandmother lay quietly. Susan could not see her grandmother's face and later she would remember that she had not heard the familiar, rhythmic sound of her grandmother's labored breathing.

Then came another burst of lightning. It illuminated everything in the room, including the form of her grandmother lying on the bed, staring at her through dead, unresponsive eyes. As she remembered it from beneath the covers of her cabin, Susan shuddered.

Again a powerful bolt of lightning flashed across the sky and she covered her ears to try to keep out the blast of thunder that followed. It seemed to shake the entire ship.

Instantly Susan leaped from her bed, threw open the cabin door and flew down the hallway to another cabin. She pounded on the door until it opened and Gene stood before her, staring in sleepy confusion. She burst into tears, unable to express herself, to explain why she was standing there.

"Susan? What's wrong? Is it Jobi?"

She fell into his arms. "No. It's the storm. I freak out when it thunders. Can you just . . . hold me till it goes away. Please."

He covered her gently with his arms. "Susan, do you have panic attacks?"

She nodded holding her sobs at bay as best she could. "I—I'm so sorry. I don 't want to sound like a baby, but—"

There came another horrific clap of thunder and she gripped him tighter, digging her fingers into his firm shoulders. "Can you ask God, please, to make it stop?"

"Susan." His voice was tender. "Everything is going to be alright. You have nothing to be afraid of. The ship is safe and you're here with me." When he felt her relax a bit, he continued, "There we go. That's better."

He brought her into the cabin, closed the door and led her to his bed.

"Please sit down for a moment. Can you tell me about this? How long have you been terrified of thunder?"

She averted her eyes, suddenly feeling stupid and childlike. "I was with my grandmother alone at night during a thunderstorm when she died. The electricity was out and there was no way I could get help." She swallowed. "I was ten at the time." She gazed up into his eyes. "To me, thunder is the hand of death coming to get someone I love."

She burst into tears, unabashed in the safe embrace of Gene's strong arms.

"It's okay to cry." His voice was soft and full of compassion. "It's okay to acknowledge the grief and injustice of it, Susan. Let it all out."

And in that instant, he closed his eyes as well. "Scott, get a hold of yourself, man. What's the matter with you? How can you be having these feelings? How can you think about kissing her? This is totally unlike you. Why do I feel like this? Why do I have the desire to kiss her? God man, she's young enough to be your daughter. This isn't like me at all."

She was sniffing with every other breath, so he handed her a handkerchief.

"Here, Susan, are you going to be alright?"

"Yes, thank you." She took the handkerchief and dried her eyes and wiped her nose. As quickly as she had broken down, she began to compose herself. "I'll clean it and return it to you."

He stood up and helped her to her feet. "Please keep it. It will be a memento to help you remember your shuffleboard teacher." He smiled as he looked into her eyes. She looked deeply into his.

"I don't need a memento to remember you, Gene." Her head tilted back and she drew a deep breath. "And I'm not going to let you forget me either." She opened the door and ran back to her room.

Chapter Ten

Gene gripped the handle on his suitcase as he stared back at the ship. He would not, he had decided, wait to say goodbye to Susan and Jobi. There were too many emotions whirling about between them, he thought. Not just those Susan expressed, but also his own inexplicable feelings.

Dr. Danfield walked beside him chatting about the port where they had disembarked.

"Not too bad, at least for this underdeveloped part of Africa, wouldn't you say Scott?"

"Huh?" Gene stopped, trying to look back over the heads of the departing crowd. For an instant he thought he saw Susan and Jobi walking down the gangplank.

"Scott, what on earth is so interesting back there?" Danfield's voice was irritated. "Did you leave something on the ship?"

"Sorta." He looked at Danfield, who gazed back with a puzzled expression. "Well what are you standing around for, we've got a job to do."

"Me? But—"

"Is that guide—Raven Jones— supposed to meet us here, by the general supply store, doc?"

"Well he said he would meet at the Taboo Hotel." Danfield pointed down the street to a tallest building near the middle of town. "I'm guessing that's probably it."

"Let's go see if we can find him and get a check for that list of supplies we drew up last night."

Scott walked swiftly toward the three story building with Danfield running alongside him and trying to keep up.

Susan and Jobi Andrews followed Scott at a safe distance.

"Hey, sis, are you going to tell me or not?"

"Tell you what, Jobi?" Susan watched the two missionaries enter the hotel.

"Why are we following Reverend Scott?"

"Well, do you remember how in his sermon he said that we

are all a big team working for God, and that we should help one another?" She smiled at her brother. "Well, Gene is going on a dangerous mission. We might be of some help to him."

Jobi 's eyes brightened. "Okay. Sure. I'm all for helping Scott. . . . But what about Granddad?"

"Well, I've been thinking about that, actually. You see, Granddad doesn't know we're coming, does he?"

"Right! So we follow Scott instead and no one will be the wiser." Jobi giggled. "We'd better call Mom and Dad and tell them we have arrived, though. Then we will be safe."

"Good thinking, Jobi." She looked around "Look, Jobi, stay here and keep a lookout for Gene. I'll go find a phone and call Dad. Okay?"

"You bet, sis. I'm a great spy!"

"Well don't get overconfident. You might slip up." She hurried away.

The hotel manager directed Scott and Danfield to a table in the bar. There sat a rather shaggy haired middle aged man, whose skin had been parched and weathered to a deep tan. Scott and Danfield made their way to his table.

"Jones?" Scott asked.

"Yeah! That's me alright. Don't tell me. Let me guess." He rubbed his unshaved chin. "Hmm. Scott. Yeh, you're that preacher. Gotta be.You fit that description sure 'nough."

Scott, not in the mood for any nonsense, leaned toward him and produced a written list. "Jones, I want you to look over this list Danfield and I made out to see if we left off anything we might need." Scott handed the paper to Jones.

"Let me see. Jeeps, yeh. Food supply for 'bout three weeks, good!" He smiled, revealing a prominent gap where a tooth was missing. "Medical supplies. Guns—with a question mark." He looked up. "What 's this here question mark fer?"

"I put it there, sir!" Danfield spoke up adamantly. "Scott feels we might have need of firearms. I say forget them. They can only cause trouble."

The gap-toothed smile emerged again, this time with a bit of irony. "Actually Scott is absolutely right, doc. Weapons are a must, if for nothing else but to protect yourself from nature. Them there wild animals ain't at all friendly. And I ought to know. I deal with this quite a lot in my business."

"And I say taking guns with us will only stir the natives up. They won't trust us. They'll think we're gonna hurt them." Danfield' s voice took on a high tone of agitation.

Jones, staring at Danfield, took his time answering. His voice was entirely serious. Any note of flippancy was gone. "Look Danfield, you are right this being a matter of trust, but not the way you think. You want to talk about the 'locals'? Because I deal with them too. And you trust them not to be trustworthy. They are completely unpredictable. Those tribes you're going to encounter do all kind of things without warning. In my experience, you have to be prepared for anything. And if they suddenly take a hankering to do me in, I, for one, want to get in on the action instead of just standing there all peaceful like a saint, just waiting to be killed!"

"All right, Jones." Scott's voice was not loud, but intense. "Did we leave anything off the list?"

"Yep." The flippant note returned to his voice. "Something very important." He turned his mug up and finished his drink.

"Well what, for heaven sakes. We haven't got all day." Danfield squirmed in his chair anxiously.

Scott motioned for Danfield to rise. "Go get us all a beer, doc, and stop being so fidgety. You're making us all nervous."

He watched the doctor, wearing a disgruntled expression, walk slowly to the bar, then rose and took a seat next to Raven Jones. "Relax. Calm down and go on."

"I hope that thar guy straightens up, Scott. The jungle is no place fer weakness, or for people who are too idealistic to be realistic. Especially when you're in BuKuba country." Jones leaned on the table and tilted his head toward Scott. "Now on the other hand, you look like the jungle type to me, Scott. All them thar muscles."

"Thanks, Jones. Although I don't plan on being Tarzan."

Danfield returned with their glasses and Scott took one of the beers.

"Thanks, doc. Now sit down and relax." He took a swallow of the cold beer. "Boy, I needed that! So tell us, Jones, what did we omit on our list?"

"Gifts, reverend. You'll find the natives far easier to handle if you have interesting, delightful gifts."

"Yes, Scott, I've read about this many times before. To show that you've come in peace and to show friendship." Danfield smiled proudly.

"Well, doc, that seems pretty trivial and manipulative to me," Scott said. "But by all means, we mustn't forget the gifts."

Jones stood up. "So when do you gentlemen want to get started? Are the rest here: Michael Sorensen and James Tabor?"

"No," Danfield said. "We received a wire that they will be waiting for us at the Babutoo village. They flew in on a private plane. It's on our way, so there's no time lost."

Scott stood as well and finished his beer. "Well let's get busy and pick up these supplies."

Concealed fifty yards away, Susan and Jobi watched Scott, Dr. Danfield and the stranger fill the Jeeps with supplies.

"Can you make out what all they're taking?" Susan shielded her eyes from the brilliant sun.

"Must .be food, medicine and I think I see . . . yeh , guns." Jobi turned to his sister. "How do we go about getting a gun?"

"Oh darn, Jobi, there has to be a way." Susan put her arms around his shoulder and held him against her. "Look. They're pulling out!"

The three Jeeps sped down the dirt street, leaving only a trail of' dust.

"Jobi, we have to think of something. Fast."

"Don't worry, sis. Just leave everything to me."

Jobi grasped Susan's hand and led her into the supply store.

"Good day, sir," Jobi said to the clerk. "How's business?"

The man behind the counter frowned at Jobi. "What's it to you, kid?"

"Well, we came to bring you some—business, that is." Jobi smiled confidently. "Our dad sent us back to get two more guns, another box of grub and one more box of medical supplies."

A smile of disbelief creased his face. "Oh, he did, did he? And just who might your dad be, sonny?"

"Well Reverend Gene Scott. Didn't you just talk to him? Our family is here to do mission work. We just arrived this morning."

Susan managed to maintain a serious, sincere expression when

92

A New Beginning

the clerk raised his eyes to her. Clearly he was still skeptical.

"Well, missy, are you the preacher's daughter?"

"Well yes sir, of course. Our dad always takes all of us with him on his mission trips. He wouldn't dream of going anywhere without the whole crew. And part of that is because he gets all excited about going into the field and forgets things or underestimates what he's going to need—like today. That's why he sent us back for what he forgot. Now if you don't mind, could we please have those extra supplies. Please. And just put them on Dad's charge."

"The whole family, huh?" His voice was ripe with suspicion. "Well, alright. Frankly I can't imagine what else you'd need these supplies for except mission work. But something sure smells fishy around here."

"I don't think there are any fish around here, sir," Jobi said. "But we will pass along to Dad how reluctant you were to fill his order."

"Just so he can assure you that we're legitimate," Susan added.

The clerk turned to his assistant. "Get them what they want so I can get them out of my hair."

"Oh, sir." Susan tried to keep her voice calm. "We're going to need an extra Jeep to carry all this."

The storekeeper's jaw dropped. "And your daddy's going to pay for all this, missy?"

"Yes. We were told to put this on the mission account."

"And who is going to drive this Jeep, missy? You?"

"Oh yes, I drive all the time at home." Susan started to show him her new driver's license before realizing he would see her last name wasn't "Scott."

"And have you ever driven a Jeep before?"

"Well not a Jeep, but a stick shift, yes. That was part of our mission training at home, to learn how to drive a standard transmission. And by the way, do you know by any chance did Dad mention which route he was taking?"

"Yeah, we actually gave him directions to the camp. We'll get it for you. . . . How is it that you don't know where you're going?" Now he looked amazed and bewildered.

"Well there's that forgetful Gene Scott again. He told us what to take but not which way to take it. And this is our first day in this mission field."

"Dad just does this kind of stuff," Jobi added for emphasis. "He's the original 'absent minded missionary.' I don't know how he survived before we came along to take care of him." He gazed at the ceiling and shook his head in mock disgust.

"Jobi," Susan said sharply, "I'm sure this dear man is far too busy to hear about our family issues. Anyway, Dad survived because of God's miraculous intervention. Now come along." She grabbed him by the arm and hurried him out of the store.

"You are amazing," she said quietly.

"Oh, like you didn't just join right in there, sis. And all on the spur of the moment. We were a great team—you know, just like Reverend Gene said. I guess we're God's secret missionary team."

The store assistant brought the Jeep around and they watched as it was loaded with their supplies.

Jobi climbed into the passenger's seat. "You have to drive off smoothly. The old clerk is sure to be watching to see if you can really drive."

"Alright. We've got to get going." Susan started the Jeep.

A marked map in his hand, the clerk walked out to them. "Here is your route. I think it's all clearly marked. And it's in English."

Susan gave him a genial smile. "You are so kind, sir. We will pass along to Dad just how helpful you've been."

"Right. Well do tell your dad I want to talk to him when comes back this way. Meanwhile, just go down the road until you come to a fork. Take the left. That will lead you to Babutoo village. That is where he was headed, right."

"That's our first stop, I think," Susan said thoughtfully.

"Thank you for your help, sir," Jobi called from the other side of the Jeep. "My father will really appreciate what you have done for him." Quietly he added, "I hope."

Susan let the clutch out slowly and the Jeep scarcely jerked as they headed down the road, waving goodbye to the storekeeper, who stood watching, hands on hips.

The village of Babutoo was a very small, dusty, cluster of dwellings at the junction of grasslands and jungle. Scott pulled his Jeep up behind Raven Jones's.

Jones emerged from his Jeep shouting. "This is probably

where you'll find Sorensen and Tabor, Scott! Good luck to you. I'm going to the one civilized location in this hovel to get a beer. If you need me fer anything, just ask anybody where the bar is."

Danfield watched him walk away warily. "I don't know how much help that man is going to be to us."

"Funny you would say that, doc. He said exactly the same thing about you. You keep worrying about things that just aren't that important." He nodded toward the run-down building in front of which they had stopped. "This must be the hotel."

Scott walked into the lobby of the decrepit structure. The fan over head turned, but threw off very little air. Scott dinged the desk bell loudly.

"Anybody here?"

A short, fat man came from the back room. "All the noise isn't necessary, sir. I'm not deaf. I take it you want a room."

"Yeh. One room with three beds." Scott produced his pack of cigarettes. "Can I smoke in here."

"Yes. Of course."

"Okay. Do you have a Mr. Sorensen and a Mr. Tabor staying here?"

"If they're in the village and they don't live here, then I reckon I do." The man smiled. "This here is the only hotel in Babutoo." He turned the registration book around. "You can look for yourself. I sometimes have trouble reading people's names. Sometimes on purpose."

Scott looked down at the dusty book. His eyes grew wide when he saw listings for "Mr. and Mrs. Sorensen" and "Mr. and Mrs. Tabor."

He restrained the astonishment he was feeling. "Are there ladies with the gentlemen, Mr.—Mr.—?"

"Rubble, Fred Rubble ." He smiled. "'Ladies,' did you say? I don't think I would call them 'ladies.'"

Scott felt his face growing hot and red. "Where will I find the rooms of Sorensen and Tabor?"

"Up the stairs to the right. Rooms 7 and 8. I'm fairly sure you're going to be interrupting some good times."

"Well, I hope they've had their fill. We're leaving in the morning."

Scott climbed the stairs without hesitation and went to room

7, Michael Sorensen's room. Danfield caught up with him just as he knocked loudly on the door.

A very feminine voice came from within the room. "Hey, Michael, don't knock the door down, sweetheart. I'm coming."

The door opened and before him stood a gorgeously sexy brunette wrapped in a towel. "Ohhh." Her voice was intended to register surprise, but she exuded only curiosity at the sight of the two strange men standing at her door. "And who are you?"

Slowly, distinctly, he replied, "The Reverend Gene Scott. I would like to speak with Mr. Sorensen. Where is he?"

Next to him he heard a soft moaning sound. He turned to see Danfield biting his lip, his eyes flowing down the shapely form of the woman.

She gave the doctor a sensuous smile. "See anything you like, sir?"

Scott pounded Danfield on his back, causing him to cough.

"Doctor. His name is Dr. Danfield. He was just examining you for obvious deformity. It's part of his responsibility as a missionary."

"Oh," Danfield said, "I'm so sorry, my dear. I never meant to stare." His face lit up an astonishing bright red.

"Oh, don 't let it upset you, Doctor, honey. I've grown used to men staring." She looked up at Scott. "Michael is in room 8, talking to James."

"Who's that you 're talking to, Jackie?"

"It's more missionaries, Ali."

A second woman, this one wearing a floor length nightgown, peeked over her co-worker's shoulder and stared into Scott's blue eyes.

"Well, hello there."

"Hello, miss. You must be James 'wife.'"

"Wife? Oh, yes. Yes I am." She laughed softly and winked at her friend, who laughed as well. "Just pop on over. I think the guys are expecting you, Reverend."

"Thanks."

Grabbing Danfield's arm, he stepped over to room 8. "Eyes this way, Danfield. We're here to do a job. So keep your mind off those ladies. I think they're spoken for by these guys anyway."

Scott knocked on the door. A tall slim man with long hair opened the door.

"You must be Reverend Scott. I'm James Tabor. Come on in, if you can stand the heat." He pointed toward the fan dangling from the ceiling. "It's not the best cooling system in the world, but I guess it's better than nothing."

"I think I would just as soon have nothing." Danfield sat down on the bed. "I don't see why anyone would want to lie here in this heat."

"You chose to come, doc. We've got bigger issues here, so quit complaining." Scott walked over to the window and looked out. "Where's your friend Sorensen?"

"Oh. He went out to get us a beer. He'll be back shortly. Just have a seat and relax." Tabor motioned toward a chair. "Hopefully it won't fall apart. This whole place looks like it might collapse any minute."

"So, Tabor, if you don't mind me asking, why did you bring your wife to Africa?" He eased carefully into the rickety chair. "I mean, there's just not much to do around here. Aren't you afraid they'll get bored hanging around the village?"

"Well . . . I . . . they—"

Michael Sorensen walked into the bedroom carrying a sack of beer. Tabor's face was filled with relief.

"Mike, this is Reverend Scott and Dr. Danfield."

"Hey, I'm glad you two made it alright." Sorensen sat the beer down and shook Scott's hand. "When do we get started?"

"In the morning. Bright and early."

Tabor tore open the sack and began handing out beer.

Scott popped open the tab on the cool can. "So Sorensen, I was just asking James why would you bring your wives to Africa. There's so little to do in the village and it's dangerous in the jungle."

"Oh. Well, Jackie and Ali wouldn't dream of letting us come without them. I mean, if you knew them the way we do, you would understand." Sorensen grinned at his friend.

"Michael's right. Why, they never let us go anywhere without them. Except of course the bathroom." Tabor laughed as if he had said something funny.

"Well, I hope for their sake, they brought plenty to keep them busy." Scott took a big sip of beer.

"Well, ah . . . Reverend Scott, they were . . . planning to come along with us." Sorensen smiled sheepishly.

"No. No way. This is where I draw the line." Scott stood up. "No way do they risk their lives going to the mission field. They go back wherever they came from or they stay right here!"

"Oh no we're not." The woman named Ali stepped through the open doorway, Jackie—now clothed in a bathrobe—right behind her. "We're going with you."

"We certainly are Reverend Scott!" Jackie's voice was silky smooth and seductive. "And that is final." She walked over to Sorensen.

"The jungle is no place for ladies, ladies." Scott bent his can and threw it into the waste can.

"Who said we were ladies?" Ali laughed coyly.

"Excuse me. Let me reword that. The jungle is no place for females. And where we are going in the jungle is extremely dangerous." Scott feigned a smile.

"If you're trying to scare us, Reverend, it isn't working." Jackie put her hands on her hips. "And I think you should know that, if we don't go, neither do Michael and James."

"Jackie, we need to listen to what Rev. Scott has to say," Michael said, pulling her down on the edge of the bed beside him.

"Oh, really? Didn't you tell me this was his first trip to Africa?" She smiled when Sorensen nodded. "Well, it may surprise you, Mr. Scott, to know that I have been on a jungle safari with my father. He even let me shoot at big game."

"I've been on several shooting and hunting expeditions too," Ali added. "And I'm good, damn good."

Tabor's eyes widened and he nodded silently.

Scott's voice was measured as he responded. "The BaKuba are cannibals. BaKuba country is no happy hunting ground. Even beyond that, there's a lot of danger involved in every aspect of this work." His voice gradually rose, as if he were concluding a sermon and coming to the most important point. "Woman only get in the way of the work we have been called here to do. I say you stay here or you go home."

Jackie's tone was tart as she responded. "And I say if we stay, the boys stay. And that, Mr. Scott, is final!"

"That works for me. All of you can stay here." The chair creaked as he rose and headed toward the door. "I'm not going to be responsible for two helpless, untrained women. I've got enough to keep me busy now as it is."

"Come on, Gene," Sorensen stood and approached him. "You're going to need our help. Please Reverend Scott, you need our help. James and I can watch out for the women. I promise you they won 't give you any trouble. At the first sign of them doing anything out of the way, we will send the back."

"We are both excellent shots, Mr. Scott. The way Mike tells it, you need all the help you can get. And if you're leaving in the morning, you don't have time to find anyone else." She gave him a seductive smile that reminded him of Gloria Weber and of Cathy, the server on board the ship. "Well, what do you say? I bet we could all have a lot of fun out in the bush."

Scott stared at her, then the others, reflecting. "I absolutely do not like this idea. Still, this mission was designed to have four workers and a guide. We all have our roles and they are all necessary. Danfield and I can't do everything. So I'm faced with a choice of canceling the mission trip altogether or being blackmailed into taking along two people who will be more of a burden than help. If I want to do what God is calling me to do, I guess I don't have much of a choice." Abruptly he turned to walk out the door, then looked back over his shoulder. "Remember that I am in charge. Be ready to leave at six in the morning. Don't bother complaining to me about anything, because I'm not listening and I told you not to go. Is that clear?"

"Oh, yes sir." Ali stood at attention and gave a military salute.

He shook his head. "As nasty as the jungle can get, we will just have to endure it." His eyes moved to each of the four. "I've given you fair warning."

Danfield, smiling sheepishly, watched him as he stormed out of the room.

"Reverend Scott always tends to make a big thing out of everything," he said, smiling at Jackie. "Speaking for myself, I'm glad you ladies are coming. Something nice to look at out there in that ugly wild wilderness."

"Why thank you, doctor. What a sweet thing to say." Jackie winked at him.

"Yeh." Sorensen's tone was cynical. "Well you can look Danfield, but hands off. He put his arm around her waist possessively. "She's all mine. Understood·?"

"And Ali is just for me." James pulled the girl onto his lap. "Frankly, I don't even want you looking all that much either."

"Oh James" Ali hit him lightly on the head. "You wonderful, skinny, lovable man."

"Don't worry, fellows. I wouldn't dream of interfering with your relationships." His eyebrows arched. "With your wives." He smiled and stepped into the hall. "Guess I'll go find my room. See you in the morning."

"Yes, good bye Dr. Danfield," Jackie called after him, then hugged Sorensen's neck. She kissed him on the mouth. "Come along, lover boy. We had better get to bed if we have to get up at the crack of dawn."

"Jackie's right," Ali said. "I believe Scott will leave us if we aren't ready to go."

"I think I like Scott," Sorensen said, leading Jackie to the door." He makes good sense, even if he is wound a little tight."

"Yeh, girls. You both would be a lot safer here." Tabor smiled at Ali.

"Nothing doing," she replied. "We're going with you—if for no other reason than to prove to that good-looking woman hater that we are capable of taking care of ourselves."

"Ali's right!" Jackie smiled broadly. "Now, come on. To bed we go."

"Sleep well kids," Tabor said as they closed the door. He turned to his paramour. "So, are we not making love tonight? Will that tire you out so you miss our departure time?"

"That's right. And the same goes for you, Romeo. I need you fresh as a daisy."

James fell back on the bed. "Shit. What's the point of going to bed if you're just going to go to sleep?"

"That sounds like something a sex maniac like you would say." She laughed and slipped off her nightgown before crawling under the sheet. "'Night, sweet one."

"'Night angel." He closed his eyes, trying to force the image of his sexy lover from his mind.

Susan and Jobi leaned their heads against the steel back wall of the Jeep. From where they had parked at the edge of the village, they could see the three supply vehicles, but they could not be seen.

Susan smiled at her brother. "Try to get some sleep, Jobi. We have to be on our toes. Knowing Gene, he's going to get up and leave early and we can't afford to let him get way ahead of us."

"I sure need some sleep after that ride, alright." He rubbed the back of his neck. "I know you got smoother as we went along, but all that jerking from shifting gears just about got the best of me."

"I know. I'm sorry. I'm not used to this standard transmission. I'll probably be better tomorrow." She closed her eyes. "Now go to sleep. And wake me if you wake up first."

"Right. . . . Good night, sis. Jobi closed his eyes and instantly was fast asleep.

Chapter Eleven

Scott made his way down the hall banging on the doors of the others in the mission group.

"Alright everybody, if you're going with me, you better fall out." He walked quickly down the steps to the desk. "Rubble, where are you?" He pounded the bell with his fist. "Hey, is anyone up around here, besides me?"

Mr. Rubble came running from his room in the back his hair an uncombed mess. He put his hand over the bell as if to protect it from Scott.

"Reverend Scott, that is quite enough. I appreciate your sense of urgency, but you must remember that your colleagues do not make up all the guests in the hotel. Others are trying to sleep as well."

Scott sighed, hands on hips and his head drooping. "Everyone is supposed to be up already." He looked at the clerk. "And I happen to know, Mr. Rubble, there' s no one here. but my little ungodly party." Sizing up the clerk, he began to laugh at the absurdity of the situation. "Well, you didn't have to get all fixed up for me Rubble."

And someone laughed behind him. Scott turned to find Jackie and Ali standing on the bottom step.

"I think Rubble is cute with his hair pointing in every direction, don't you Ali?"

Jackie smiled over at the blushing fat cheeks. "Oh, most certainly." She winked at Rubble. "I certainly hope we have time to eat some breakfast before we depart."

"Of course," Scott said. "Why shouldn't we eat, since we're waiting on half the group." He turned back to Rubble. "Could you get us some breakfast please?"

The clerk turned wordlessly and disappeared.

Scott looked at the women. "So where do we eat around here?"

"You mean you haven't eaten in Mr. Rubble's fine dining room, Reverend Scott?"

A New Beginning

Jackie took one of his arms and Ali quickly took the other.

"Please allow us to show you 'Chez Fred.'"

They led him into a tiny room with three bare tables.

"Isn't it swell?"

Scott pulled out chairs for the woman. "It serves its purpose, I guess." He sat down and leaned on the table. "So be straight with me, why are you two so determined to go on this mission? Do you really not grasp just how dangerous this is going to be?"

"Our going makes as much sense as your going. Could you explain your reasons for going in a way that would make sense to us, Scott?"

Rubble appeared holding a tray with six unappetizing plates. Jackie took them from him.

"Thank you. We'll just leave them all here. The guys will be down shortly."

Scott grimaced as he tasted the food. "Well, ladies, what are the chances I can talk you out of going? I'm not saying this as a male chauvinist pig. I'm talking about your welfare. I'm saying this for your own good."

"Thanks for caring, but we really can take care ourselves."

"Oh, what's the use? Women never listen to me anyway." He reached for the salt. "I expect this will help the flavor of breakfast. Nothing could hurt it."

"Not the best breakfast I ever had," Ali said, swallowing a bite of the lumpy eggs.

James and Michael joined the group. Danfield came down ten minutes later.

"What took you so long?" Scott, impatient and ready to leave, stood up.

"Couldn't get my hair to do a dern thing," Danfield laughed.

"You 're worse than any woman I ever waited on." Scott walked toward the door, calling back over his shoulder. "Well, don't be a sissy about eating, Danfield. What I don't need on this job is a sissy shit getting in my way."

Sorensen and Tabor, who choked on his coffee, erupted in laughter.

"Scott, please, no more funny remarks while I'm eating." He cleared his throat.

Jackie and Ali stood up laughing.

"Wait up Scott, we will go on out with you," Jackie said. "Hurry Michael, I'll be waiting."

He winked at her. "Okay, hon."

Susan and Jobi watched as Scott stepped out of the hotel with Jackie and Ali.

"Who are those women, Jobi?"

"How should I know? Am I a mind reader all a sudden?"

"Scott didn't mention anything about women on the trip." Susan gritted her teeth. "Oh, I wonder who they are?"

Sorensen, Tabor and Danfield stepped out of the door of the hotel.

"There's the doc and two more fellows."

Jackie took Mike Sorensen's arm and James Tabor helped Ali in a Jeep. Susan heard herself sigh in relief.

"See, sis, nothing to worry about. "Jobi gave a relieved laugh as well.

"Thanks, Jobi, but I was never worried." She motioned to the backseat. "Why don't you get us out something to eat?"

"Good idea. I'm starved." Jobi reached in the box and pulled out a bag of donuts. "How about this?"

"That's perfect! I'm starved too." She took a big bite of a doughnut, never taking her eyes off Scott. She sat up straight when she heard Scott yelling to his party.

"All set? Let's roll these wheel."

When she saw the Jeeps moved at a steady pace down through the middle of the little village, Susan started the motor of her Jeep.

"Hold on Jobi."

"Don't worry," he laughed. "I intend to hang on for dear life!"

"Ha, ha!"

Susan jerked the gear into second as she made her way through the village, following Scott's dusty path.

The road to BaKuba was bumpy and the further they got from Babutoo the thicker the growth hung around and over the road. They rode for several hours until they came to a river. Raven stopped the lead Jeep and pointed across the river.

"After we cross that there river, Scott, we are in BaKuba country." He spat tobacco juice. "Better tell them fellers to take it

104

easy crossing this river. They wouldn't want to get stuck in there with them crocodiles lying over there jest waiting fer their supper."

Scott gazed at the motionless gray shapes of crocodiles lying along the river bank. He stood and turned around.

"Alright, listen to me. See this river? Well that's our only way of getting in to BaKuba territory. Now I want you to follow close behind Jones and me. And be careful that you don't drowned out your motor." He pointed to the crocodiles on the bank. "They're not particular what they eat, as long as it's fresh."

Ali turned back to look at the trailing Jeep for Jackie's reaction. Jackie made a face back at her."

"I don't think I want to serve myself to those fellows for lunch. Do you?"

"No way." She turned to Tabor. "Keep this baby going, or I will faint and you'll have two problems."

"Where's that brave hunter who could take care of herself?" Tabor teased her.

"James, this is no time to be cute." She slapped his knee. "Now get serious and get us through the river."

"You ready back there?" Scott shouted. "Better have your guns ready."

"Thanks," Jackie mumbled quietly, her eyes wide.

"All ready back here Reverend." Sorensen looked at Jackie and smiled. "Take it easy, baby. I'll get you over there, safe and sound."

"That's my Michael. I know I can depend on you, sweetheart." She kissed him gently on the lips.

"Come on. Let's go." Scott waved the go ahead and Jones drove the lead Jeep slowly into the water. Tabor followed and Sorensen took up the rear. The crocodiles scarcely moved, only lifted their heads to watch as the Jeeps made their way slowly through the water.

Jones laughed. "Look at those bastards, just waiting for a chance to snatch a free meal."

"Well, I don't have anyone to spare, so they had better look elsewhere for their meal."

Scott looked back to gauge how the rest were coming along. At last, Jones pulled out of the water, followed by the other two Jeeps.

Scott laughed. "We made it! But we got a lot more work cut out for us."

"You had better believe it. That little river crossing is nothing compared to what's waiting fer you out there." Jones nodded toward the thick jungle.

"We better move a little further before it gets dark Jones." Scott turned back to the others and called, "We're going just a little further. Then we'll break out the tents. Let's keep moving."

"Good ideal!" Ali shouted back, then turned to Tabor. "James, I sure don't want to camp by this river and wake up with one of those fat crocs staring at me."

"Well you are a looker." When she reacted in surprise, he laughed and said, "Me either, baby. I'd rather be safe in the jungle with the lions and snakes."

Ali trembled. "Oh, shut up!" She pulled her knees up under her arms and tried to relax.

They had gone about a mile when Scott noticed a large washed out place in the road ahead of them.

"Better take it slow here, fellows," he called. "There's a big hole across the road and you could get hung up if you're not careful."

Jones guided his Jeep as far to the right as possible and stopped. "Scott, if some of those branches were cut back a piece, we could pass right through."

"Alright"

Scott got out of the Jeep with a bush knife and started hacking the thick vines.

Michael called to him from the back Jeep. "Want us to help Scott?"

"I've got it."

The incredibly sharp blade in Scott's sure grip slashed through the undergrowth effortlessly.

Jackie walked up to Ali and leaned against the Jeep.

"Would you just look at those muscles."

"I am." She smiled back at James who was busy chatting to Mike. "He certainly has got what it takes."

"He certainly does. That 'Great Scott' is all man." Jackie laughed. "Could you imagine having that beside you in bed?"

"Could you imagine having that inside you in bed?" Ali took

her friend's hand. "We're awful! If James and Mike heard us talking like this—"

"I know. They would feel like killing us . . . until we changed their minds," Jackie laughed. "Can we help it that Scott is so damn sexy."

"Yeh! And a man of God too. That we can't forget. . . . Even though I keep trying." Ali smiled at him when Scott looked back their way. "All finished, Scott?"

"Right." He laid the knife in the back of the Jeep. "Alright, let's roll!"

He jumped in and Jones drove around the hole in the newly made path. The rest followed closed behind.

Susan pulled to a stop when she reached the river.

"Now what—a dead end?"

"Can't be, sis. They had to come this way." Jobi looked up and down the river and then across toward the far side. "Hey, I can see the road. It continues on the other side."

"You mean I have to drive this Jeep across the river?" She swallowed.

"Looks like it." Jobi smiled at his sister. "You can make it, sis. Come on, where's the old Andrews spirit?"

She sat up straight. "You're right, Jobi. If Reverend Gene made it, so can we. He would want us to be brave, right?"

"Right." He watched her as she sat staring at the water. "So, what are you waiting for?"

"I'm going, I'm going." She closed her eyes. "Oh please, let us make it. Let us make it." She started across the water slowly trying to aim straight for the road—which seemed like an eternity away—waiting on the far side. "So far so good."

"Oh yeh!" Jobi gripped the edges of his seat, eyes wide, as he suddenly saw the danger lying on the river bank.

"Jobi?" Susan laughed softly. "I guess it could be worse."

"You bet it could," he swallowed, "because we are not alone."

"Huh? What do you mean, Jobi?" Susan glanced over at her brother.

"Just keep looking straight ahead, sis, and no matter what you do, don't stop this Jeep till we get out of the river."

Her voice dropped to a whisper. "Why, Jobi. What is it?"

"Crocodiles. Sunning on the bank."

"Oh!" She gripped the wheel and drew a quick breath. "Please, let us make it. Oh Gene, how I wish you were here."

"It's alright, sis, we're almost there." Jobi began to pat her shoulder, patting harder the closer they drew to the shore. "Just a little further." Involuntarily, he rose in the seat, looking out the passenger window at the ground beneath them as they rose out of the river. He sat back down with a huge sigh of relief. "Congratulations, you made it!"

Despite the roughness of the road, Susan shifted into a higher gear and drove away from the river rapidly.

"The further away I get from those crocodiles, the safer I'll feel."

"Yeh. You and me both." Jobi laughed sheepishly. "They didn't look none too friendly."

"I'll take your word for it. I was trying to avoid eye contact." She laughed softly.

The sky was beginning to grow dark and the vines hanging thick overhead made it hard to see the road.

"We have to stop soon, Jobi. It's getting hard to make out the road."

"Don't you think we should get as close to Scott and the others as we can?" He gazed around them. "It could get dangerous out here at night."

She looked around and nodded in anxious agreement. "I suppose you're right I would feel safer if I knew Gene were in shouting distance."

She drove more slowly as the darkness closed in on them rapidly. Dusk had obscured the washed out area of road when they came to it and she ran right into it, the Jeep stalling immediately. Susan remained calm. She tried backing up and easing forward, but the vehicle simply would not budge.

She looked at Jobi in defeat. "It's stuck, Jobi. What are we gonna do now?"

Jobi was also trying to remain calm. "I guess the best thing to do is to wait until morning. Maybe we can see better then and we can figure a way to get out." He took his sister's hand. "It's gonna be alright, sis. Reverend Scott can't be too far in front of us. Hey, they probably stopped hours ago."

"Yes, of course they did." She smiled at him. "We'll get this Jeep going first thing in the morning."

Scott had awakened early and was almost finished preparing breakfast when Sorensen and Tabor emerged from their tents, walking lazily toward him.

"That sure smells good, Scott," Tabor said, standing above him and stretching. "Anything we can do to help?"

"Yeh, hand me them plates." He pointed to a box. "Mike, you can pour coffee for everyone. Speaking of which, are they up?"

Sorensen laughed. "Oh you bet. I rolled Jackie out right behind me. And she wasn't too happy about it either."

"How touching." Scott chuckled. "So have the little ladies decided yet that they should never have come along.?"

"Don't be silly, Reverend. I'm overjoyed." Jackie stretched her arms above her head. "Give me the outdoor life any day."

Ali stepped out of her tent wearing a short set that matched Jackie's.

"Now I feel cool as a cucumber. Although soaking in a hot bath would be nice."

"No baths for a while, ladies." Scott looked up from the fire at them. "Do you plan on wearing those outfits in this particular jungle?"

"They beat wearing those pants we wore yesterday. I nearly burned up." Ali sat down on a log.

"What 's wrong with these shorts anyway?" Jackie joined her friend. "Tarzan wore practically nothing. And look at the natives. They dress very cool."

Scott nodded slowly in disbelief. "You have no idea what a secure feeling it gives me, knowing I'm surrounded in the heart of the jungle by a bunch of people who were educated at the movies."

Danfield, who had been standing in the doorway of his tent door listening to the conversation, stepped toward the fire. "You know they're absolutely right, Scott. Tarzan never wears any more than a swimsuit. Less, actually." He laughed.

"Very well, suit yourselves, ladies. Wear those fancy little shorts all you want. I'm sure it will make the day for all the disease carrying mosquitos. And assorted other biting insects." He swallowed the rest of his coffee. "Hurry up and finish breakfast.

We've wasted enough time talking already."

Quickly he began to disassembly his tent.

"If you wait for me, Scott," Danfield said with his mouth full, "I'll help you."

"Just keep eating, doc." Scott said quietly. "I'll be finished before you are. Anyway, if you take it down as well as you put it up, I don 't want your help."

Susan opened her eyes slowly. She stared up at the huge snake hanging in the tree overhead. Her eyes grew huge as she gripped Jobi's arm and whispered.

"Jobi. Jobi don't move a muscle."

"Huh?" He shifted and rubbed his eyes. "What is it?

"Above us. In the tree." She swallowed. "Do you see it?"

She realized, when he jerked and froze, that he did.

"I see it alright. . . .What we do, sis?"

"I'm going to start the Jeep, nice and slow. Maybe the noise will make it crawl away."

"Yeah, or maybe it will crawl down to see what's going on." He stared helplessly at the enormous serpent. "I wonder if this is the kind that poisons you with its venom or wraps itself around you and smothers you?"

"Well, we can't just sit here until we learn firsthand."

She turned the key and the Jeep fired to life. She looked up

"Well, it still hasn't moved. I'm going to get us out of this hole."

She jammed her foot to the floor and let out the clutch. The tires only spun deeper into the soft earth. Susan pulled the gear shifter into neutral. She exchanged looks with her brother.

"Boy, Jobi, if we weren't stuck before, we really are now."

"And the snake is getting restless." Jobi inched closer to his sister ". It's beginning to crawl down the tree."

"Quick, Jobi. Hand me that pistol. Hurry."

Susan shut off the ignition and took the pistol from Jobi's trembling hand. She pointed the end of the barrel at the dangling head and pulled the trigger. There was the unbelievably loud report of the gunshot, followed by the heavy thump of the snake falling on the hood of the Jeep.

". . . Is it dead?"

It was only when she turned to Jobi that she realized he had his eyes covered.

"I'm pretty sure." She climbed out of the Jeep to get a closer look. "Well, it's not moving and you can see daylight through the hole in its head."

Jobi uncovered his eyes and sat up straight. His expression was joyous. "Pretty good shot, sis."

He climbed out and studied the tires, deep sunk in the dirt.

"Too bad your driving isn't as good."

"Very funny." She frowned at the partially buried Jeep.

Scott and Sorensen looked up from their packing when they heard the shot ring out.

"What was that?" Scott faced the direction of the shot.

"What do you mean, what was that? Aren't you the ex-Marine? You don't recognize a gunshot?"

"Yeah. I know that sound very well." He stood, hands on hips, facing the direction of the gunfire. "I guess that's the last thing I expected to hear."

Sorensen watched Jackie as she came running to him. He took her hand and she pressed herself against him.

"Who did that shooting?" Her voice was full of anxiety. "It couldn't have been one of us." She had a death grip on Sorensen's hand.

"No, it came from down the road. About two miles would be my guess." Scott was already climbing into the rear Jeep. "I'm going to see who took that shot. The rest of you wait here."

"Hey, Scott, don't you think I should go with you.?" Sorensen walked toward him. "What if you need some help."

The doctor, leaning against the trunk of a tree, said, "Let him go with you, Scott. What if it's a set up."

"You have a point, actually. Okay, what about you, Danfield?" Scott started the motor. "You can come."

"Me?" His voice rose with alarm, then dropped. "Ah, ah—I still have to pack some of the . . . .well, my stuff." He motioned toward his tent, still fully assembled. "Medical supplies is what I'm trying to say. You know I would go, but since this young man is not doing anything at the present, well I thought—"

Scott smiled grimly and opened the door for Sorensen. "Let it go, Danfield. Okay, Michael. Hop in. We're wasting time."

They took off down the bumpy road. Five minutes later the stranded Jeep came into view."

"Look, there, Scott. Another Jeep. The shot must have come from here."

His military training and experience took over and Scott immediately took in the whole area. "I don't see anyone. Do you?" he asked tersely. He stopped his Jeep slowly, rolling up to the washed out area, but leaving plenty of room to drive away quickly."

"Nope. Maybe they're hiding."

"Maybe." Scott scanned the jungle around them. "I'm sure they heard us driving up."

Sorensen noticed the snake on the hood. "Check out this massive python. That must have been what the shot was for."

"Yep. Whoever did that is pretty good shot." He drew a deep breath and called out, "Hey! Is anyone around here?"

Instantly Susan and Jobi Andrews popped up from behind the Jeep. Gene's mouth dropped open in astonishment.

"My god, Scott, it's a couple kids." Sorensen stared at them in disbelief.

Gene Scott drew a deep, measured breath and tried to remain as calm as possible. "What in the world," he asked slowly, "are the two of you doing here?"

"Hi, Reverend Scott," Susan said softly "Aren't you happy to see us?"

Sorensen turned to Scott, amazed once again.

"Am I happy to see you?" He repeated her question. Slowly he shook his head, uncertain as to how to respond.

"We sure are happy to see you." Jobi laughed sheepishly. "We sorta got stuck."

"We can see that, kid." Sorensen leaned toward Scott and said in a curious voice, "Well, Scott, you seem to know these two. What are they doing here?"

Gene shook his head. "I have no idea. But I intend to find out immediately." He motioned for them. "Don't just stand there trying to act innocent. Come over here."

Susan and Jobi looked reluctantly at one another and walked slowly to Scott.

A New Beginning

"What are you doing following us?"

"Well, you said we should help one another Reverend Scott," Jobi said, trying to sound matter-of-fact, "so we came to help you."

"Help me? Is that what you're doing now, helping me? Did you think getting in my way was going to help me? And now I have two more really big things to worry about. Was that supposed to help me?" His eyebrows arched.

"We won't get in your way." Jobi smiled without conviction. "There are a lot of things we can do to help you."

"Yes!" Susan said brightly, holding tight to her brother's hand. "I heard you say yourself just a second go what a good shot I am."

Gene's head dipped to one side incredulously. "Well if we had come out here to shoot the natives, you would be the ideal missionary. Only I don't think that's what we had in mind."

"I love children," she said, her voice a little less certain. "I—I can help teach the native children too."

"Uh huh. Does your granddad know you chose to follow me instead of going to visit him like you were supposed to?" He gazed into Susan's fearful eyes. "What about your parents? Do your mother and father know what danger you're in?"

"Well—"

Susan was interrupted by Jobi. "Sure they do! We sent granddad a wire and we phoned Mom and Dad."

"Is that so, Susan?" Gene could not help but glance down at her form in nice fitting shorts. He looked back up to her eyes. "Well?"

"Oh, a—yes, of course." She squeezed Jobi 's hand. "I phoned before we left that first town."

For a time, he said nothing. Then, hands on hips, he shook his head. "Well, I can't let you go with us, even if you're telling the truth. It's way too dangerous for children."

Her expression changed to indignation. "Well we can 't very well stay here," she snapped. "And it's plain to see I can't move this da—" She caught herself. "This wonderful Jeep." She looked down at her hands.

"Sis is right." Jobi stepped up close to Gene. "And I don't think walking back is so great an idea either. If the sun don't get

113

you, then the crocs will. You know, crossing that river"

"Well, you have to admit they have a good point, Scott," Sorensen said. "I think you have to let them come along with us. They can't stay here. And what are the chances somebody is going to come along and give them a ride."

"Well . . ." Scott thought over the possibilities.

"We promise not to get in your way or cause you any unnecessary troubles or worries, Reverend Scott." Susan said, her voice firm and proud.

"Actually what I'm inclined to do is get your Jeep unstuck and watch you drive back across the river. . . . The problem is, it's really irresponsible of me to let the two of you go back through the jungle without supervision." He sighed. "So I guess I don't really have any other choice." Scott stared down at her. "And I don't want to sacrifice this mission trip to take you back personally. So here is the plan. I will expect you both to listen to me and do as I tell you."

"Are you going to help us get the Jeep unstuck?" Jobi asked.

Gene shook his head. "I'd have it out in thirty minutes if I had a wrecker with a wench. Just using shovels and limbs, that's an all-day project."

Silently he helped them into the Jeep. "Michael, will you put their luggage and guns in.

"What about the food they brought, do we have the room?"

"Not with two extra butts taking up space. Anyway, I think we have enough."

He climbed in behind the wheel and backed the Jeep into an opening in the undergrowth where he could turn around. He looked over his shoulder to Susan and Jobi.

"Oh, one more thing. If you have any suggestions about how we should be doing things based on what you've seen in a movie, forget it. I have enough actors in the crowd"

Sorensen laughed. "Come on, Scott. Even Tarzan had a chimp who followed him everywhere. Anyway, Jackie and Ali are really trying Scott. They're really great gals."

"Maybe so, Mike. The problem is that, just like most women of any age, they never listen."

Sorensen laughed, but Gene Scott said nothing all the way back to their encampment.

Chapter Twelve

Raven Jones checked the guns to be sure they were loaded when he saw the Jeep returning.

Tabor, flanked by Jackie and Ali, stood curiously waiting to meet the Jeep when Scott and Sorensen pulled up at the encampment. They stared incredulously at Susan and Jobi sitting in the back seat. Finally Jackie smiled at them.

"Hi kids, what are you doing here?"

"Same thing you are." Susan stood, impatient to get out of the cramped back seat. "We're here to help Reverend Scott."

Tabor spoke to Scott as he opened the door. "Who are these kids and what do they mean they're here to help?"

"Their Jeep got buried in that hole in the road we drove around. They were stranded by themselves." He glanced at Susan "I didn't feel like we could leave them there."

"I guess not. This isn't the busiest highway I've ever been on," Tabor said, "but that still doesn't explain who they are or why they're here."

"Of course you were right in bringing them here," Ali said. "Is anyone going to introduce them?"

Gene shrugged. "All right. Everyone, this is Susan and Jobi Andrews." He helped the brother and sister out of the Jeep. "They were traveling on the same ship that brought Danfield and me here."

Danfield, who had been lurking in behind the other Jeeps, spoke up, "Oh yes, I remember them now." He shook his head. "It's ridiculous to think they could help us, Scott. We can't take those children with us. You know perfectly well where we're going is not suitable for children."

For the first time Scott smiled at Susan.

"I am sorry, Danfield, that you feel so strongly against taking these 'children' with us, but I'm afraid we have no other choice."

"The whole idea is absurd. It's unheard of!" The doctor's face grew red. "Perhaps it's time to think of cancelling the whole mission trip."

"They're going, doc." Scott turned to Sorensen. "Would you check to make sure everything's ready to go?"

"You bet, Reverend." He slapped his hands together. "Come on, James. Let's find Raven.

"Reverend Scott," Ali said excitedly, "did you see that movie where these two children were trapped alone in the jungle. They were chased by wild animals. They nearly starved to death. Why, if it hadn't been for John Wayne—"

"Oh I saw that one." Jackie tugged her arm. "What was it called? 'Jungle Lost' or maybe 'Lost in the Jungle'? Something like that."

"Yes now that I think about it, maybe I did see that." Ali stood beside of Danfield. "But wasn't it Gary Cooper who save them?"

"No , I believe it was John Wayne. Or maybe it was Cary Grant."

"Maybe it was the Three Stooges," Scott said absently. "They made a jungle movie. You three seem to have this all down pat." He jumped into the lead Jeep. "It's past time to go. One of you kids can ride with us in the front Jeep."

Susan pushed Jobi toward him. "Go ahead, Jobi. I don't think I want to sit anywhere near that man right now."

"Okay, sis, if you're sure." Jobi ran up to the Jeep and climbed in beside Danfield. Susan got in the back of Sorensen's Jeep, sitting behind Jackie.

Scott signaled for the little convoy to proceed. "Let's make dust."

They had ridden for several hours, slowed by the undergrowth crowding the road, when Ali leaned over towards Tabor and spoke softly. "James, do you feel as though someone is watching you?"

"No." He shrugged, then glanced at her. "Do you?"

"You may think I'm joking, darling, but I can feel eyes staring at us." She looked around in the thick jungle surrounding them. "They're out there somewhere, I just know it."

At the same time, Jackie moved over close to Sorensen and whispered loudly. "Mike, someone is out there in those bushes."

"Did you hear something, sweetheart?" He looked around.

"No, but I can just feel eyes peering at me." She turned around to Susan. "Do you feel as though you're being watched."

"Yes." Susan swallowed. "I have been feeling that way for the past half hour. I think something or someone has been following right alongside us, hidden, and watching our every move."

"Well, if both of you feel that way, maybe I had better warn Scott to be on the lookout."

Sorensen beeped the Jeep's horn. Scott looked back, then motioned for Jones to stop. The Jeeps stopped in a little cluster.

"What is it Mike?"

"Could you come back here for a minute."

"Scott climbed out and walked back to them."

"The girls feel like we're being watched. I thought I should warn you just in case," Sorensen said quietly. "Never hurts to be prepared."

"Well the girls are correct, Mike. We are being watched." Scott leaned casually on the Jeep. "They're out there alright. Been following us for some time."

Jackie squeezed Sorensen's hand. "What—what do you think they're up to? Do you think they're planning to attack us?"

"Not likely. The Lavites are a curious bunch. They mostly want to know what we're doing here." He looked back at Susan "How's it coming, Susan?"

"Fine, thank you Reverend Scott." She shifted her feet into a new position. "Is Jobi giving you any trouble ?"

"Not really. Jobi is not the trouble maker. He just likes to ask a lot of questions."

"Don't most kids?" Susan asked airily.

"You ought to know," he said tersely. "Michael, we'll just keep moving at a slow pace. They won't show themselves till they're ready. Just be ready for anything." He started to walk back to his Jeep, then turned. "And keep those guns down. We don't want to provoke any trouble."

Susan watched as Gene stopped and explained the situation to Tabor and Ali. She thought, "I know he thinks I'm just a kid. That's what he keeps saying." She dropped her shoulders. "Oh Gene, why can't you feel like I do?"

Susan sighed, louder than she had intended, and Jackie smiled back at her.

"Hey, pull yourself together kid. Everything is going to work out fine."

"I hope so." She smiled, thinking, "Between Gene and me."

117

The Jeeps began rolling again slowly and it wasn't long before they came to a stop. Natives had encircled them, holding spears pointed down to the ground. Scott extended his hand in the natives' peace sign. He climbed slowly out of the Jeep. Susan sat·up in her seat and took a deep breath. One rather good looking native—not much older than she was, she thought—stepped up to face Scott.

Unsmiling, focused intently on Scott, he said, "What you do here?

"We have come as friends. To bring gifts and share knowledge with the Lavites, your people."

"You say you come as friend. Show me gift." His face remained unchanged and unfriendly.

Scott turned to Danfield. "Hand me that box of candy bars."

"But Scott, why not give him something that looks costly, candy is just—"

"Don't argue with me, Danfield." He held out his hand.

"Sir, they always give the natives the most costly—"

"You hand that candy down fast, doc. I'm losing my patience!" Scott gripped the candy box and turned back to the tribal spokesman. "Eat one of these. They taste very good."

The Lavite took a piece out and handed it back to Scott."

"You! Eat first!"

Scott nodded. He stuffed the candy in his mouth. "Mmm. Very good."

The young man's eyes narrowed. ". . . I try." He stuck the candy in his mouth. Instantly his expression softened. "That is good."

The Lavite standing next to him reached for a piece of candy and the speaker slapped his hand away.

"Wait." He stared at Scott. "What name?"

"Scott. What's yours?"

"My name Rama. You follow. I take you to Father. He chief of our tribe, Chief Takama."

He motioned to the other Lavites and they started walking past him. Four clustered behind Sorensen's Jeep.

"Drive. We walk ahead. Okay?"

"Fair enough."

Scott climbed back into the Jeep. He looked back to see how

A New Beginning

the group had endured the encounter. His eyes met Susan's and the same feeling that descended upon him the moment he saw her aboard the ship fluttered in his stomach.

"Oh Susan" he thought, "why did you follow me? I don't understand and I can't cope with this strange feeling I have for you. Didn't I have enough to worry with without trying to sort out this feeling that grips me whenever I'm around you."

He felt a tug at his arm. "Reverend Scott, this isn't the cannibal tribe you told us about, is it?" Jobi asked anxiously.

"No Jobi." He rubbed the boy's head. "Just try to look relaxed. Everything is happening the way it's supposed to so far."

"Well Scott, I think when we get to the village, I should be the one to talk with Chief Takama. "Danfield pulled out a cigarette.

"Put that cigarette up and listen to me." Scott frowned at the doctor. "I lead this group and I'm perfectly capable of handling Chief Takama. If I need your help Doctor, I'll ask for it."

He climbed out of the Jeep when they reach the Lavites village and smiled down Rama. "Which way to your father, Rama?"

"I take you. Rest get out and follow Bamik here." He patted the arm of the smiling man beside him. Rama looked at Susan when she stepped down from the Jeep. "Hummm!"

Scott followed his gaze.

"Rama, take me to your father."

He frowned at Susan, who was returning Rama's smile.

"Oh yes. This way, Scott. I take." He looked back at Susan as they walked toward his father's hut. "Who girl dress like yellow bird?"

"Why do you ask?" Scott realized he was gritting his teeth.

"I like. Very pretty." He smiled at Gene. "Pretty, yes, Scott?"

"Yes, yes she is." Gene stopped in front of a hut. "Is this the right place?"

"Yes. I go see if my father can speak now." He slipped through the door. Several minutes passed before he stepped back out. "He see you. Come."

Scott followed Rama into the hut. Chief Takama sat smiling upon a rug made from a leopard skin. He motioned to Scott with his hands.

"Scott, please to sit." the chief said.

Along with Rama, he sat in front of the chief.

119

"My son say you come as friend to our people. What do you want, Scott, in return."

"Just your friendship, Chief Takama. We only want to help show your people things to make life better for them. And at the right time, if we can, we want to bring peace to the valley of BaKuba. We will need your help and cooperation in bringing the Karubi tribe around to see it our way, so all can live in peace." he waited a minute for a reply. "Does that sound acceptable to the chief?"

"Good friend, Scott." The chief studied his face. "You welcome here. But Karubi's will not listen. They kill my people if we even cross to their side. "

"I know it will be difficult, but my heart tells me we can do this. I hope you trust me." Scott leaned toward the chief, conspiratorially. "Your people remain in danger as long as you and the Karubi 's fight each other. We can help, given a little time."

"Very well, Scott. "Do what you will to help my people." Takama patted his knee "You are the first to offer help to us."

Scott stood. "I will do all I can to help your people, Chief Takama. My friends who have come with me will help to in every way they can as well."

The three of them stood and walked to the door, made of vines tied together.

"My son, Rama, will show you and friends where you can sleep. "

"Thank you for trusting us. "Scott touched his joined hands lightly and followed Rama back to the Jeeps, where the rest of the party stood waiting, trying to ignore the unflinching gaze of the gathered Lavites. They took in every word as Gene spoke.

"Rama is going to show us our huts. When you get there, just take the things you need. "

"I need something for these bites. "Jackie scratched at her legs

Scott laughed. "You 'll find something in the medicine box. Try long pants from now on. I think somebody mentioned that this morning."

"Very funny, Reverend Scott." Jackie walked over to the Jeep to find the medicine box.

Gene looked around to find Susan. Rama was helping her with her suitcase.

"I've got it, miss."

He smiled and she returned it.

"Thank you, Rama. You 're very kind."

"I like to help a pretty girl." He took her hand. "Rama will show you to your hut. Uh, what name?"

"Susan Andrews." She laughed softly. "Jobi will stay with me. He's my brother." She waved Jobi over. "Come along, Jobi. This is Rama and he is going to take us to our cabin—I mean hut."

"Hello Jobi. Nice to meet brother of pretty girl."

Rama led them toward a row of huts.

"That s sweet, Rama. You're very nice." Susan smiled when she saw Gene watching them. She took Rama's hand again and said, "Shall I help you learn anything?"

"Oh, yes!" Rama said eagerly. "Anything you teach, Rama will learn."

Gene came to them and took Susan's arm. "I would like to speak with you, alone."

"Later, Reverend Scott. Right now Rama is being nice enough to show me to our hut." She got close enough to Gene to whisper. "We have to keep them happy, don 't we?"

"Well that depends. Just how happy are you planning to make him?" He shook his head. "You get too chummy and you might regret it later."

"Oh Reverend Scott, don 't be silly. I'll take care of myself. Remember, you've got enough worries." She caught up with Rama and followed him into the hut.

". . . Shit." He shook his head. "That girl."

"My, my Reverend Scott!"

He turned to see Ali standing behind him. She smiled at him.

"Let's watch that kind of talk. We don 't want to teach the natives our bad habits."

He pointed to the hut. "Bad lessons? That Susan, she' s making a mistake by leading that boy on. It could very easily cause a lot of trouble."

"Now, Scott, what harm can it do?" Jackie joined them as they walked toward the huts, and as always joined in on Ali's side. "She's just being a typical, friendly teenager."

"Friendly teenager? Just like in America?" Gene chuckled ironically. "There are many different ways to be friendly, 'Mrs.

Sorensen'. I'm not sure either of those two teenagers understands what 'friendly' means in the other's culture."

"Susan can take care of herself," Ali said. "Besides, I think that young man Rama is very sweet and helpful."

It was at that instant Rama emerged from Susan's hut laughing.

Ali smiled. "You see? They seem to be hitting it off real well."

"Yeah," Gene responded dryly. "There will be some hitting if he's not careful. This could undo everything we're trying to accomplish." His face was colored with anger.

"Really, Reverend Scott" Jackie gave him a puzzled look. "I don 't quite understand why you 're getting so uptight."

He gazed down at her. "Like you didn't understand why it was so dangerous, until we got surrounded by people with spears—who are the nice ones? Or you couldn't understand why not to wear shorts? . . . Susan is a very young and innocent girl. I—" He stopped when he saw the smile on Jackie's face. "Well, I wouldn't want her doing anything to get herself hurt. And I don't want her disrupting our mission work. That's all."

Rama waved for Scott and the others-to follow him. He showed them to available huts and told them they would eat shortly.

After he had stowed his few belongings, Gene walked to where Rama had directed they would be fed and found a place to sit. Most of the others had already arrived, all except for Susan and Jobi. She came up behind him and tapped him gently on the head.

"Hello, teacher."

He looked up over his shoulder and saw her smiling down at him. She sat next to him, rubbing his arm gently.

"You don't mind if I sit next to you, do you?"

"No, of course not." He returned her smile and looked around for her brother. "Where's Jobi?"

"Wouldn't you know it. Jobi has already found himself a friend. Rama's cousin, Datari." She pointed to the two boys coming toward them. "There he is. He's about Jobi's age too, I would guess."

"Yeah, pretty close to it." Gene smiled as Jobi sat across from him. "So, Jobi, how's things going?"

"Couldn't be better, Reverend Scott. Datari has got a neat

collection of things," Jobi said excitedly. "You should see them. Wow!"

"Nothing compared to what Rama got." Datari smiled at Gene and Susan. "You got some pretty good collection there too, Reverend Scott."

Gene glanced at Susan, who was laughing behind her hands. Jackie smiled at her and whispered, "So, Susan, what are you so overjoyed about?"

"Oh, it's nothing, really." She looked up at Gene and smiled. "But then maybe it is something."

Gene frowned. Then a sly smile came to him.

"Jackie, how old would you figure Susan to be?"

He smiled at Susan, whose face instantly became a light pink as she looked down at her hands.

"Oh gee, I would say around sixteen. Seventeen maybe." She turned to Ali. "What would you guess?"

"Yeh, sixteen, most likely."

"Yes, that's what I thought too," he said guilelessly, "but would you believe that she's really almost thirty." He gave her a fatherly pat on the head when she feigned a smile at him.

"Oh, come on, Reverend Scott, that's over the top. Don't tease a girl about her age."

"No, it's the truth. Go on. Ask her." He gazed at her. "Tell them, Susan." He sipped from his drink before looking back at Susan, who sat quietly staring at her plate. "I think she's mad at me cause I told you how old she is. . . . Almost thirty."

"Don't be silly Reverend Scott, I'm nothing of the kind."

"You mean you're not mad at me, or you're not almost thirty?" He winked at Jackie and Ali, who did not respond.

"I—ah—well."

She looked to Jobi for help. He was busy talking to his new friend and hadn't been listening to what was said.

"I'm certainly not mad at you. And, to be completely candid, I'm not the one who said I was almost thirty." She stood and handed her plate to a native girl. "Thank you. It was very good."

"Finished so soon?" Gene's eyes moved up her legs as she rose. He pulled them away when he saw Jackie and Ali watching him from the corner of his eye.

"Ah yes, Reverend Scott. I think I'll turn in early tonight. I'm a little tired from all the riding. And shooting deadly thing that needed shooting." She walked quickly toward her hut, calling over her shoulder. "Jobi, come on to bed."

"Coming." He got up and walked over to Gene. "Good night. Good night, everyone. See you in the morning."

"Goodnight, Jobi." Gene stood. "We all better turn in too. We've got a lot of work cut out for us and we will be getting up early. Goodnight all."

Jackie frowned. "Rev. Scott, I see no reason why you should have embarrassed Susan like that! In short, sir, you were a total jackass! Goodnight."

He turned and walked to his hut.

"Come along fellows," Ali said. "You heard Reverend Scott say 'early', and when he says 'early', that's exactly what he means."

Together the two women walked toward their huts, whispering about Gene and Susan and laughing.

"Jackie, thanks for letting Scott have it," Ali said softly. "I think there are feelings going on between those two."

Chapter Thirteen

The next day, Scott divided the mission group into sections. Jackie and Ali were put with the women, to help them learn how to do things like sewing, washing, cooking with variety and good grooming hints. Sorensen and Tabor were assigned to show the men of the village how to plant drought and insect resistant crops and to build things that would be useful. Doctor Danfield was in a special hut set up for him to examine and treat natives who had various ailments. The tribe's shaman was persuaded to assist Danfield. It wasn't long before he grew enthusiastic about Danfield's abilities and began to ask about the various medicines the doctor had brought along with him.

For his part, Scott gathered the children of the village with the assistance of Susan and Jobi

"I'm going to teach you a little song so that we all can sing together." He patted Susan's arm. "I'm going to ask Susan and Jobi to help me teach it to you. It's called 'Jesus Loves the Little Children.'"

A small hand shot up from the back. "Yes?"

"Who Jesus?" a young voice filled the air.

"A very special person. He's the Son of God."

"God? You mean Tamoo?"

"What's your name, sweetheart?"

Gene walked to her and sat down in the middle of the children.

"Lela." She looked down at her hands and smiled shyly.

Scott lifted her face, his hand under her chin. "Well Lela, the God I know is the one and only God. He made everything that lives."

"Did he make me?"

"Oh yes. He made all of us. We're all his children."

"Where does he live? Can we see him?"

"Well, you can't see him standing like a man or walking about. But you can see him working through people."

"Like you?" Lela smiled up at Gene.

He shrugged. "I guess you can say like me." He patted her head.

"Yes, you can." Susan walked over next to him and squeezed in between him and the child.

"Reverend Scott is a perfect example Lela. He goes around doing good deeds and helps other people find their way to God. "

Lela looked up at Susan in awe. "Do you work for God too, Susan?"

"I do now." She smiled at Gene. "It's Reverend Scott and the Andrews all the way, working for God day by day." When he smiled, she patted his hand. "Am I right, Gene?"

"Ah . . . now would you children like to sing that song?" He looked down at the children to avoid Susan's smiling eyes.

"Tell us about Jesus." Bemeo, a native boy who had joined up with Jobi and Datari, crawled over next to them.

"I tell you what, first I'll tell you all about Jesus, then we will sing the song," Gene replied, smiling broadly. "Fair enough?"

"I like!" Bemeo punched Datari playfully on the arm. "Pretty good man, huh, this Scott."

"Yeh! I like much." He hugged Jobi's shoulder. "But Jobi, he my best new friend."

"Thanks, Datari. I think you're pretty cool too!" Jobi laughed.

The children sat quietly listening to Scott as he began telling them all about the life of Jesus.

Jackie held a dress as Tari, the native girl slipped her arms through the sleeves.

"Perfect fit, Tari. It's lovely on you, too. Don't you think so, Ali?"

"Oh Tari, it's beautiful." Ali stood up, stretching as she finished hemming another girl's dress. "Okay, Bunoke. Let's see what it looks like as you move and stand. Go walk over by that tree."

The native girl twirled around.

"Oh Miss Ali, it beautiful!"

"Tari's beautiful too, no?"

Tari smiled at her mother who sat quietly on the ground watching.

"Yes, very." She smiled at her daughter.

Michael Sorenson, who had been observing the interaction, came to Jackie and kissed her.

"Hon, I found out where you can take that bath you've been wanting." He pointed down at a path. "At the end of that path there's a water fall, very small and perfect for taking a shower."

"Oh Mike, you're a real doll." She hugged his neck tightly. "I've been dying to take a. bath."

"Well, you've put in plenty of work for one day." He smiled at her and turned. "I've got to go help James keep the men occupied. See you later."

"Hold on. Where's my kiss?"

She pulled him close to her, He took her in his arms and kissed her tenderly. The native girls stared in surprise. They whispered to one another as Sorensen made his way back over to the men.

After he was gone, Tari touched Jackie on the arm. "Why Jackie and Mike do this 'kiss'?"

"Because it shows affection. It shows that you care for that person very much." She smiled at the girls. "So don't you kiss?"

"Not kiss, but like to learn." Bunoke laughed "You teach us how."

"Well Ali, what do you think?"

"Well Jackie, I think as a matter of principle everyone should know how to kiss. After all, it is one of the nicest things people can do." She giggled. "But girls, we have to use our men to demonstrate how it's done."

"Yes, and you must bring your fellows so that they can watch too." She winked at Ali. "I wonder if Susan would like in on this lesson?"

Ali laughed. "We can ask her about it when we go down to bathe." She turned back to the girls. "We will teach you tonight. It's always better at night, although it's pretty doggone good anytime."

"Yes, we could have a party first to celebrate everything you have already learned." Jackie clapped her hands together joyfully. "You could wear your new dresses and Ali and I can help you fix your hair."

"Good! Good!" Tari said, clapping her hands in delight. "My Montu will like kiss."

"Oh I'm sure of it."

Jackie walked down the path. She saw Susan swinging one of the native children.

Joan Byrd

"Susan, hey. We found where we can take a bath. Want to go with us?"

"Sounds heavenly. I'll be right there." She hurried into her hut and came back carrying a towel and bathrobe. "I sure could use a good bath. Where are we going?"

"Mike says there's a perfect place down this path."

The three young women made their way slowly down the shady walkway. They could hear the gentle waterfall and smiled as they removed their clothes when they reached the isolated, small body of water surrounded by trees.

Jackie smiled at her friend and winked. "Susan, we're going to give the native girls a special lesson tonight in how to kiss. Would you care to get in on it?"

After the momentary shock, Susan reflected on the possibility. Silently she asked herself, "Would it be possible to persuade Scott?"

"Well, what do you say?" Ali asked. "Maybe you could persuade someone to be your partner."

"I think that would be·fun." She giggled girlishly as she stepped into the refreshing water. "If he will do it, of course."

"He? Who, is 'he'? Reverend Scott?" Jackie asked coyly, as she let the water run over her shapely body. "Or have you got somebody else picked out?"

"Well, ah . . ."

"Come on, Susan," Ali said. You can tell us. We're your friends." She filled her hand with shampoo and lathered her hair.

"Plus, we know all the ropes for catching the right man," Jackie added conspiratorially. "In case you need a little help from your friends."

"I would like very much to get him interested in me," Susan said, lathering her legs. "But I'm sure he thinks of me as nothing more than a child."

Ali gazed at Susan's figure. "Trust me, sweetie. You're not a child. With a little devilish strategy, you could make him see you in a whole new way."

Jackie stepped out of the water and toweled off. "For instance, tonight, wear something very sexy."

"Yes, and when you start the kissing action," Ali said, "do some little things to reassure him that you are totally a grown-up woman."

A New Beginning

Susan stopped and looked at them, mystified. "Like—ah what kind of little things?" Susan wrapped her robe around her.

"Play with those darling little curls on the back of his neck, play in his ears." Ali laughed. "Oh, and if he begins to breathe heavy, get your hands up his shirt and gently rub his chest."

"Trust us, Susan, all these things work beautifully."

She stood still, imagining herself doing to Gene as they had suggested. She smiled. "Yes, well Delilah persuaded Samson, didn't she?" Susan laughed. "Only I'm not sure I have anything really sexy to wear."

"Jackie, I bet we could find her something to wear in our things."

They started back down the path toward the village.

"Yes, I know just the thing. You remember the red one: low cut, long, with the slits on either side?"

"Oh, Jackie, that one would be perfect." Ali smiled at Susan. "Come with us to our hut. We'll help you get ready. It will be a big challenge hooking a preacher. That is who we're talking about, Susan. It's so obvious when we see you look at him."

"Yes, but I think that goes both ways," Jackie said as they entered their hut. "I believe he already has something there for Susan."

Susan caught her breath. "Why do you say that?"

"Oh, I can just tell when someone feels something for someone else."

". . . Do you really think he feels something for me?" She couldn't contain the excitement that gripped her heart.

"Well, tonight is a good test to find out. I mean with the way you're going to look, and if you do what we tell you, I'm sure he will reveal some of the true feelings he has for you."

Susan smiled, and said to herself, "Gene Scott, tonight will be one night I shall always remember, for it will be our first romantic scene together. I intend to make you suffer plenty when we're close and we're kissing."

Gene sat quietly in the noisy circle, watching as Susan walked toward him. He could feel the pounding of his heart in his throat and chest when she stopped in front of him. His eyes moved slowly up her body until they rested on her face. She smiled down at him and his lips melted irresistibly into a smile.

"May I join you Gene?"

"Back on first name basis again." He took her hand to steady her as she sat down, revealing most of a shapely leg. "Where did you get that outfit, Delilah?"

"Oh, do you like it?" She ran her tongue over her upper lip.

"It's . . . a . . . very pretty." He turned away to look at the chief, who sat next to him. "Chief Takama, I hear we're having a big party tonight."

"Yes, that right. My daughter Remali is very happy. She say that we learn good lesson tonight." He laughed heartily and took a big sip of his drink.

"Lesson? Really? What sort of lesson?" He wore a puzzled expression.

"Later we see. Right now, my son will do Lavite dance for you." He clapped his hands and drums instantly began beating in rhythm. Rama leaped into sight from a nearby hut, dressed in an ornate tribal costume and began dancing. Another native emerged, dressed as a lion chasing a native girl. Rama acted out killing the lion and rescuing the girl in distress. After the demonstration was over, all the mission workers applauded loudly.

Jackie stood up and waved her hands for silence. "Now we would like to show you how we dance in America. And this is something everyone can dance to. It's lots of fun." She pointed out the portable record player Sorensen was holding. "We have brought our music to help show you. Start the music and come here, Mike. Ali, James, anyone who wants to try. Just stand up with your partner and watch how we do this."

Sorensen took Jackie into his arms tenderly and started dancing to the smooth, rhythmic music of "Chances Are," by Johnny Mathis. Several couples rose and began to mimic the dancers.

Standing Susan touched Scott's shoulder lightly. When he glanced at her, she said, "Let's dance."

"I—I don't dance too hot," he stammered. "You've heard of people with two left feet. Well that's me they're talking about."

Her eyes sparked. He couldn't resist the smile that came to his lips.

"No, I won't take 'no' for an answer." She tugged on his arm

A New Beginning

to help herself stand. "I want to dance with you, Gene."
He heard the doctor chuckle. "Go ahead Scott. After this day's
work I need a good laugh."
"Very funny, doc." He looked up at Susan. "Don't you think
it would be better if you could find someone else to dance with?"
"I will." Danfield hopped up and grabbed Susan into his arms.
"Prepare yourself for a romantic whirl, sweetheart." He gripped
her tightly around her waist.
Gene glared at him. "Damn." He stood up and tapped Danfield
on the shoulder. "You know, you're right. I really should dance
with her, doc. Better you should have something to laugh at than
to be laughed at."
Danfield reluctantly let go of the girl. He sank back to the floor
wordlessly.
Susan smiled with great satisfaction. She put her arms around
Gene's neck. He stood staring at her, unsure of where to put his
spare hand. She pulled it down with his other hand and placed it
on her back at her waist.
"Relax, Gene. Just enjoy yourself."
"What kind of dancing do you call this?" he whispered in her
ear.
"Oh please."
She laughed softly and he cleared his throat when Danfield
gave him a resentful look.
"This is the way everyone dances now, luv. Look at James and
Michael. See? They're doing fine."
He watched the other men. Tabor's hand kept moving down
Ali's back.
"Well Gene, do you see." Susan held his eyes with hers. "It's
easy."
"Easy? Yes, I can see. It's a very easy way to get yourself into
a lot of trouble if you're not careful."
The song ended and fast music began to play. Gene Scott
pulled away.
Susan grasped his hand. "What's wrong, Gene. Are you
chicken to try this one?"
"You kids can have this one. I'll stick to the slow ones." He
sat back down. Susan stood above him, looking down.
"Don't give up until you try. It's lots of fun and not hard at

131

all." Susan tugged on his hand, trying to get him to his feet without success.

"I dance with Susan." Rama had appeared beside them suddenly. He took her hands in his. "Susan teach Rama this dance, yes?"

She turned away from Gene and smiled at the chief's son. "I'd love to Rama, both the fast and the slow kind. How's that?"

"That good. Rama like."

They moved away to the center of the dance. He caught onto the swift beat quickly.

"How Rama do?"

"Rama do very good." She laughed and took his hands in hers when the slow music began. "Now Rama, put your hands around my waist like this." She slid his hands around until they met behind her back. "Got it?"

"I got it, okay."

Gene could see Rama squeeze Susan tightly in his arms. He lowered his head and talked himself out of balling his fists. He gripped the bench beneath him and gazed around at all the other dancers.

Remali, the chief's daughter touched Scott's shoulder. "What wrong, Scott? Who mad with?"

He looked up at her, restraining his emotions and forcing a genial smile. "No, Remali. I'm not angry."

At that instant Susan and Rama passed close to him, within his field of vision. Gene felt his teeth clench.

"Scott dance with Remali." She held out her hand.

"Remali, I really am not good at dancing. Why don't you ask—"

"My friend Scott," Chief Takama stood beside him, "please honor me and dance with daughter Remali." He put his hand on Gene's shoulder. "I go to my hut now. Please you to keep my daughter happy."

With that he turned and walked away before Gene could say anything. He looked up into the smiling eyes of Remali.

"Dance now."

Scott stood and began to dance when he noticed Susan and Rama were missing. His eyes darted around the crowd, but Susan was not there.

"Excuse me for a moment, Remali." He walked over to Jackie and Michael. "Did you see which way Rama took Susan?"

"No." Jackie craned her neck around. "Did he take her somewhere?"

"Yes, and if he tries anything—" He cleared his throat. "What I mean to say is, if something happens between them, it could undo our entire mission effort." He saw Jobi and Datari coming out of one of the huts. "Excuse me while I look for them."

He walked toward the boys. Jobi smiled as he saw him approach.

"Hi, Reverend Scott. You look like you lost something."

"What? Ah—Jobi, have you seen your sister within the last minute or so."

"So you did lose something." He pointed to the last hut in the row. "Rama took her into his hut. Better go get her before something happens."

"Well nothing better happen or I'll—" Gene grew silent when he heard Susan.

"Rama, please let me by." She feigned a laugh.

Gene ran to Rama's hut and burst in. He heard Susan give a sigh of relief.

"What 's going on here?" He tried to keep his voice calm.

"Rama was just showing me the collections he's made." She swallowed anxiously.

"Yes, Rama like Susan. Think take Susan for wife." Rama took her hand.

"What?" Her voice was full of alarm. "No! You can't! I can't!" She threw a panicked look toward Gene.

"I'm afraid you can't have Susan for a wife Rama," he said, speaking not with anger, but complete authority. "That's out of the question. It's not how we do things in our way." Gene took her hand and pulled her next to him.

"Man can take any woman in village for wife when she no belong to another man. I then take Susan." Rama said adamantly. He frowned at Gene. "I claim her."

"Well you can't have her, Rama." Gene responded more loudly than he had intended. "That's not our way and she's—well she's—"

"I'm Reverend Scott's woman, Rama. I belong to him."

She gripped his arm and he stared down at her in amazement. Rama, astonished stomped his foot.

"Scott, is she your woman?"

He looked helplessly from one to the other. "Ah—well—ah—"

Susan gazed into his eyes with equal parts of desperation and determination.

"Yes, Rama, Susan is my woman."

For an instant, only an instant, Rama's face registered angry disappointment. Then he shrugged. "Oh well, easy come, easy go." He laughed. "Sorry, didn't know Scott."

Gene nodded, mumbling to himself as he turned and pulled Susan with him out of the hut, "You're not the only one."

He glared at her as they walked away. "I warned you to leave him alone. I knew something like this was going to happen."

She tilted her head to one side so she could see his face clearly. ". . . You are jealous, aren't you?" She laughed girlishly.

"Jealous? Jealous? Let me tell you what I care about. I care about this mission and its success—something you obvious could care less about, otherwise you wouldn't have led that boy on. You understand nothing about the culture of these people. You've just been asking him to do something dramatic like that."

Her smile broadened. "You are jealous."

He sighed. "No. You are a child. Come along. We have to get back with the others."

"What's the matter, Gene. You aren't afraid to be alone with your woman, are you?" She remembered the advice Ali and Jackie had given her and tried to run her fingers up his arm.

"Cut out the Delilah bit, Susan. We've just seen how you react when you're alone with a man who really wants you all the way."

He saw the little group of mission workers gathered in a circle as they made their way back to the community dance. He pulled Susan to a stop beside them.

"So what's going on here?"

"Oh, you two made it just in time." Jackie said and smiled at Susan. "We're about to teach the young people how to kiss?"

For the second time in a few seconds, Gene was astonished. "What? Teach them to kiss? Why?"

"Don't tell me you don't even like to kiss," Tabor said, slapping him on the back.

"What is going on? Why is everyone trying to ruin my mission trip?"

"This wasn't our idea, Reverend Scott," Ali said. "The young people asked us to show them."

"Just out of the blue," Gene asked incredulously. "Knowing Americans are over-sexed, they wanted a demonstration? This is outrageous."

"Maybe I was wrong," Tabor said. "Maybe he doesn't like to kiss."

"I'm sure he does," Susan said, taking hold of his arm again as she winked at Jackie. "And we're glad to help with this demonstration."

This time it was Gene tipping his head to look at Susan. "Ah, no! I'm sure you four can teach them kissing and a whole lot more without our help."

He had started to walk away and take Susan to her tent when Ali grabbed his shirt.

"Hold on there, Reverend. We really do need you. We figure it will be easier to divide them into three groups. That way they can see better."

"Ali's right, Scott. Just a kiss or two on those luscious lips of Susan can 't kill you," Tabor laughed.

"This is a terrible idea," Scott said. "Don't you care at all what sort of example you are setting—"

"What's wrong, Scott?" It was Rama's voice. He had come upon them silently, listening to the conversation. "You, no kiss your woman?"

"Rama is right, Gene. I am your woman, remember." Susan put her hand on his bewildered, out-maneuvered cheek. "Of course we'll kiss. We want to show these young people a true, affectionate kiss—just like it says in the Bible, 'Greet each other with a holy kiss.'"

The other mission workers studied Gene and Susan with great curiosity.

Ali whispered to Susan, "You're his woman? What did we miss?"

Susan smiled. "Funny how things work out. I'll explain it all later."

Jackie smiled. "I can't wait to hear this. Okay, everybody.

We're going to divide into three groups. Mike and I will 'teach them' over in front of our hut. James, you and Ali just keep your group right here." She smiled coyly at Gene. "And Reverend Scott, you and Susan can go over there, next to your hut."

He was amazed again at the way Susan pulled him toward his hut. He could hear the sounds of young people whispering as they followed closely behind. How, he wondered, could he get out of this without losing honor in the sight of the villagers. When they stopped in front of the hut and turned, he saw dozens of curious, delighted eyes upon them. For a minute he stood and watched, afraid to look at "his woman."

Rama stood closest to them. With a great smile, perhaps thinking of what it would have been like if he had been in Gene's place, he spoke up. "We ready, Scott. Hit it."

There was no way out of this, he realized. Strangely, a part of him felt tremendous relief.

"Well . . .ah . . . first you take your woman in your hands, like this."

He pulled her closer. Her eyes twinkled with delight.

"My Delilah," he thought silently.

She looked at the group and said, "Like this, girls."

She put her hands around his neck

"Well?"

He could smell the sweetness of her breath.

She whispered. "Go ahead. Teacher."

He heard his voice, as if entranced. "Then you press your lips to her lips . . . like this."

He kissed her gently. She sighed and he felt her relax in his arms. He straightened, only to feel her pull him back to her.

"Let's show them again," she sighed.

Gene kissed her again, this time longer and more tenderly. He felt her fingers tease the curls on his neck. He drew a deep breath and pulled himself away from her.

He swallowed. "So, did everyone . . . did everyone catch on?"

"Do it one more time." It was Remali, Rama's sister. "Just to make sure we got it."

"Ah . . . sure. But just one more time."

He looked down to see Susan staring into his eyes. The feeling descended upon him again, the feeling he experienced the first time he saw her on board the ship, the feeling that had fluttered within his chest again and again in the few days he had known her, the feeling he had pushed away and denied until this moment when he could no longer deny it—and no longer wanted to.

Gene took her into his strong embrace and kissed her with passion, with a fire he had never allowed himself to feel. It was a kiss that cut them off from the rest of the world. In the instant their lips met, no one else existed. So captivated were they in their embrace that they did not notice the rest of the young people silently walking away and leaving them alone in their intense intimacy.

Gene's tongue found its way in Susan's mouth. Her heart beat wildly as she let her hands find his chest. His breathing grew heavy, as did hers, and she could feel him swelling as he pressed his body tightly to her. He pushed her away and leaned against the hut.

"Oh my God," he said slowly. Then, looking up at the girl, he said quietly. "Susan, you'd better to go in to bed now."

She wore the expression of someone completely possessed by love. "Alright, Gene." She touched his face with sweet tenderness and walked quickly to her hut.

Jobi had been watching—and timing—the final kiss, as he and Datari looked on.

"Wow, Datari. Reverend Scott kissed sis for eight minutes. Wow!"

"Hey Jobi, your sister. She's headed to your hut."

Susan walked toward her hut swiftly.

"Better get the fellows ready," Datari said.

"Right!" Jobi glanced at the boys gathered in silence around him. "We're going over to my hut, fast and quiet."

"Remember, we must look like sleep, okay?" Datari smiled. "Must fool Miss Susan. Got it?"

"You bet!" Bemeo giggled. "Think it work?"

"Sure. Sis won't know where else to go. She'll have to turn in to Reverend Scott's hut."

Jobi laughed as he and the other boys raced out the back and piled into his and Susan's hut. They lay down and shut their eyes just in time. Susan stepped into the hut and looked around at all the sleeping boys covering her small, thatched floor. She picked

Joan Byrd

Jobi out of the crowd and tried to rouse him.

"Oh it's no use. He'll never wake up." Her shoulders dropped in resignation.

She stepped back outside so she didn't wake the boys. "Now what? Everyone has retired for the night. I can't possibly go to Jackie and Mike's hut, or to James and Ali's. After all that practice kissing, I know they are busy at." She smiled. "The only place left for me is Gene's. . . . Wonder how he's going to take this?"

She made her way slowly to Scott's hut and paused just outside. From the darkness, Rama stepped up behind her and tapped her on the shoulder. Susan gasped and jumped.

"What Susan do out here, late. Must be in bed."

The memory of their first encounter flooded her mind. "I—well, I needed to talk with my man." She swallowed and twisted the ring on her little finger. "I just came over to see him."

"Oh, Rama see. Go ahead, pound on hut. Rama wait, so no harm come to missy." His eyes wandered down to her legs.

"Oh that won't be necessary, Rama. I'm perfectly safe." She gave him a phony smile.

"No, Rama wait until you safe." He knocked on the door to Gene's hut and Susan shut her eyes in anticipation.

Scott opened his eyes slowly and sat up. The knock came again, so he crawled out of bed and opened the door. The first thing he saw was Susan, smiling shyly at him.

"Susan," he asked sleepily, "what in the hell are you doing here." Then he saw Rama standing behind her and remembered the problem she had with him before. "Is there anything wrong? Dear?"

"Yes, could I come in?" She gazed at him with pleading eyes. "Please?"

". . . You're sure this can't wait until morning?" His gaze shifted from Rama to Susan and back.

"Gene. Darling. Please." She reached out for his hand. "It can't wait. Honest."

"Scott, you make your woman beg all night?" Rama shook his head. "Take her now. Not be stupid."

Gene looped his arm around her waist, pulled her inside and shut the door. Inside, he stared at her, waiting for a plausible explanation.

138

"What's so important that it couldn't wait until morning? Did you get yourself in more trouble with that, lover boy Rama?"

"No." She felt herself trembling. "I just don't have anywhere else to go."

"What's wrong with that nice hut you share with Jobi? Not good enough?" His jaw set. Somewhere deep within himself was the recognition that the alternative to being angry at seeing her in his hut so very late was to start kissing her again.

"Actually it's not okay, Reverend Scott." Her voice was louder than she had intended. "It is filled to the brim with little boys!"

Gene instantly pulled her closer and put his hand against her mouth.

"Oh Susan, not so loud." When her excitement abated, he let go of her. "What are those boys doing over there. Why didn't you just run them out?"

"They're asleep. Jobi must have invited them in and they must have fallen asleep." She walked to the door. "I don't think you're in a very hospitable mood. I'll find somewhere else to go."

"Hold it right there, young lady." He took her arm. "Exactly where do you think you can go?"

"That I don't know, but I do know when I'm not welcome." She felt her heart begin to beating rapidly as Scott maintained his tight hold on her arm.

"Susan, don 't be so childish."

"Me? Gene Scott, just turn loose of my arm l I don't need to be made fun of by you or any other man.

She tried to jerk her arm away, but Gene held it tight. "Susan, you're not going anywhere, because there is no where you can go." He loosened his hold on her arm.

"I could go to Doctor Danfield's hut." She put her free hand on her hip.

"Like hell you will. I know what that dirty doctor wants with you."

He stared into her eyes. The taste of her lips rushed back to his memory. She felt tears coming quickly and turned her face from him.

"Susan." His voice grew tender, "I never meant to be harsh with you. You can stay here. There's plenty of room for both of us."

She looked down at her hands and smiled shyly. "I wouldn't have bothered you if it hadn't have been necessary."

"I know Susan." He patted her hand gently. "You can sleep in the leaf bed. I'll sleep over by the door."

"On the ground? Oh I couldn't take your bed, Reverend Scott." She sat down on the earthen floor. "I'll sleep by the door."

"Nothing doing, young lady." He raised her to her feet." "Since you're my house guest, you'll sleep where I tell you to sleep to." He smiled.

"A house guest? More like an intruder, I'd say." She laughed. "I couldn't take your bed, I just couldn't."

"Well you had no other choice in coming here, and now you have no say in where you have to sleep. So stop arguing, and get in that bed." He pulled up the sleeves of his pajamas. "Or do I have to put you in there myself?"

Susan focused on his pajamas and a wry smile crossed her face. "Do you always sleep in pajamas?"

"Doesn't everyone?" A wave of embarrassment swept over him. He wanted her to avert her curious eyes. "Stop changing the subject and get in that bed. "

"After you." She motioned toward the bed.

"Susan." His voice was low and stern.

"Look, Reverend Scott, we're both mature enough to go to bed together and just go to sleep. I see absolutely no need for either of us to sleep on a damp floor."

"Oh you don't?" He gazed around the room as if looking for some kind of help.

"Nope. Now if you would be so good," she said in a perfectly calm voice, "be so good as to turn around until I get undressed ·and under the covers."

She began undoing her dress and Gene quickly turned his back to her.

"Susan, where is your pajamas?" He stared at the wall in front of him.

"I wasn't able to step over a dozen sleeping boys and unpack them before I came looking for a place to sleep. I'll just have to sleep in my underwear." She slipped beneath the sheet. "Alright, you can get in bed now."

"Susan, I don 't think—"

"Gene, please shut up and come to bed, so I can get some sleep. If I didn't know better I'd say you were afraid of me."

"Afraid?" he mumbled to himself. "It ain't you I'm afraid of." He slid slowly onto the very far edge of the bed, as far from Susan as he could get without falling on the floor. "Good night Susan."

"I don't bite," she whispered.

"I might. Now good night."

Gene's heart pounded wildly in his chest. "Oh God," he asked himself silently, "why do I feel this way when I'm near her, when I see her, when I kissed her?" He closed his eyes tightly. "Oh God, help me."

"Good night, Gene." Her voice was soft and alluring in the darkness. "I hope you dream about me." She laughed girlishly. "And I hope I dream about you."

"Go to sleep and stop chattering like a squirrel. I've got to get some sleep and so do you. We've got a busy day tomorrow."

He lay still, trying to push everything out of his mind that would keep him from falling asleep. Only his mind could not block out the image of Susan's face, the moment before he first kissed her. When finally sleep overcame him, even his dreams were filled with her.

Chapter Fourteen

Scott opened his eyes slowly and stared down at Susan's breast moving in peaceful sleep. She had kicked the covers off during the night without realizing it. She rolled over and put her hand on Scott's chest. He swallowed and reached for the covers. As he reached down, his eyes followed the contours of her body. She was more of a woman than he had pretended to himself she was. Quickly he covered her and rolled out of bed. He pulled his pajamas off and picked up his pants. Susan opened her eyes and gazed up at the strong body before her. A smile of approval came to her lips.

"Mmm." She sighed softly and Scott jerked his pants up and twirled around. "Good morning, Gene." She smiled brightly.

"How long have you been awake?" His hand shook as he yanked the turtleneck over his head.

"Long enough." She giggled girlishly and rolled out of bed, causing Gene to turn away instantly. "What's wrong? I saw you in your underwear. Underwear is clothes too, you know. Mine covers as much as some of my bathing suits. A little more maybe."

"I'm sure of it. It figures," he muttered. "Always the temptress, aren't you?"

"Oh, come, come, Samson." She laughed when Gene glanced over his shoulder at her in bewilderment.

"Does my Samson not know that his Delilah will eventually get him to give in to her?"

Gene shook his head in astonishment. "I seriously don't have time for this nonsense, Alice."

He shook his head and gazed out the door of his hut. Jackie, Ali and their men were sitting around an open-air table eating their breakfast. Jackie waved at Gene with a smile.

He returned the greeting as he mumbled softly, "Oh shit."

"Very funny, Gene Scott. I'm going to prove to you that I'm no Alice. Sooner or later you will believe me that I'm all woman."

Susan stood behind him, peeking around his shoulder. She saw the others watching the hut, waiting for Scott to come out.

A New Beginning

"Well, what are we waiting for? I thought you said we had lots of work to do."

"We do."

He gazed back at her with uncertainty. She responded by giving him a push out the door and following along beside him. The two couples outside looked at one another in stunned surprise. "Good morning, everyone," Susan said as if nothing unusual had transpired. She piled some food onto a plate and handed it to Gene. "Beautiful day, isn't it?"

Jackie looked at Ali and winked. "It certainly is Susan. Beautiful and exciting."

"I'll say exciting". Ali suppressed a laugh. "So, how do you feel today, Reverend Scott?"

"Tired. I didn't get much sleep." Suddenly realizing how it must have sounded, he added, "I mean I couldn't sleep because it was . . . hot."

"Yeh, I bet it was pretty hot," James Tabor nodded, his eyes widening as he bumped Scott's shoulder.

"No, I mean, the night was hot, I—"

"Hey, I understand. Believe me man, I grab it." Tabor smiled at his plate. "You don't have to explain anything to us."

"No, you don't understand." He looked around anxiously at the group. Most wore knowing smiles. "Nothing happened. Nothing. Everything was completely innocent. You see, Jobi—"

"Gene, they said they understand." Susan put her hand on his arm. "Now, dear, just relax. They're all lovers too."

His jaw dropped. "Susan!" He stared at her. "Susan is trying to be very funny today. Nothing but one wisecrack after another. She doesn't understand how important it is to be clear that nothing happened between us."

"Eat your breakfast, Scott," Michael Sorensen said, patting him on the back. "You can 't win when it comes to women. Especially with that young vixen. You might as well let them have the last word and just live with it."

"Mike's right," Tabor said. "Women have a way of turning everything around so it's just the way they want it." He smiled at Ali. "Ain't that right beautiful?"

"It's because we always know best honey," she said coyly, returning his smile.

143

"Well, not for me." Scott stood and dropped his plate on table. "All this being dominated by the fairer sex is making me crazy. It's turned my mission trip into a soap opera. And I can tell you that, in the unlikely event I ever got married, I would definitely wear the pants in the family. I can't handle being led around like a love-struck puppy. I expect my woman to be all woman, and for her I'll be all man."

Jackie giggled. "That wouldn't be difficult for you, Scott." She took her plate and stood. "I bet you're man enough for any woman."

"Oh, yes," Susan said casually, "that man is all man." She walked toward her hut to change out of the evening gown she still wore from the previous evening. "Every beautiful inch."

Scott closed his eyes and put his head in his hand. After a moment he realized he needed to reassert control of the group and their mission. He cleared his throat.

"All right, that's enough of this crap. Michael, you and James come with me. We're getting together this morning with Danfield and Jones." He looked at Jackie and Ali. "I'd like you girls to continue teaching the women. And tell Susan and Jobi to help the children. Everybody got it?"

"Sure, but what are you going to do?" Jackie took Michael's arm and turned him toward herself.

"We're having a meeting. Now please do as Reverend Scott asked, alright, hon?"

"Alright, Mike." She kissed his cheek. As the men walked toward Danfield's hut she mused, "I wonder what they're up too."

Ali followed her back to her hut and flopped across the bed. "What makes you think they're up to something?"

"Oh, I don't know. It's just a feeling. I mean, why should they have a meeting without us? We've done just as much work as they have around here, right?"

"You're damn right." Ali got up and tied her hair back. "Oh well, you know men. They're always trying to sneak around and plan things behind our back."

"Well, they won't get by with it for long." Jackie smiled at her friend. "Mike and James will tell us—with just a little feminine convincing, right pal?"

"Absolutely, girlfriend. When Jackie Beason and Ali

McConnell start their feminine charms to working, they can get anything they want."

Scott pointed out the Karubi village on the map.

"It will take us a good day to reach Karubi territory from here. We better plan to get up extra early in the morning, before the girls awaken. I hope everyone here understands this will be dangerous enough without them wanting to tag along."

"I agree," Sorensen said flatly. "Jackie must not find out that I'm leaving though, or she will insist on my taking her." Michael stared at James. "So don't tell Ali anything either. They keep no secrets from one another."

"Don't worry. I don't want anything happening to my woman." James pointed to the road on the map. "Are we taking the road? I mean it looks as though they would spot us coming like the Lavites."

"Chief Takama has chosen some of his best men to go with us" Scott replied. "They will guide us through the jungle after we have driven just as far as possible. Then we will hide our Jeeps by the side of the road."

"Sounds good Scott, but—ah—don't you think someone should stay back and see that the women are protected. "Danfield lit a cigar. "I mean, leaving them unprotected around these natives could be dangerous."

Scott gazed at him. "And who did you have in mind Danfield?"

"Well, you fellows can probably shoot better than me . . . . and someone might get sick here and need me." He shrugged and laughed sheepishly.

"It's a lot more likely one of us would get hurt—or wounded—out there in the jungle, Doc." Scott stood up. "Sorry but you're going with us."

"But what about the women?" Danfield hopped to his feet.

Scott laughed. "As I recall they said, 'We are capable in protecting ourselves.' The more I've gotten to know them, the more I'm convinced that's the gospel truth. The Lavites have more to fear from them than they do the Lavites."

Sorensen patted Danfield on the shoulder. "Jackie can handle things pretty good, Doc."

"And I'm sure if anyone gets sick, they can hold out until you

145

return, Doc." James chuckled. "Think how long they waited before you got here."

They followed Scott outside. He frowned up at the fierce sun.

"Be ready to leave about five in the morning, and be careful that you don't wake the girls."

"Don't worry, Scott. Jackie and Ali sleep like logs." Michael wiped away the sweat streaming down his face. "Boy, when it gets hot here, it gets hot."

"You can say that again." James lifted his hair in both hands. "If this is any example of what hell is going to feel like, I for one don't care to go."

"No one does." Scott leaned back, looking at Tabor's heavy, long locks. "If you put your hair in a ponytail, it might help." He chuckled and walked away.

"Ho ho ho." James walked lazily beside Mike. "I sure hope Ali don't start asking me questions about our meeting."

"Well, they probably will ask. So don't give in and tell her. Make something up if necessary."

"What happened to what you said about honesty is the best policy?"

Mike shrugged. "Well my friend, there comes a time when one must lie a little to prevent those he loves, from getting hurt."

"Sure. That makes sense." James sat down on a log. "Better get up a good story for them. It might be safe if we had the same one."

"You have a good point there. They discuss everything and you know they're going to compare notes." Mike sat down beside his friend and rubbed his chin. "We could tell them Scott wanted to tell us about his dream to build a church here."

"Yes, and that he thought we should start on it tomorrow morning."

James laughed and nodded. "That way if they do hear us leave, they won't get to suspicious. And that probably wouldn't make them too eager to come along, either."

"Of course they might think getting up before the sun comes up might be a little weird." Mike stood up. "Better still slip out at five. But the church story is great." Mike started toward the garden. "Well, back to school."

"Yeh, lift that hoe. Move that plow." They went off laughing.

Scott walked over to where Jackie and Ali where showing the women how to wash and iron. Ali took the iron off the hot coals and started ironing a cotton shirt.

"See how easy the wrinkles come out." She took a deep breath as she set down the heavy iron.

"Easy, huh?" Scott smiled at her.

"Well, this is not the most modern iron in the world." she protested. "I don't see how women used to keep using their wrists back when they had to use flatirons like this."

"They were stronger." He said casually, avoiding the peevish look he got in return. "Where did Susan go with the children." He looked around. "I get nervous when I can't see them anywhere."

"They went for a little hike." Ali slumped wearily onto a log. Continue with your ironing, ladies. I'm going to take five."

" . . . By the way, which way did they go." As casual as Scott tried to appear, his serious expression belied the concern he felt.

"Well, they went down that path, the one that leads to the little waterfall."

He sighed, shaking his head. "Doesn't she realize the jungle is no place for her to go frolicking about." When he noticed Jackie's coy smile, he stammered. "I mean she shouldn't be taking those little children out there. There are so many things that can hurt them."

"These children live here, Reverend Scott. I'm sure they know which part of the jungle is safe," Jackie said. She sat down next to her friend. "I don't think they went that far."

"How long have they been gone?" He looked down the path and back at Jackie.

"Oh, I'd say it's been about three hours, wouldn't you, Ali?"

"Has it been that long?" Ali looked at her watch. "Boy, time does fly when you're busy."

"Three hours? Seriously? They've been out long enough." Scott hit his hand against his leg. "I'm going looking for them. Be back later."

"Sure, Reverend Scott. Take all the time you need," Jackie called after him as he headed down the trail.

Ali watched Scott disappear down the path.

Jackie continued, "Poor man, doesn't even realize or want to admit he has deep feelings for Susan."

"Yes, but I guess it's the age difference that holds him back."
Ali stood up and wiped off the back of her pants. "Well, back to
the old iron."

"Yeh, let's go to it." Jackie said, standing up. "Do you suppose
Scott will be mad when he finds out they've only been gone thirty
minutes?"

Susan looked around with frustration bordering on alarm. Lela
had vanished from the group when the children had stopped to
watch a troop of monkeys playing in a tree.

"Oh, where can she be," Susan wondered aloud. "She can't be
far. Okay, we will have to split up and look for her. If something
was to happen to her, Gene would never forgive me."

"Don't worry, sis. We'll find her." Jobi noticed his sister's
hand trembling and took it in his. "Right, Datari."

"You bet. Miss Susan, we find Lela." He motioned for the
group of children, who stood watching in anxious silence, to
gather around him. "We find Lela. She got to be close by."

"Datari is right," Susan added, "but we must remain calm and
stay together in groups." She looked down at the smaller children,
their big eyes stared back fearfully. "We all don 't need to go out
in the bush searching. Jobi can go with me. Datari you can take
the older boys. And the rest of you remain right here where it's
safe. Everybody understand?"

"Me understand," a small voice rose from the small children.

Susan smiled. Then she grew serious as she and Jobi began to
walk slowly through the jungle, calling out to the missing child.

"Lela! Where are you? Lela, can you hear me? It's Susan."

A small voice cried out from a short distance. "Help me,
Susan."

"Did you hear that, sis?" Jobi froze in place.

"It came from that direction, Jobi!" Susan ran toward the
sound. "I'm coming, Lela. Keep talking. Where are you?"

"Over here, Susan, over here!" Lela cried out from the depths
of the pit she had fallen into.

Turning her neck in every direction, Susan could not see the
little girl. As she turned about, she too stepped into the concealed
hole in the overgrown trail, landing heavily in crumpled heap in

the darkness. Lela ran to her and threw her arms around her.

"Susan! You come! You come!"

She spat dust and twigs and tried to decide if she was injured. "Yes, Lela, but I'm afraid you're not much better off." She gathered herself and called up to Jobi. "Jobi, are you up there?"

"Where are you, sis?"

"Stop! Just stop wherever you are and don't move. Look down. Lela and I both fell into a pit. Be careful, Jobi. This hole is deep, too deep to climb out."

Jobi's head appeared in the circle of daylight above them. He looked down at his sister and Lela.

"You have to go get help, Jobi."

He put his hands on his knees, staring down into the hole helplessly. "Are you alright, sis?

"I think so. Go get Reverend Scott." Her voice was anxious as she gazed up at her brother. "Hurry, Jobi. Go now."

"Okay, sis, don't worry. I'll bring him back. Just stay calm and don 't go anywhere." For an instant the absurdity of his words caused a look of confusion to flash across his face. Then he disappeared, running away to find Scott.

"Don't go anywhere?" she mumbled, shaking her head. "You be careful, Jobi!" Then she turned and smiled at the frightened child. "It's alright, Lela, everything is going to be alright. Reverend Scott will be here soon to save us. You'll see."

Relief washed across the child's face. Lela hugged Susan tightly.

Scott stopped when he reached the children sitting on the logs near the waterfall. They looked up at him wordlessly.

"Where's Miss Susan? Is she not with you?"

"Not with us now," a little boy said, standing up. "Gone to fine Lela. Teni watch children. Teni brave, yes?"

"Yes. Teni is very brave. Which way did Miss Susan go? Which way, Teni?"

"Miss go that way." Teni pointed down the path.

Datari emerged from the bush and came up behind Scott. "Reverend Scott, did Jobi and sister return?"

"Datari." He took the boy by the arm. "Can you tell me what happened here? What's going on?"

149

"Lela got lost from us. We try to find her." He pointed to the path from which he had come. "We no find that way."

"Reverend Scott!" It was Jobi's breathless shout. He ran right up to Scott and bent over at the waist, hands on his hips as he caught his breath. "Boy am I glad to see you!" He paused again to catch his breath.

"Where's Susan? Is something wrong?" Scott kept his voice as calm as he could. He put a hand on Jobi's shoulder. "Where is she, son?"

"She fell in a hole on the trail. That's what happened to Lela first. They're both okay, but they can't get out."

Scott looked at Datari. "I want you to lead these children back to the village. No detours and stay together, okay? Jobi, take me to her now. Hurry!"

Scott followed close behind Jobi as they raced through the dense jungle. Jobi slowed when he came to the spot where the unseen pit waited. He held out his hand so Scott would not stumble into it.

Above her, Susan heard a noise. She called out softly, "Jobi, is that you?"

She breathed a great sigh of relief when Jobi's head appeared, gazing down at her.

"Oh, thank God."

Then she caught her breath when Gene appeared beside her brother. She had expected him to be furious. Instead, she saw worry—and then a quick smile cross his face. And, despite her predicament, joy and another powerful emotion she had scarcely felt before burst within her. Susan felt the heat of tears forming in her eyes.

"Just hold on, Susan," came the marvelous voice she had come to adore. "I'll get you out of there right away."

Within a minute he had found a rope-like vine, cut it to the right length and tied a loop into it.

"Take the loop in this and tie it around Lela. I'll pull her up first."

Susan pulled the green rope gently snug around Lela's waist. "Now you're set. Be a big girl. Reverend Scott is going to pull you up out of the hole."

"I be big girl." Lela gave a bright, confident smile and gripped the vine with both hands.

Susan glanced up. "All ready down here, Gene. Pull her up."

The little girl floated effortlessly through the pit to jungle floor above. Scott removed the vine and dropped it back for Susan.

"You alright after this big adventure, Lela.?" He hugged her and kissed her cheek.

She nodded, looking back down into the pit, concerned now about Susan, who had tied the vine around herself and gazed up, waiting patiently to be rescued.

"All ready to come out of the rabbit hole there, Alice?"

She frowned. "Yes, Mad Hatter. I'm all ready."

He pulled her up gently, hooking his arm around her middle when she was close enough to reach. For a time he just held her close to him, their faces inches apart, their eyes locked.

"Are you okay?"

"Now I am."

"Well that's good because you had me worried sick. I should've left you down there for getting me upset like this."

She held onto him tightly and he kept her in a close embrace as well. When he noticed Jobi smiling at them, he finally let her go. He picked Lela up and sat her on his shoulders.

"Alright, let's go."

"Wait a minute." Susan sat down on a rock. "Where's my kiss?"

"What? What kiss?" Gene turned to Jobi and thumped him on the head when he laughed.

"Well, when you helped Lela out of the hole, you kissed her."

". . . Right, maybe I did, but she's a little girl."

"Yes," she stood and brushed the dust off her pants, "but you keep telling me that I'm just a little girl."

"And every time I do, you inform me that you're a grown-up woman." He laughed and put his hand gently against her cheek. "Although falling into the hole like, Alice, was a very childish thing." He kissed her on the cheek.

"Oh, very funny. That wasn't the kiss I wanted and you know it."

Susan quietly led them down the path back toward the village. As they walked, she suddenly became aware of a movement in

151

Joan Byrd

bush beside her. Instinctively she froze, extending her hands so the others stopped as well.

Gene tilted his head to side and asked mischievously, "What's wrong, Alice. Hear something?"

"It's not funny." Her voice was low and soft and she remained motionless. "There's something in that bush."

"I heard it too." Jobi said, quickly pointing to the movement of the dense foliage. "You see? There it goes again."

A male lion appeared, silent and still, staring at the four who stared back at him.

Shivering, Susan whispered, "What are we going to do, Gene?"

Lela started crying. Scott handed her to Susan.

His voice was quiet and full of authority. "Now listen to me, when I engage this lion, no matter what happens, you take Lela and Jobi and run back toward the village. Make sure all the other children got back safely. . . . Do you understand."

"I hear, but I'm not going to leave you." She touched his hand for an instant. "I won't. I won't. There has to be some way I can help."

He set his jaw. "Why is it every time you help me, I get in a jam? . . . For God's sake, Susan, for once just do as I say."

That was the instant the lion chose to dash toward them. It made for Lela and Jobi, the smaller ones who would be easier to kill and carry into the jungle.

Scott anticipated its charge and seized it as it made to go by him. He grabbed and twisted its head back violently.

Susan pushed Jobi and Lela back toward the bush. Lela grabbed her, climbing up her back, closing her eyes tightly. Susan and Jobi inched toward the undergrowth, staring in horror and awe at the struggle happening before them as Scott fought savagely with the lion.

He had gripped the lion's jaw and with an unrelenting grip began literally to tear the beast apart. He jerked the lion's head swiftly, brutally to one side and suddenly the animal quivered and fell limp. In the silent minute that followed, Scott fell to the earth, watching the carcass to make sure it was dead.

When he managed to stand, the children ran to him, throwing their arms around him.

"You shouldn't hold me," he said wearily. "I'm covered in blood."

"Oh Gene . . ." Sobs began to wrack Susan's frame. "I've never been so scared. I can't believe you killed him. Thank God you're alright!"

"Yes. I guess I am alright." He extended his arms, badly clawed. "It's kind of a miracle I guess."

Susan studied his wounds. "Oh Gene, you're hurt."

"It's nothing, Susan. Just a few scratches." He put Lela back onto his shoulders. "Come on. Let's go."

"We have to clean and dress those wounds as soon as we get back to the village." Susan examined his cuts as they walked along.

"I'm sure Danfield can fix me up. It's time he earned his keep." He smiled at her.

"Nothing doing," she said firmly. "I'll take care of you. After all, it was my fault you got hurt. "

"I'll not deny that, Alice." He gazed up at the sky, suddenly extremely weary.

Lela rubbed his arm. "Strong. Scott very strong to kill big lion with only hands."

"Yeh, just like Samson in the Bible," Susan said.

For an instant their eyes met, filled with the irony of the moment. His gaze took in her face and her body and his stomach lurched strangely as he thought, "Yes, my little Delilah. . . . I know you're no damn Alice in Wonderland."

Chapter Fifteen

Dr. Danfield rolled over and tried to open his eyes when Reverend Scott tapped him on the shoulder. "Wh—what do you want, Scott?" he mumbled sleepily.

"Get up, Danfield. You know why I'm here. We have to get going." He pulled the limp doctor out of bed and set him on his feet. "Come on, man. I haven't all day."

"Couldn't you wait until the sun came up at least. I just got to sleep a few hours ago." He sat back down on the bed and Scott yanked him back to his feet.

"Stop acting like a baby, Danfield and get a move on. You're wasting time. Do not lay back down." Scott stormed out of Danfield's hut and met Michael and James at the Jeeps. "We don't need but two Jeeps. The natives are going through the bush and are going to meet us later on the road."

James climbed behind the wheel of the second Jeep. "Who will guide us, Scott?"

"The chief is sending his son Rama. He will help speak for us. I don't speak too much of the native language."

"Huh. Neither do I." James laughed and took the rifles Michael handed him and laid them gently in the back of the Jeep next to Jones.

Rama made his way quickly toward the Jeeps. He smiled at Scott as he took a bite of his banana. "*Bwana* want a banana?"

"No thanks, Rama. I got all the banana I need." He looked toward Danfield's Hut and slapped the side of the Jeep "Shit. That Danfield is going to slow us up."

He strode to the hut and pushed his way through the door. Danfield sat dressed on the bed. He looked up with a sick expression.

"Scott, I'm sorry. I just feel terrible. My stomach is acting up and I don't think I'll be able to go."

"Enough bellyaching, Danfield. Remember what Jesus said, 'Physician, heal thyself.' Get your ass out to that Jeep, right now."

Scott jerked him to his feet and pushed him out the door. He picked up his medicine bag and shoved it in his hands.

"The fresh air will do you a world of good."

"But, Scott, I—" He gazed into Scott's angry eyes. "Alright, alright. I'm going. Don't expect me to be too helpful."

"I expect you to do your job. You're an essential part of this team. Healing people physically opens a door for us to minister to their souls." Scott handed him a banana. "You'll be fine after you eat something. This will do for a start." He fired up the Jeep. "The funny thing is, every woman in our group has to be tricked into staying here." He shook his head.

Rama took the seat next to Scott as he put the Jeep in gear. Danfield climbed in the back seat and tried forcing the banana down. Scott gave the signal and the Jeeps pulled out of the village.

Susan opened her eyes slowly. The sun streamed in the window, covering her bed in brilliant light. Jumping up, she stood hands on hips trying to wake fully and wiped the sweat from her forehead with the back of her hand. She smiled at the sight of her sleeping brother.

"Hey, sleepy head, get up. It's too hot to stay in bed. Besides we should get busy with our work." She looked out the door at the busy village.

"Why?" Jobi wiped the sleep from his eyes and rolled out.

"It seems late. The native people are already doing their daily chores." She studied the village grounds. "Funny I don't see any of our group anywhere. . . . Hey, Jobi, come here."

He came to her side instantly.

"The Jeeps are gone. . . . Two of the Jeeps are gone." Her voice was uncertain, anxious.

"Probably had to go after more supplies or something." He stretched, lifting his arms above his head. "I wouldn't worry about it, sis?"

"Well, maybe so, but I think I'll go find out, just to be sure."

She walked to Jackie's hut quickly and banged on the door. "Jackie! Are you up?"

Jackie came to the door. "Mmmm. What?"

"Sorry to wake you, Jackie, but I was wondering if you knew who has taken the Jeeps out this morning. "

Jackie's eyes fell onto the one remaining Jeep. She stared at it for a minute, then raced to Ali 's hut, talking to herself as she went. "Oh they wouldn't! They couldn't!"

Ali stepped out into the bright sunshine. "Who wouldn't and couldn't do what?"

"Mike and James, Ali. Two of the Jeeps are gone." She took her friend's arm and turned her so she faced the road and one remaining vehicle. "Don't you remember how funny they acted last night? Mike kept telling me how much he loved me and that he always would no matter what happened."

"James said things like that too, but I just thought he was being a little more romantic than usual." She twisted the ring on her finger.

"Do you think Reverend Scott went too?"

"We can probably find out from the chief," Susan said, louder than she had intended. "I mean, he would come closer to knowing where the men went, right?"

"Sure, kid." Jackie put her arm around Susan's shoulder. "Let's go have a word with good old chief Takama."

The three girls walked quickly to the chief's hut and rapped on the door.

"Who knock?" an old voice called from within.

"It's Jackie B—uh, Sorenson, and the other two ladies are with me."

The old chief opened the door and smiled at them. "A good morning, *mooie meisie*." He motioned for them to enter. "Come in, please."

"Chief Takama, what does *mooie meisie* mean?" Jackie smiled.

"*Mooie meisie*. It mean 'pretty girl'." He laughed and sat down. "What can Takama do for you?"

"Do you know where the fellows went in the Jeeps?" Ali looked around the small hut.

"Didn't they tell you?" The chief's eyes narrowed.

"They—ah—probably didn't want to wake us." Ali smiled at the old man. "They told us if we ever wanted to know their whereabouts, to—ah—ask you."

"Oh! Takama see. Takama help *mooie meisies*." He stuck a nut in his mouth and cracked it with his teeth. "Scott take Jeeps and go to Karubi village."

A New Beginning

"What?" Susan exclaimed. "We have to go help them!"

"There nothing *mooie meisie* could do. Better stay in village with us. Jungle no place for you. Karubi village worse danger for you."

"Thank you for telling us, Chief Takama." Jackie nodded in respect, then turned toward the door. "We can take care of ourselves and we won't do anything foolish. You needn't worry about us."

The chief shook his head skeptically. "Good. Chief got enough to worry 'bout." He dismissed them with a wave as they walked from his hut.

"What are we going to do," Susan asked fretfully. "Gene—I mean, Reverend Scott is in danger and I'm sure he needs our help."

"Don't worry Susan, we intend to do all we can to help," Jackie said with authority. She went into her hut and popped out a moment later with a pistol. "Now listen, you two. This trip must be pretty dangerous or Mike would have let me go."

"Right!" Ali agreed, walking to her hut. "I'll get guns for Susan and myself."

Jackie looked at the girl anxiously. "Can you shoot a gun, Susan?"

"Actually I can shoot pretty well. At least I think I can. I shot that stupid snake right through the head."

Jackie got in behind the wheel of the remaining Jeep. "That's good to know. Just make sure you point in the direction of what you're trying to shoot and not at anybody who's friendly."

"Okay." Susan climbed in the back seat. "Although I might shoot Gene for going off without telling us about this trip."

They laughed in the moment of respite—until she saw Jobi running toward the Jeep.

"Oh great," she muttered.

"Hey, sis, where are we going?" He started to climbed in and stopped when he saw Susan's upturned hand. "What are you doing?"

"You have to stay here, Jobi. We're just going for a little ride, ladies only." She tried to sound as natural as possible.

"Oh no you're not! You're going to find Scott and the others. Aren't you?" Jobi waited for his sister to answer. "Well, aren't you?"

157

"Alright, alright. But you have to stay here," she said firmly. "It's too dangerous for us to take you."

"No way! I want to help Reverend Scott too!"

When he tried again to get into the Jeep, Susan pushed him back, got out herself and took his arm. "Jobi, remember what mom told you. You have to do what I tell you. Now I'm telling you to stay here!"

"But, sis, if it's as dangerous as you say, it's not just Reverend Scott I want to help. I don't want you to go in that jungle without me to help you either."

"Look, Jobi, your sister is right," Jackie said. "We're just going to watch them from a distance to make sure everything goes alright. You can stay here with your friend and help out in the village, like yesterday. I'm sure Reverend Scott would appreciate it a lot more."

He frowned at them, doubtful. Turning to Susan, he asked, "Really?"

"You will be helping him a lot by staying here and helping teach the children." Susan rubbed the top of his head lightly. "Alright?"

"Well, alright, but you be careful sis." He hugged her. "Hurry back."

"We'll get back just as soon as we can Jobi, you don 't have to worry about that." Ali laughed as she handed Susan the guns and climbed in.

"Let's roll, as Scott would say."

"Great!" Jackie slapped the wheel. "No damn keys!"

"Well where could they be?" Susan sat up closer to Ali and Jackie.

"Probably in Scott's pocket," Ali mumbled. "Now what?"

"Excuse me, but maybe I could help." Jobi smiled at the bewildered girls.

"How could you help us kid? "Ali lay her head on the dashboard •

"What are you talking about Jobi?"

"Well, do you remember that day Dad took us out into the desert in Uncle Mark's Jeep?" he smiled.

"This is no time to be remembering the good old days, kid," Jackie grumbled.

"I remember, Jobi, and Dad lost the keys and had to start the Jeep without them!" she said excitedly. "Do you remember what he did?"

"I think so. I watched him as he fixed the wires under the hood and then it started. Bang! Just like that!" He clapped his hands and laughed.

Susan jumped out and opened the hood. Jackie and Ali climbed out and ran to the front of the Jeep.

"Kid, are you sure you know what you 're doing?" Jackie looked in under the hood. "I wouldn't want you to get hurt monkeying around under there."

"It's a cinch." He reached in and started moving around a few wires as Susan held him up .

"Don't touch anything that will shock you, cause I'll get it too!"

"No sweat, sis." He looked up at Jackie. "Got a bobby pin or something small?"

"Sure kid." She pulled a bobby pin from her hair. "Here it is."

"Good. Take it and put it in the switch and when I say 'turn,' turn it."

"With a bobby pin?" she laughed.

"Just do it, Jackie. Anything's worth a try." Ali patted her friend's shoulder . "Are you sure this is going to work?"

"Don't ask me how, but it worked when dad did it." Susan smiled sheepishly. "Maybe we could say it's a miracle."

"I think we could use one right now," Jackie called and she stuck the pin in the switch and shook her head . "A stupid bobby pin."

"All set, Jackie?" Jobi called from under the hood.

"Yeh, kid, I'm ready with my trusty little bobby pin."

"Alright, turn!" After a few tries, the engine fired up.

"See, what did I tell you!" Jobi laughed and Susan hugged him.

"Oh Jobi, sometimes I don't know what I would do without you?"

"Okay, girls, hop in." Jackie called and winked at Jobi. "I wouldn't have ever believed that stupid bobby pin trick, but thanks, Jobi." "

"Just look after my sis and Scott." He waved as the girls sped out of the village and onto the dusty road which headed toward Karubi country.

Scott held up his hand for the Jeep behind him to stop. A native came running down from a small hill toward them shouting
.
"*Bwana Bwana Kuya apa! Mambo!*"

"What's he saying, Rama?" Scott jumped down from the Jeep and Rama walked beside him toward the native.

"He say, 'Sir, sir, come here.' Trouble. Must have spot some Karubis."

Jones whispered to Scott, "These natives are afraid of the Karubis. They might run back to their village."

Scott took hold of the native's arm and patted his back. "Does he understand English?"

"Yes, Scott. He just frighten. "Rama smiled at the native. "Luta, no worry . Tell Scott what saw."

"Luta saw four Karubis, *Bwana*! On other side of *kopje*."

"Where in the hell is Kopje! "James stepped up beside Scott.

"*Kopje* mean hill, Master James." Rama smiled. "Did Karubi see Luta?"

"No see Luta? Out on hunt, for meat I think. "His hand shook the spear in his hand. "Luta. Go back to village. "

"Luta, there's nothing to be afraid over. We need you. If we stick together, we can bring peace to your land." Scott patted his arm.

"Luta stay with Scott." he smiled. "*Bwana*, you brave, Luta not."

"To tell you the truth, Luta, Scott is a little afraid too." Scott led the native over to the Jeep. "Who wouldn't be if they thought they might be someone's next meal?"

Luta laughed and was joined by the others. Scott looked around and pointed at some of the bushes on the side of the road.

"We'll hide the Jeep there. Better go the rest of the way on foot."

"You mean, we have to go wading through this jungle on foot? "Danfield moved nervously in his seat. "Scott, there's snakes out there, and I for one don 't care to get bit!"

"I suppose you had rather drive in and have the Karubi's shoot you down like an animal or capture you and cook you alive." Scott got in and edged the Jeep into the cover of the bushes.

"Come on Danfield, don't be so hard to get along with." Michael got the guns out and handed them around.

"I told you Scott, the jungle is no place fer a coward." Raven Jones strapped the gun over his shoulder. "He should have stayed home and knitted with the rest of the ladies." James and Michael started laughing.

Danfield stepped down out of the Jeep. "Oh, very funny" he mumbled. "You'll find that walking can be dangerous in this animal invested jungle!"

"We know all about the animals Danfield! Just get your gun and your bag and get moving." Scott's eyebrow flew up.

"I'll not carry a loaded gun, I refuse." he grabbed his black bag from the Jeep. "Do you realize all the accidents that happen when people carry loaded guns, do you?"

"Danfield, I detest cowards And sissy shit cowards are the worst kind!" He gave the doctor a push toward the others and he fell at Mike's feet. Scott yanked him up. "Forget the damn gun and just get your ass moving. You 've wasted enough time already." Scott pushed past him and made his way to Rama. "Alright, Rama, which way. "

"This way *Bwana.* " Rama looked over at Danfield and smiled and started walking toward the hill.

"I wonder how long the fellows have been traveling" Ali looked around the thick jungle. "They must have gotten up way before daylight. "Jackie held on tight to the wheel as the Jeep jarred them over the rough road. "I hope they stopped for lunch. Maybe we could catch up."

"I think it's better if they didn't see us." Susan bit her lip. "Reverend Scott would be angry with us if he knew we were coming."

"Well, what Scott don't know won't hurt him." Jackie laughed. "I would just love to prove to that man that we can take care of ourselves."

"I agree Jackie. He's so sure we will get ourselves into trouble."

Ali laughed. "He thought he had us stopped by taking the Jeep key."

"Yeh, that dear sweet Jobi. I could just kiss him." Jackie

161

smiled back at Susan. "He's a little doll."

"He's a pretty good kid, even if he is my brother."

She laughed and stopped suddenly when they saw six painted natives jump out the bushes at them. They all screamed in unison and grabbed a gun. Susan's hand shook as she pointed it at the natives running toward her, shouting and waving a bush knife. She closed her eyes and pulled the trigger. A scream rose from the native as he fell to the ground. Then, Jackie shot one of the natives as he made a dive for her and Ali slung her rifle around and struck another one on the head. Susan looked overhead and screamed when she saw two more getting ready to jump down into the Jeep. Jackie and Ali looked up and began shooting. One of the natives fell dead in the Jeep on Jackie.

She started pulling herself from under him and screaming. "Get off me, you bloody bastard."

A native grabbed her arms and pulled her out. "Let me go! Mike!" she screamed till her throat felt like it was tearing in two.

"Take your hands off her!" Ali slung back her rifle, but a native on the other side grabbed it and pulled her off with it. "Don't you touch me....you.....you...."

"Susan! Run!"

Jackie bit the native and tried to free herself. He yelled out and slapped her across the face. Susan jumped down from the Jeep and started running off into the jungle. Two Karubis threw a net down over her as she ran under them. She screamed when they lifted her up and started carrying her back toward the Jeep.

"Let me down!"

She closed her eyes and tried to picture herself waking up in bed and hoping that this was only a nightmare. She pictured Gene's face in her mind then suddenly opened her eyes.

"Oh Gene, please, where ever you are, my darling Gene, help me," she whispered.

Scott and the others had abruptly stopped when they heard the screams and the gunfire in the distance. Scott's eye fell on Mike and James. He grabbed his stomach and swallowed.

"My God, it's Susan!"

"You think it's the girls?" James's face turned pale, "Oh God, it can't be."

"It was female screaming alright," Jones looked through the thick vines behind them. "Some kind of trouble. Could be Karubis or some kind of animal after them. There were too many shots for it to have been an animal. It had to be the Karubis."

Scott 's eyes showed fear and he began to breath heavily. "We have to go see!"

"Wait Scott!" Danfield grabbed his arm, "It could have been an animal. They could have been frightened and kept firing. Scared people do that!"

"He could be right." James bit his lip. "You know how women are."

"Yeh *Bwana*, James right." Luta tried to smile. "Danfield orda know how coward act, he one."

"Well, I..." Danfield looked up at Scott. "But women do crazy things. I say we go on ahead. They probably got frightened and went back to camp." He laughed. "I saw a movie once when these two women were out—"

"Shut up Danfield. I don't want to hear about your damn movies! I'm going to find out what has happened to Susan!"

He started running back through the jungle, Mike and James took off behind him, followed by Rama.

"Scott, you fool, come back here!" Danfield shouted. Don't leave me."

Raven Jones grabbed Danfield's arm. "Calm down Doc, you can't stop a man when he's out of his mind over a broad." He slapped Danfield's shoulder. "Now come on. Scott and the others can catch up later."

"I am not going with you, Mr. Jones. "Danfield's hands shook as he held tightly to his black bag. "I....I...shall wait for Scott."

"Suit yourself, Doc, but if any wild animal comes to get ye, I hope that there little black bag is enough to knock 'em out." Jones laughed and started walking on through the jungle, followed by the natives.

"Jones!" Danfield hurried to catch up. "I....I....can't be left alone, unprotected!"

"Then come on and shut that there trap of yorn!" Jones slapped Danfield's face lightly and continued on through the jungle.

"Slow down Scott!" James panted as he tried desperately to keep up with Scott's long steps. "I'm going to be so tired ...when...we...get there...I ain't going to be worth shit!" He swallowed and kept running.

"How much further do you think, Scott?" Michael sounded out of breath.

"How the hell do I know, just keep moving for Christ sake!" Scott kept his eyes strained straight ahead.

"Scott run like cheetah." Rama run slowed down a little. "I....can't go much more."

He felt as though he was dying inside. "Oh God," he thought, "Don't let anything happen to Susan, my Susan."

"If Scott keeps going at this pace, I won 't be able to fight off a mouse." James stopped suddenly, as Scott stuck out his hand. "What is it?"

"Quiet. There they are!" Scott gritted his teeth. "Damn it! They've got them alright."

"Are they hurt?" Michael tried to look over Scott 's shoulder.

"No, I don't think so." Scott balled up his fist. "But those bastards are shoving them around! I'll kill them!"

He started to move out from the bushes when Rama stopped him.

"No, *Bwana*," he whispered loudly. "If you charge now, they will surely kill the girls. We follow close, keep eyes on them. They no try to kill now. Wait for big party tonight."

"Why wait until they get into the village with all those other devils?" James tried to get by Scott, but he grabbed fast to his arm .

"No, James, Rama is right. Tonight we can get them. The natives probably celebrate by drinking strong drinks."

"Scott right, they drink much pompe. Get much drunk." Rama laughed.

"Then we just rush in there and take them, us against all those drunk wild natives?" James leaned on his gun. "Can't be done."

"We 're going to do it damn it!" Scott knocked the gun out from under James' arm and he almost fell over. "We have to! Now, for God's sakes, let's go before we lose them. Rama, go tell Jones and Danfield we will meet them outside the village."

"Aren't you afraid we'll lose them without Rama to guide us

through this damn jungle?" James jerked the gun over his shoulder.

"I think we can find the village of the Karubis seeing as now they will be leading us there themselves." Scott waved Rama on, "Meet you when we get there. "

"Right, Scott, be careful."

Rama was lost in the jungle within seconds.

"Alright you guys, let's go before we lose those damn Karubis!"

The Karubis lined the village street as the girls were pushed past them. They stared up and down each girl and several fat tribesmen licked their lips. Jackie felt the chills run up her spine as she whispered back to her friend.

"Look at them, checking their supper over! The dirty filthy vultures."

"Oh, do you think we have a chance to get out of this, alive and in one piece?" Ali swallowed.

"God only knows." Jackie closed her eyes. "That damn Scott was right! Why didn't we listen to him?"

"He was right about the shorts too. I thought I was going to die from all those bites." Ali looked down at her feet. "But stupid me, I was too proud to admit it. I was in misery."

"Yeh, me too. Oh now I would even welcome his I told you so." She looked back at Susan, who was looking around at all of the staring eyes. She glanced over and tried to smile through her fearful eyes." Oh poor kid, I wish we hadn't brought her. "

"She wanted to come Jackie. You know how she feels about Scott."

The natives pushed the girls down at the feet of the chief. They looked up into his dark, focused eyes.

He smiled and said, "*Mooie meisies! Mumrnm!*" he rubbed his stomach and Ali gagged.

"Ohhhh! I think I'm going to be sick."

"You and me both." Jackie squeezed the other girls' hands. "The fellows have just got to save us from these creeps."

"Reverend Scott will, I just know it!"

Susan felt her heart beating in her throat. She had never felt fear like this. She might die never knowing what it would be like to belong to Gene. To have him make love to her, to feel his body next to hers. She closed her eyes to blot out their current situation. Gene's face came into focus in her mind and her lips melted into a smile.

Jackie punched her arm. "Hey, Susan, are you alright?"

Huh?" Her eyes snapped open to see Jackie. "Oh, yes....I was thinking about...I was..."

The natives pulled the girls to their feet and dragged them over to a nearby spot where three posts had been erected in front of a enormous pot. They tied the girls each to a post. The chief walked over and pointed to the pot and rubbed his stomach.

"Mmm, *biyampe*."

"Oh, what the hell are you talking about, you big creep!" Jackie turned her head and looked over at her friend who was laughing. "How can you laugh at a time like this?"

"I wish that old fat king or whatever he calls himself, knew what you said." She looked back at the chief and smiled. "I hope you choke over us and die."

He laughed and rubbed his stomach again.

"Boy, that old man has a one-track mind." Jackie laughed to herself and looked toward Ali and Susan. "At least he's not a sex maniac.... I hope."

"Yeh, me too! I'd prefer getting ate up by him rather than raped by him." Ali nervously laughed.

Susan shivered and closed her eyes as she thought, "Oh Gene, save me, please God, let him save me from this crazy blood thirsty people!"

"Jackie?" Ali nodded toward Susan. "I'm worried about that kid. She's scared out of her wits."

"She's not alone, believe me." Jackie looked at the pot that held danger for them, "I just don't want those devils to know I'm scared."

"Yeh, They would eat it up with a spoon." She shivered, "Oh, why did I have to say that?"

Susan laughed softly and Jackie and Ali looked at her.

"What's wrong kid, what's funny?" Ali smiled as Susan opened her eyes.

"These stupid natives will really be sorry when my Gene comes to rescue me." She smiled at the other girls. "He will save us, you know. I really believe that, more than anything. He will save us."

"I sure hope so, kid. I could use saving right now." Ali laughed and stuck her tongue out at the chief. "Take that, fatso."

The chief waved to the group of natives standing around and they followed him, except for two guards that sat down in front of the girls. They could hear the natives mumbling in a circle but it didn't matter to them that they couldn't make out what they were saying. They wouldn't have understood it anyway.

"I suppose they're planning a big party and we're the refreshments." Ali faked a smile at the guard who was staring at her, smiling.

"Well, I hope whoever eats this little appetizer keels over dead."

Susan looked over at the crowd. It began to break up and the natives dispersed in all directions. Then the drums began beating and the girls looked at one another.

"That must be what inspires them." Ali looked up into the darkening sky. "It's getting dark. I guess they're planning a late supper."

"Let's hope they skip it all together." Jackie breathed heavily and dropped her shoulders. "I use to love being invited to parties, but this is one party I'd just as soon skip."

"Yes, being part of the menu is no treat." Ali glared at the staring guard. "Just what the hell are you looking at? Are you trying to figure out which part of me you are going to take?" She faked another smile. "I hope you get a bone in your throat!"

"Ali, for God's sake! Stop saying those eerie things." Jackie looked around. "If the fellows are around, they sure are staying hidden."

"Oh, that stupid James probably got the beat of that drum in his ears and thinks he's in some swinging night club."

Ali's eyes moved about the village and came to rest on a group of women walking toward them. "Huh, I wonder who they are? "

"Maybe they are the chefs." Jackie turned up her nose. "Woops. Bad thing to say."

"Talk about me."

Ali laughed and one of the women slapped her across the face. "What was that for, you bitch?!"

Ali slung her arms around wildly as the women jerked off her clothes and put a skimpy little outfit over her naked body.

"This just isn't my style, ladies. Now if I could just have my own back…."

They glared at her as they tied her back to the post and then they repeated the same thing with Susan and Jackie. They frowned at the guards who were leering at the shapely bodies of the three captives.

Jackie laughed. "The old biddies are jealous of us."

"I believe you're right."

Ali chortled as one of the women slapped the guards face and yelled something at him. He laughed and spit on her. She stomped away, followed by the other women. The guards stared at them and a smirk came to their lips. "Mmm."

"Your fat ass chief will get mad at you if you mock him." Jackie tried to loosen the ropes behind her. "Boy, those old bats really tied these things."

"Oh shit, what are we going to do?" Ali bit her lip.

"Just stay calm. The fellas have to be out there somewhere. Probably watching us right now." Jackie murmured softly. "I hope."

Susan closed her eyes. "Oh God, then Gene saw me…naked."

Scott gritted his teeth and silently mumbled to himself. "Damn!"

"Where is them old hags taking their clothes?"

James watched the captives. "Hang in there, Ali, your man is right here."

"Rama, why did those women take off the girls' clothes and replace them with those bits of nothing?" Scott's eyes fell on Susan.

"That dress for offer to God. All sacrifice wear them when given to *Maka*." Rama's eyes looked around the village and fell on Susan. "Mmmm, *mooie meisie*."

Scott 's eyebrow flew up as he punched Rama's arm, nearly knocking him over.

"Rama, go place the men in fours around the village. We will encircle it and make it seem like more men up here. Tell them to wait quietly until I give them the order to move in. Got it?"

"Yes, *Bwana*." he smiled up at Scott. "Missy Susan got great body"

Scott jabbed his finger into Rama 's stomach. "Now look! You had better keep your eyes off my woman or I'll bash your head in, understand?" "

"Got ya, *capita*." Rama jumped away from Scott. "Yes *Bwana!*"

"What the hell does *capita* mean?" Scott whipped around to peer down at Rama.

"It only mean 'boss'." Rama laughed and ran into the heavy vines.

"Well Scott, Susan your woman huh?" Michael smirked over at James.

"Why the hell not?" Scott slapped his back and laughed. "At least that's what we must keep that jerk thinking. He wants Susan for his own, the slimy creep."

"What do we do now?" James sat down on a rotten log and nearly fell through. "Shit!"

"Cool it James! Those Karubis hear like an animal." Michael helped his friend up.

Rama slipped up behind them, and Scott sensing him, whipped around and grabbed him by the neck.

"No *Bwana*, it Rama!" he rubbed his neck when Scott released him.

"What the hell are you slipping up on us like that for?" Scott looked Rama up and down in disgust. "I could have easily killed you."

"True, *Bwana*, but didn't." Rama nodded thankfully. "Men ready for Scott to give order." Rama stepped up closer to Scott and studied his face.

"What in the shit are you doing?" Scott stepped back.

"I knew I saw face like yours before." Rama uttered, "You *Maka*."

"I what?" Scott whispered loudly.

"Your body, your face, strong. Yes, yes, you *Maka*." Rama shook his head, " *Maka*, alright."

"You mean that Scott looks like that statue of their God *Maka*?" Michael's eyes widened. "Could we see it closer? I think ...I have just come up with the solution to our problem"

"What the hell are you talking about?" Scott frowned at Mike.

169

"If that statue of their god does look like you, then we could pass you off for him! Scare the living daylights out of them!" Mike exclaimed.

"Mike is right, Scott. Those natives will be so drunk by then, it would be a snap." James patted Michael 's shoulder. "Way to go, brains."

"What do you think, Rama? Do you think it could work?" Scott inquired of him hopefully.

"Yes, Rama think it work." He looked over Scott's body, "But first must change clothes. Must wear native dress, like *Maka*."

James laughed, "This I got to see. "

"Shut up, James." Scott gritted his teeth. "What sort of dress Rama?"

"Like native men wear." His eyes danced with laughter. "Hope we find man big enough to take off of."

"A regular old Tarzan, huh Scott." James hit Scott's arm and hurt his own hand. "Shit Scott, you're solid steel."

"Let's have a look at this statue."

Scott followed Rama closely. Rama pointed down at the huge statue resembling Scott. The three men looked a one another.

"That son of a bitch looks just like you Scott!" James carefully studied the statue of *Maka*.

"Yeh, too bad it didn't look like you!" Scott faked a smile. "But then I don't guess skinny gods are in these days."

"Very funny, Scott." James slumped down on a log. "How do you go about getting your...dress?"

"I'll simply borrow one from one of our natives down there." He looked around at the natives below him. "There's a big one. Now if we could just lure him out in the jungle."

"Easy to do, Scott!" Rama pointed at himself. "Rama get big Karubi to come out."

Rama crawled into a cluster of bushes near the big native to hide. He began squealing like a pig. The native rolled his eyes over toward the bush and smiled. "Mmm, *iyampe.*"

He began walking slowly toward the bush. Rama backed away slowly, further out into the jungle, keeping a safe distance between him and the hungry native. Scott slipped around behind him and grabbed him around the neck. He cut off the big native's wind with his strength and he fell to the ground unconscious. Scott dragged him over to Michael and James.

"Let's get him undressed and hide him here under those bushes." He cut a piece of vine and bound the native's hands and feet." There, that orda hold the pig."

Scott took off his clothes and put on the skimpy little bottom. He rolled his eyes at James and Michael who was laughing. He eyed them in disgust, including the smiling Rama.

"I'm glad—out of all this crap we're in—you fellows have something to laugh about," he mumbled. "Damn, if I don't look pretty."

"Like a true god. Oh great *Maka!*" James laughed. "I don't believe I've ever seen anything as funny as this in my life."

"I think he looks pretty good James." Michael tilted his head, "You do have the makings for a good Tarzan."

"Can you yell like him Scott?" James held his stomach as he laughed.

"I don't know about my yell, Tabor, but I might try out my powerful swing on you." Scott looked frustrated. "Now what, brains?" he said glancing over at Mike.

"Well, wait until they start the ritual. Then you climb up on that big cat, and do your thing." Mike's eyes danced in the moonlight. "Simple."

"Sure. What did you have in mind that I do?" Scott now glowered at Michael.

"Whatever it takes to convince them you are *Maka.*" Michael smiled sheepishly. "Just scare the hell out of them so they'll lose their appetite."

James started to slap Scott's arm, but dropped his hand. "You know, you are a dead ringer for the old fellow."

"Alright, now listen." Scott motioned them closer. "I climb *Maka* and come out with this angry bit while you fellows close in, being prepared for anything. Got it?"

"You bet, *Capita.*" James smiled over at Rama. "Pretty good, huh, Rama?"

"Not bad, Mr. James, not bad!" Rama laughed and Scott frowned in their direction.

"You can practice your Bantu language later Tabor."

"Sure thing, beautiful legs." James turned his head to keep from laughing.

"The trouble with this group that I'm stuck with is that everyone is out to steal Bob Hope's job." Scott slapped James lightly on the knee. "Straighten up, Tabor, and cut out the cute remarks about the way I look."

"I'm sorry. Continue with the plans." James yielded to Scott.

"Michael, you and Hope here, stand behind the statue. Rama, you stand with three other men on the other side, directly in front of it. Tell Raven Jones to take the left and another group, the right."

"Will do, *Bwana*." Rama nodded to Scott. "You act well now."

"Don't worry, I'll be up there acting as though I knew the Oscar was waiting for me to pick it up." Scott patted Rama's shoulder. "Good luck."

Rama waved and hurried off to tell the plans to the other men. The beat of the drums remained the same so they waited until the rhythm changed and the natives began their dancing and shouting.

Scott tried to see Susan from this side of the village, but his view was blocked by huts. He pictured her in his mind as the village women ripped off her shorts and top, then her underwear. He felt his heart beginning to beat faster and he swallowed hard.

He thought, "God knows I better get that picture out of my mind, especially in this outfit." He looked over at Michael and James who was busy in their own conversation. "And those two would really rib me if I started showing."

One of their natives came running out of the bush near them. "*Bwana, Bwana!*" he stopped in front of Scott breathing heavily, "*Kuya apa, kuya apa!*"

"What's he saying Scott, do you know?" Michael stared at the frighten native.

"He said, come here. He wants us to follow him. It must be some sort of problem." Scott looked around the village below them. "You both stay here, I'll go see what the problem is. If they start the ritual, come find me" Scott raced off quickly behind the frightened native.

"*Bwana* must hurry!" the native called breathlessly. "Snake kill Luta if not hurry!"

"Which way, quickly!" Scott raced ahead and stopped suddenly when he saw Luta caught in the grip of a giant snake.

172

"Oh my God!" he reached for his hip gun and realized he was wearing nothing but the native bottom. He looked over at the native shaking next to him, "Hand me your knife!"

"No, *Bwana* can no save Luta now!" the native's eyes were wild and frightened.

"Give me that damn knife!" Scott shouted and grabbed the knife out of his pouch.

He raced over to Luta and pulled the snake off. Luta fell as the snake began wrapping its slimy body around Scott's neck. He felt his oxygen being cut off as his hands gripped tightly to the snake head. In his mind he saw Susan and he knew he must free himself of this snake to save her.

"You damn serpent, sent from Satan! You dare to come between me and my task to God!"

His strength grew to double as he pulled the snake free from his throat and stuck the knife through its head.

"Go back to your master and burn in hell!" He flung it to the ground and helped Luta up. "Are you alright, Luta?"

Luta's eyes were wide as he looked fixedly at Scott. "Luta see, Luta no believe! *Bwana* kill deadly snake with hands and knife."

"See Luta, it was my God—our God—who gave me strength to win."

"Your *Vidye Biyampe!*" The other native peered at Scott, then down at the dead snake.

"What did he say Luta?" Scott pulled the knife out of the snake's head and handed it back to the native.

"You're Great One. Your Lord, good!"

"Yes, very, very good!" Scott smiled and looked back toward the village. "Come, we must hurry back before the ritual begins." Scotts legs carried him quickly back to where he had left James and Michael.

"You got back just in time. They're starting something now down there!" James looked up at Scott. "Did you straighten the trouble out?"

"Yeh."

Scott's fist balled up when he saw a tall native push Susan down in front of the statue. "That bastard! That's one ugly face I'll keep in mind."

"Yeh, look at those big jackasses pushing my woman around!"

James started to walk forward and Scott pulled him back." Let me go! I got to help Ali!"

"You will, but not by going in there like an idiot and getting yourself killed." Scott let him go and appraised the back of the statue. "Well, here I come *Maka*." He looked over at Michael and James, "You fellows be ready."

"Got ya Scott!....I mean *Maka*."

Michael held tight to the gun in his hand. Gene Scott climbed to the top of the statue and peered around its giant head. He could see Susan well from up there. She appeared to be holding up fairly well, considering the danger she was facing.

"Oh please" he thought, "Don't call my name when I stand up."

Scott looked towards the heavens with a whisper on his lips. "Stand by me, Lord." He closed his eyes and swallowed. The sweat ran down his face and his heart was pounding wildly. There was a distant rumble in the sky and Scott looked upward.

"Thunder, what luck!" he whispered between his teeth. At the first loud crash I'll stand up. That orda do it!" He laughed softly and winked up at the sky. "One big team working together."

Suddenly there came a loud crash of thunder and Scott stood up and shouted, "*Maka Mambo!*"

The natives began backing away from the statue. Their eyes filled with fear as they stared up at Scott, his hands outstretched over them.

The chief's eyes opened wide and his mouth fell open. "*Maka Maka!*" He fell to the ground. "*Maka, Kuya apa, Karubi!*"

"What's he saying?" James whispered in Michael's ear. "Do you know?"

"*Kuya apa* means come here, so he must be saying, '*Maka* comes here, to Karubi.'" Michael's eyes were on Scott.

"Makes sense."

James looked up at Scott who stood strong on the arms under the statue's giant head. The girls couldn't believe their eyes as they gawked at the half-naked Scott. Susan couldn't pull her eyes away from the man she had fallen for. His strong body had her in a trance and she felt her scared body relaxing. Their eyes met for a brief moment and she desired to hold him and let him embrace her in those strong arms.

174

He surveyed the natives, who were shaking with fear on the ground. He looked up and luckily in the tree just over head, there were vines that he could use to swing down from the giant *Maka*. He grabbed hold of one vine, swung down and landed at the feet of the Karubi Chief. The chief jumped back and lay on the ground under the shadow of Scott's large figure.

Scott stared into the chief's eyes as he spoke, "Can you speak English?"

The natives, barely lifting their heads from the ground, peered nervously at Scott. The chief's mouth dropped open and he stuttered, "huh."

Scott looked around at the nervous tribe. "Does anyone of you speak English?"

"One, great *Maka*," a native of about nineteen years spoke up softly, "What is it you want of us?"

"Let these girls go for a start!" Scott pointed at the three captive women. His voice was loud and the natives shook. "Then peace between you and the Lavites"

"But great one, why you ask your people to do this?"

"Your people will surely burn in hell if they keep worshiping that stone and eating people," Scott shouted. "There is only one God! He looked around at the natives at his feet, "One *Vidye*, one Lord, one Father, One *Tata*!" He pointed at the statue, "And it's not that piece of stone which you worship. It is the maker of this world, the maker of you!" he pulled the native boy upright, "What is your name?"

"Katanda, *Bwana*!" he swallowed. "Chief my father. "

"Tell your father and your people everything that I have told you. Tell them we have come not to hurt them or to take from them anything they own. Tell them we come as true friends. We want to help bring you to God, the real and only God. The God who gave you life, who sends you rain, and sun, and everything you have."

The native told his people everything Scott had said. The chief talked to Scott and his people then Katanda repeated his father's words.

"My father say, strong man came into village with no weapon. Just his God as his spear. He say your heart is good to want help his people find peace with the Lavites. No man come to Karubi with this in their heart. What your name, brave worker of God?"

175

"Scott, Reverend Gene Scott. Tell your father that we have taught the Lavites many things that help them. If your people will sign a peace agreement with the Lavites, they will show you how to do these things too."

Katanda repeated Scott's word and the chief smiled and spoke more, then Katanda turned to Scott. "Father say, Scott, he like you. Will sign agreement. Getting tired of waiting for visitors to come to Karubi. Need change."

The chief pulled his son over and whispered in his ear, "Father want know if Karubi tribe can't eat people."

"Right, no more people or else ..." Scott threw a stick in the fire in front of the statue, "That is what will happen to you when you die."

Katanda's eyes grew big as he told his father about burning if he ate any more people. The chief walked over to Scott and spoke softly. Scott looked over at Katanda.

"Father say, we eat no more people. He afraid of fire." Katanda laughed. "Tell Scott truth. Me no like people meat anyway.'

Scott laughed and patted the chief and his son lightly on the back. "I have friends around your village. Can they come in?"

"Yes. Scott bring in your friends. I tell father."

Katanda told his father while Scott waved to his friends. "Come on, it's safe."

Then he turned to attend to Susan. She smiled gratefully at him as he lifted her to her feet and untied her hands. He grabbed her tightly in his arms.

"Are you alright?" he breathed heavily.

"I am now." She felt his bare skin next to her body. "I knew you would come, I just knew you would save me!"

"Oh Susan, why did you follow us? Why?" His hands moved slowly up and down her back. "What are you trying to do to me? Worry me to death?"

"Gene, I was afraid for you. I...I wanted to help you." She swallowed as her heart beat wildly from the sound of his breathing in her ear.

"Help me? If anything had happened to you, I..." He pulled himself away from her and gazed into her eyes. "I feel responsible for you kids."

"Gene Scott, do I look like a kid?" She put her hands on her hips.

Scott 's eyes fell down the shapely body in front of him. Her breasts could be made out easily through the thin cloth. His eyes fastened on them. He spun around, startled, when Rama touched his shoulder.

"Chief Marui say he go back to Lavite village to speak with my father and sign. paper. Rama's eyes dropped down to Scott's bottom and he smiled.

Scott gritted his teeth and whispered between them, "Damn Delilah." He quickly sat down on the statue's feet and looked up at Rama smirking. "You want me to knock you on your ass kid?"

"Rama not do nothing." He admired Susan who stood gazing at Scott. "She will make man hot easy. Not Scott's fault he desire woman."

"Round up everyone who is going with us." Scott requested. "I'm going to get my clothes."

"We not leave till morning, jungle no place to go walking at night, *Bwana.* "

"Tell them to get some sleep then. We 'll be leaving at the first sign of dawn."

He started to go into the bushes and Susan ran up and grabbed his arm. "Where are you going?"

"To get my clothes. I don't like to run around bare butt." He pushed her hair gently out of her eyes, "Like some people I know."

"I can't let you go out in that jungle alone. she looked up seriously in his eyes, "I'll go with you."

"Like hell you will!" he sounded back.

"But it's dangerous out there. You shouldn't go alone." She tilted her head and swallowed.

"My dear sweet Susan, I feel much safer in that jungle than I do standing right here." His eyes studied her body, then he closed them and turned his head away. "Now stay here and go to bed!"

"But..." She clung to his arm.

"That's an order young lady!" He softened and took hold of her shoulders. "With me in this Tarzan outfit and you in that jungle princess outfit, I feel very uncomfortable. It makes being mischievous too convenient."

"Yes, I see what you mean." She smiled, now surveying

Scott's body. "Mmm how easily one could just reach in and take hold." She smiled slyly at Scott. "Are you sure you don't want me to come with you?"

"Now more than ever, young lady," he patted her cheek. "I already conquered the Devil's serpent today." He looked down at Susan, "I'm not so sure I could conquer his temptress."

They stared at one another silently for a moment. Scott's admired Susan's lips as she gently licked them. Slowly, he moved his head down until his lips found hers.

"Get some sleep, Susan sweets."

He turned quickly and disappeared into the jungle. Susan smiled to herself and clutched her heart.

"I love you Gene Scott," she whispered and turned and glided slowly to where Jackie and Ali where waiting.

Chapter Sixteen

The natives began working together after the peace agreement was signed. Scott said that after they built a church between the two villages, his party would pull out. He smiled down at the two chiefs as the truck he had sent for brought in building supplies.

"Now we can start building that church."

"Good!" Chief Takama smiled at Chief Marui. "Build church. *Kanisa*, church."

"Oh, *Kanisa*, church!" Marui laughed. "*Biyampe*."

"Yes, *biyampe*, good!" Takama looked at Scott. "We get many men to help Scott. Get done much fast."

"Good." Scott patted his back. "There will be other missionaries coming in when we leave. They will bring you the word of God and teach you the Bible in both English and Kiluba. They will continue the work we have started here."

"Yes, chiefs." Danfield smiled as though he had achieved everything himself. "We did all the hard work, made it safe for the others to follow up our work." His smile faded when he saw Scott staring at him.

"We'll prepare to leave the village and start on the church shortly. Have your men ready." Scott walked over to where his group awaited his instructions. "Michael, you and James will go along with me. We start building today. Jackie and Ali, continue with the women, for if all goes well, we will be leaving soon." He looked down at Susan who was smiling broadly at him. "Susan, you and Jobi can take the children as usual. Stay out of the jungle. I don't have time to be saving anyone today."

"How long will you be gone?" She looked deeply into his eyes.

"I will probably remain at the building sight until we have completed it." His gaze took in the figure before him. "We'll set up tents, so there will be no time wasted in moving back and forth."

"You mean Jackie and I will be separated from James and Mike?" Ali asked.

He patted her gently on top of her head. "With all the men we have helping us, we shouldn't be long. Don't worry. It's not going to kill you to be away from one another a few days."

"Haven't you ever loved anyone before Scott?" Jackie put her hands on her hips.

"Yes, very much." He glanced at Susan. "But you know the old saying, 'absence makes the heart grow fonder.'"

"I hate old sayings." Ali put her arms around James. "Miss me, will you?"

"You betcha I will babe." He kissed her. "I'll let that old hammer fly."

"Can I come?" Susan grabbed Gene's arm. "I can do little things for you."

"I just bet you can." Scott laughed. "I want you here with the children."

"But I want to go with you." Her eyes looked pleadingly into his.

"Nothing doing, young lady." He took her shoulders in his hands. "You have to learn that you don't always get everything you want."

"Come on, Susan, listen to Scott for once." James laughed. "After all, he knows with you around, he won't get any work done."

A smile flashed across Susan's face. Scott frowned at James.

"Alright, Tabor. Get in that Jeep and cut out the cute remarks."

"We'll keep a close eye on him, Susan. Make sure he doesn't go running around the jungle dressed like Tarzan." Michael winked at Susan.

"Alright you guys, move!" Scott looked at Ali and Jackie, trying to avoid Susan's eyes. "Watch after Susan and Jobi. You know how kids are. Never know what's in their minds."

Susan gritted her teeth. "I hope you think about me so much you hit your—your finger instead of the nail." She turned and walked quickly to her hut.

"Better watch that hammer, Scott." Jackie touched his cheek and walked away. Scott got in the Jeep mumbling to himself.

"Women always sticking together. Shit, a man don't stand a chance."

"Did you say something, Scott?" James slapped his shoulder and grunted. "Shit! I keep forgetting that hurts."

A New Beginning

Scott laughed and started up the Jeep. "Let's move it."

At the end of four days the fellows pulled in to the Lavite Village. They were dusty and dirty from working straight through. James climbed down from the Jeep and stretched out his long slim arms. "Boy, it's great to be back." He looked around the village. "I wonder where my woman is?"

"I don't know James," Mike said, "but I intend to get a bath before Jackie sees me looking like this." He walked to his hut and came out with clean clothes and a bath towel. "Anyone care to join me?"

"You can count me in." Scott walked over to his hut to get some clean clothes.

Danfield came into his hut and sat down on his bed.

"Where's everyone, Danfield?"

"They took the children on a picnic."

"They who?" Scott picked out his clothes and turn to face the doctor.

"All the women." He stretched out on the bed.

"Has everything been alright? No troubles?"

"Nothing I couldn't handle." He sat up. "Oh, there is one thing I've been keeping my eye on."

"What?" Scott stared at Danfield impatiently.

"That kid Rama, why did you send him back to the village?"

"Because he got sick. He wasn't doing anything but lying around and complaining." He looked at Danfield curiously. "Why, what's he been up to?"

"Well he hasn't been sick. I just don't like the way he's been looking at that Susan girl. He sure has been helping her do everything and, when her back's turned, he watches her constantly. You know what I mean? He looks at her real hard."

In a fluid motion Scott jerked Danfield to his feet. "You mean to tell me he's been messing around Susan? And you let him?"

"Nothing has happened yet. Well—I don't think nothing has happened." He swallowed. "Why are you getting so mad at me?"

"I feel responsible for that girl. If that little bastard has tried anything with her, I'll kill him." Scott's eyes burned into Danfield's. "Where is he now?"

"How should I know?" Danfield pulled away from Scott. "Get

181

Joan Byrd

ahold of yourself, Scott. I think you're going mad!"

"Now look, that kid could be getting herself in a tight squeeze." His voice was grim. "I don't want to see her get hurt. Did Susan go on the damn picnic too?"

"Yes, I assume so. That's probably where you'll find Rama too. He never lets her out of his sight for long." Danfield stepped to the door, then looked back. "I wouldn't worry much about the picnic. Jackie and Ali are with Susan."

"Hmm! Well, I feel they would protect her better than you, Danfield."

Scott stormed past him and joined Michael and James.

"What kept you, Scott? Couldn't figure out what to wear?" James said, chuckling. "I kinda like your Tarzan outfit."

Scott glared at James and started on down the path out of the village.

James shrugged and turned toward Michael. "What's got his hair up?"

Michael nodded. "I don't know, but I bet Susan is involved in it someway." He hustled along the path and caught up with Scott. "Is there some trouble?"

"Yeah. Remember how Rama got sick and I sent him back to the village? Well he only pretended to be sick so he could come back to the village to make time with Susan." Scott's stared straight ahead.

"I see. Well, you have overestimated Rama, but don't underestimate Susan. She's a pretty smart kid, Reverend. I think after all that's happened before, she will keep her cool." Mike stepped into the water.

Scott yanked off his dirty clothes and threw them on a nearby rock.

"Sometimes she does things just to be nice," he said, "and Rama accepts them for something else."

"Any idea where they are now?" Michael lathered up his tan arms and chest.

"They've gone on a picnic." Scott disappeared beneath the water and came back up shaking. "Oh shit! That's cold."

"Speaking of picnics, I bet Rama has been having a real picnic with you not around to get in his way." James laughed, then stopped abruptly when he saw the furious look on Scott's face.

182

A New Beginning

"Cool it, man. I was only pulling your leg."

"If you know what's good for you, Tabor, you will keep your smart-ass remarks to yourself." Scott rubbed the wash cloth over his arm and slapped it in the water.

Susan stopped quickly when her eyes fell on the Jeeps. "They're back." She grabbed Jackie's arm. "They're back. Scott came back."

"You're right." Jackie looked around, trying to spot Michael. "I don't see any of our guys, though. Do you?"

"I don't see James." Ali stretched up on her toes to have a better look through the crowded village street. She noticed Danfield standing in his door way. "Let's go ask nosey Danfield. He'll probably know where they are." She led the way to the doctor. "Excuse us, but can you tell us where our men are?"

"I'm man enough for you, sweetheart." He smiled, gazing at her bare legs.

"I doubt it." She feigned a smile. "Now, can you tell us where they went?"

His eyebrows arched. "Very well. Based on the direction they were going and what they took with them, I think they went to take a bath."

"Thank you, Doctor Danfield." Ali turned toward Susan and Jackie and made a face.

Sneaking down the path, the three girls slipped up on the bathing men and stared through the bushes.

Ali punched Jackie's arm. "I say, this is very interesting."

"Boy, it makes me impatient and in a hurry for the night to come." Jackie looked at Susan who stared continually at Gene. "Scott does have a great body. What I can see of it looks terrific."

Susan frowned at her. "Well, let's make sure what you see now, is all you see of it."

Jackie giggled and winked at Ali. "I do believe our little Susan wants to claim Scott for herself."

"I love him." Susan looked at Jackie, her expression totally serious. "I really love him, very much."

"I believe you Susan." Jackie caressed her cheek. "I was only kidding around. I didn't really mean anything by it. I love Michael very much too."

183

Joan Byrd

Susan's eyes dropped to her hands. "I'm sorry. I didn't mean to sound so possessive."

"Hey, I've got a great idea!" Ali said, giggling. "Let's go pay a visit to our fellows and make them think we're going to steal their clothes."

Jackie laughed. "I can just see Scott 's face. He's so serious about everything."

"Do you think we should? I mean Gene can get pretty angry when you play tricks on him." Susan looked at the girls.

"Oh, come on Susan. That's all the more reason to tease him. It's only in fun." Jackie put her hand on Susan's arm. This will be hilarious. You can make the rules up. He'll do just about anything to get his clothes."

Susan smiled, considering the possibilities. "Let's do it. This sounds better and better every second."

They crept toward the water and each picked up their man's clothes. Just as they did, the fellows noticed them and looked at each other helplessly.

"Hey, Jackie, what gives hon?" Michael smiled at the woman he had missed for four days.

"Why didn't you fellows let us know you were coming back?" She rubbed the towel gently across her chest. "We would've been ready for you."

"And how were we supposed to let you know, by telephone or air mail maybe?" James punched "Mike's arm. "Good idea, huh? You should've thought of that."

Michael groaned. "Brilliant, James."

"What's wrong with you, Gene Scott? Lost your voice?" Susan gripped his clothes, holding them prominently in front of her.

"This is not funny, young lady." He stared at her, his expression a mixture of relief, annoyance and longing. "How about if you 'ladies' put down our clothes and go wait for us in the village?"

"Should we do what Scott wants?" Ali winked at Susan.

"You know how you keep telling me I can't have everything I want? Well you have to learn, Gene," she said, smiling triumphantly, "that you don't always get everything you want either."

184

"Susan, that is not funny." His jaw tightened. "I'm tired. I've been worried about you—all of you. And I'm in no mood for silly games. Put those clothes down right now and go back to the village before I get out and—"

"Get out?" she said excitedly. "Get out and do what, Gene?"

The women laughed out loud and Susan grinned at them.

"Susan, I—If you don't . . ." He looked down at the water and mumbled to himself. "Women always doing stupid things."

"Scott, maybe if James and I could get our women to leave, Susan wouldn't be so tough to handle." Mike squeezed his shoulder.

"Well, it's worth a try."

Michael waded near the girls. "Jackie, I'm getting all wrinkled in here. Hand me my clothes or I'll have to come out and get them."

A look of delight crossed her face. "Oh Mike, I can't have you getting all wrinkled up. Come on out." She stepped back with a smile.

"Susan, unless you and Ali want to get flashed, better turn around. I'm getting out."

When he actually did start out of the water, Susan turned quickly around.

Ali laughed, hands on hips and said to James, "Are you climbing out too, lover?"

"Why the hell not?" he laughed. He made his way quickly to the edge and climbed out. "Hand me my clothes, babe."

"Here you go." She handed him his clothes and helped him slip them on quickly. "Come along, dear. Susan and Gene can take care of themselves."

The two couples walked up the path toward the village laughter trailing behind them. Susan stood smiling at the helpless Scott in the water. She sat down on the rock next to his dirty clothes and crossed her legs casually.

"Oh, these are yours too, aren't they?" She pulled them next to her. "I'll wash them for you when I wash out mine."

"Susan, would you be a sweetheart and follow those folks to the village?" He edged closer to the shore. "I really would like to get out of here."

"I'm not stopping you, Gene. How can little bitty me stop a

185

great big man like you, huh?"

He stared at her, disgusted. "Alright, Miss Smarty Pants, ready or not, I'm coming out."

Her eyes widened as she tried to decide if he was bluffing. "Alright. Good." She stood up. "Too bad I don't have my camera."

"Susan!" He slapped the water in frustration. "Have you been playing little games like this with Rama too?"

"Rama? Why would I do that. He means nothing to me." She tilted her head oddly as she looked at the man before her. "You, on the other hand, I don't mind teasing at all."

"I—I've been told that Rama has been spending a lot of time with you. Is that true."

As they stared into each other's eyes, Susan recognized her opportunity. "Well, he's been very nice in helping me with the children." She hugged Gene's clothes. "Why, I do believe my darling reverend is jealous."

"Enough of this game, I'm losing my patience."

"What game, Gene? I'll have to look at you sooner or later." She wet her lips. "And you will have to look at me."

"Susan, I'm in no mood for your Delilah act right at the present. I've got work to do. And sitting around in this water on my ass is not getting it done."

"Oh, my dear, dear Gene. Must you think about work all the time?" She shook her head and smiled shyly. "You just came back from four straight days of hard work. I can think of better things to do."

"So can I," he muttered angrily, "as soon as I get out of here. I'm going to start by giving you the spanking you've been needing, young lady."

"Gee luv, that might hurt. I mean, your big hand on my little bitty bottom." She laughed. "But at least that would be a start in the right direction."

His jaw dropped open in amazement. "Oh! Susan, what on earth is wrong with you?"

"There's nothing wrong with me, Gene." Her voice had become serious. "You're the one who's afraid to be honest."

"Honest? Susan, when I say something I honestly mean it." He gazed back at her. "I'm not hiding anything."

"Oh." She smiled and glanced toward the water that concealed half his body. "Then stand up."

He shook his head slowly. "Susan, Susan what am I going to do with you?"

"I can imagine plenty of things".

She turned when she heard someone come up behind her. Rama stood smiling at the scene before him."

"What matter, Scott? Why not come out of water?"

"Scott is afraid of me, Rama." Susan giggled.

He frowned at her. "Susan, would you please be quiet."

"Oh? He afraid of you, huh?" He considered Scott before him, half concealed by the water. "Scott man in fighting. Scott man in building. Scott man in hunting. But when it comes to Scott woman, Scott not much man."

Susan sighed, nodding. "Well Rama, he is rather hard to persuade to do anything. I've been standing here waiting for him to come out for fifteen minutes."

"Susan," Scott said between clinched teeth, "you're talking way too much."

"Oh Gene, darling, I can think of so many better things to do than talk if only you would just get out." She smiled despite the anger in his eyes.

"Susan need real man. Rama real man. Susan need Rama, not Scott."

"Uh, no." She turned to Scott, who had closed his eyes and was shaking his head. "Aren't you going to say something, Gene?"

"Rama challenge Scott to be man of Susan's." The boy smiled at Susan. "Rama make Susan happy."

"Scott makes Susan happy." She hugged the clothes tightly to her chest.

"Rama," Gene's voice was measured, "Susan is mine. You should go find yourself another woman."

He stretched his hand out. Susan handed him his clothes and turned her head. He slipped out of the water and pulled on his clothes.

"A challenge is not necessary. I don't intend to give Susan up."

"Sorry, Scott. Rama see Susan need man. Scott no make woman love. I challenge you to battle of strength. Winner prize, Susan."

187

"Oh no. This can't happen." She grabbed Scott's arm. "Please, Gene, do something."

"This challenge you're suggesting Rama, it's ridiculous and out of the question." He glanced at Susan, her eyes wide with fear. "Even if I did accept the challenge, you couldn't win her no matter how hard you tried."

"Rama think he can." He smiled brightly, staring at Susan. "Rama try extra hard for Susan."

"Damn it, Rama, you are not getting my woman." He grabbed Rama. "You need to forget you ever made that challenge."

Susan's heart melted as she asked herself silently, "Oh Gene, do you really mean these things, or are you just pretending for Rama's sake."

Rama's face hardened in seriousness. "Rama fight. Rama not give up chance to win. Susan. Rama go tell father about challenge. He make everything ready for night." He turned abruptly and walked away.

Scott's eyes followed him until he was out of sight, then they fell on Susan.

". . . Oh Gene, I'm so sorry! I've gotten you in trouble, haven't I?" Her eyes fell to the ground.

"I'm not sure what kind of contest Rama has in mind, Susan, but he probably knows how to do it very well." Scott took her hand gently. "Well, what's done is done. I guess I fight."

"Oh God, Gene, if it's dangerous--oh if anything happens to you, I'll just die." Tears flooded her eyes as she buried her head on his chest. "It's all my fault you're in this stupid mess."

"I'll not deny that. You did keep talking when I told you to be quiet." He patted her head. "Look, Susan, there's nothing going to happen to me. Do you take me for a weak sissy?"

"No! Oh no, Gene! You're the strongest man I've ever seen in real life." Susan looked back toward the village. "He did say a contest of strength, didn't he?"

"That's right." Scott started toward the village. "Now we'll have to find out just what kind of contest it is."

Susan ran along beside him to keep up with his big steps. Many of the villagers had begun gathering for the contest. Michael and Jackie walked out to meet Scott and Susan.

"Scott, what's up?" Michael asked with a puzzled expression.

"This whole place is buzzing. Some kid came around saying there was going to be a contest between you and Rama."

"What's this all about?" Jackie asked, looking around at the agitated crowd. "It must be something pretty good to excite everybody this way."

"Rama has challenged me to a contest on strength," Scott said absently, taking in the swelling mass of spectators.

"Strength?" Jackie laughed. "Is Rama crazy? He doesn't have a chance."

"There are more than one kind of strength, luv." Mike put his arm around Jackie's shoulder. "There's physical strength and then there's mental strength." He turned to Scott. "What exactly is he challenging you for? What's the prize?"

"Susan," Scott said flatly. It was at that instant he saw Rama as he made his way toward them. "And I'll fight him all the way to hell before I let him lay one lousy finger on Susan."

Jackie smiled at Susan, who stared in terrified disbelief and awe as Rama approached Scott.

Rama, wearing a confident smile, glanced at Susan as he punched Scott on the shoulder. "All ready, Scott?"

"Ready, Rama." Puzzled, he gazed at the boy, up and down. "You should know, son, I'm fighting to win, so you had better pick out something where you won't get hurt."

"Rama no scared of you, Scott." He gestured toward his father who sat on a wooden chair, silently observing them. "Father ready. Contest start." He called to the gathered villagers. "Everyone be seated please."

In an instant the whole village found places on the ground, waiting expectantly. Susan sat next to Jackie and Ali. She twisted her ring and bit her lip nervously. Jackie slipped an arm around her shoulder.

"Hey kid, pull yourself together. You've got the best man around here fighting for you. Better be glad it's Scott instead of Danfield."

"Oh gross! I'd prefer Rama over that creepy doctor." Susan stared helplessly at the man she loved. "Oh Jackie, it's all my fault he's in this terrible danger."

"Now, now calm down, Susan, maybe it won't be all that dangerous. I don't think Rama would pick anything he couldn't

Joan Byrd

do. And anything he can do, you know Scott can do." Jackie pulled her close. "I think they're about to begin. We'll soon find out."

"My people and my friends, your attention please." Chief Takama motioned for silence. "My son has challenged Reverend Scott for the love of Susan. Now we see which man have strength enough to win her." He winked at his son. "I be judge of contest."

"Now wait just a minute, Chief Takama." Jackie stood up, hands on hips. "That will not be fair. How do we know that you will not choose your son without giving Scott an equal chance?"

"Jackie's right chief." Ali hopped up and stood beside her friend. "We want to find the strongest, not the favorite. With one judge—well it just isn't democratic."

"Okay, missy, okay." The chief glanced toward his son and shrugged in resignation. "They right, Rama. Must be judged fairly. Scott my very good friend. We owe him much. No do him wrong." The chief turned toward the girls. "Pick one judge among you and he sit next to me."

"Michael, you do it." Jackie pulled him to his feet. She whispered, "And see to it that Scott wins."

"I'll judge fairly, just like Takama." He went to the chief's side. "I guess I've been selected."

"Good choice. Sit down." The chief addressed Scott. "Must put on Lavite bottom, my friend. It custom to fight in one."

"Oh great," Scott mumbled. "I still have the one I wore when I was *Maka*. Is that one alright?"

"It perfect!" the chief laughed and motioned Scott away. "Hurry. Everyone excited and ready for contest."

Scott hurried away and returned quickly dressed in the short bottom. The native women giggled and whispered to one another as they stared at him wide eyed.

Susan frowned and hit the ground with her fist. "Why don't they stop staring at Gene like that?"

"Can you blame them?" Ali said as she patted Susan's hand. "He's better to look at than most."

"Yes, I suppose. Well, okay, it's obvious. But they don't have to look so darn close."

Her eyes met Gene's. A smile crossed her lips. Spontaneously she blew him a kiss.

"Good luck, Samson."

"He returned her smile. "It's all for the heart of Delilah." Turning to Rama, he said, "Okay, let's get this contest over with. We've got packing to do."

Exuding confidence and smiling at his father, Rama said, "I ready anytime."

"Okay, my son. Rama pick for himself, lifting heavy rocks." He pointed at a pile of rocks, placed in order so that each one was progressively heavier as they proceeded. "Rama see how big a rock he can pick up and hold overhead."

Rama walked over and started picking up the rocks, beginning with the smallest. He successfully picked up the first three, but when he tried to lift the fourth, he dropped it. He smiled and glanced at Scott.

"You try that one."

Scott immediately stepped over, picked up the rock Rama had dropped and held it over his head. To his surprise, the village people began clapping. Rama motioned for them to stop.

"Scott think smart? Pick up last rock."

Scott gazed at the final, largest stone and then at Susan. She tried hard to smile reassuringly at him. He flexed his knees and, with a fierce groan, lifted the rock slowly off the ground. Susan sat up on her knees and bit her lip. Gritting his teeth, Scott slowly lifted the massive rock over his head and dropped it quickly. The villagers leaped to their feet, cheering. Rama motioned them down.

"Scott not win yet." Rama's voice was defiant. "Next the strength of the mind." He looked at his father. "Tell Scott about next contest, Father. Maybe he rather just call it quits after he hear about it and give me woman."

Gene's voice was equally strong. "Let's hear it, Takama." He winked at Susan. "I'll do anything it takes to keep my woman."

The chief smiled. "Scott very determined. Very well. The last part of the contest will rely on your strength to withstand fear. We have prepared a large box in which you and Rama will lie down. You will be tied down. Then we shall put certain poison snakes in with you. Your only chance to survive will be to lie perfectly still and not move for fifteen minutes." In the silence, the chief's laugh was shrill and eerie. "First man to move or beg to be let out will lose contest. And Susan, it fair to tell you some of the snakes are not poison enough to kill you, just make sick. But then some very deadly and will kill you right away." Takama gazed at Scott. "Scott still want to do this?"

"For Susan? Yes! Bring on the damn snakes." He strode toward the box.

"No!" Suddenly Susan was on her feet, running to Scott and grabbing him around his strong waist. "Please don't do it, Gene! Please!"

Everyone watched silently as Gene gazed at the terrified girl he had grown to care for so very much.

He lifted her chin gently and smiled. "Hey, where 's my strong hearted Delilah? Have you no faith in me?" He kissed her cheek and whispered in her ear, "God will be with me. And I'll concentrate on you."

She stared up at him. "Well, no matter what happens, don 't you dare move. Not one little muscle."

"As long as you're not lying beside me, I think I can control all my muscles." He laughed as she blushed. "Now, please, go back over with Jackie and Ali. And you keep still, too. I wouldn't want to upset those little snakes."

She bit her lip and squeezed his strong hand. Silently she mouthed, "I love you."

Their gazed locked, Scott's breathing grew heavy. He put his fingers on her cheek.

"Go on, Susan. Let's get this over with."

"Alright Gene, but please, be careful." She made her way slowly toward the women, glancing back toward Scott.

He nodded toward her and lay down in the deadly box next to Rama.

The chief motioned to the native holding the box of snakes. He slowly opened the container and let the snakes slither into the enclosure with Scott and Rama. Susan's heart beat wildly in her throat. Jobi came to her, sat down and squeezed her hand.

"Sis, why is Reverend Scott in this trouble? Why does he have to do this?"

"Oh, Jobi, it's all my stupid fault! Rama thought Scott didn't love me enough to be my man. So he challenged him." She took a deep breath. "If anything happens to Gene, I just want to die!"

"It's alright, sis. Nothing is going to happen. Scott is the bravest and strongest man I've ever met—or read about for that matter."

Datari had followed Jobi to Susan's side and he spoke up. "Rama pretty brave too, friend Jobi." He smiled at Susan.

"Please Datari, instead of discussing your cousin's bravery right now, can we please just pray they both get out of that box without getting bit? I'm fond of Rama, but I'm in love with Gene."

"Datari understand. Hope Scott win for you." He stared at the deadly box and shook his head. "Just glad Datari not in there."

"Oh, Gene." Her hand quivering, Susan looked down at her watch. Only five minutes had passed since the snakes had been placed in the enclosure. "Oh, time, please hurry." She swallowed and buried her face in her hands.

Inside the box, Scott lay still. His eyes shut, he tried to think only about the moment he would get out. Silently he counted the seconds as he felt the cold bodies sliding over him. He had never liked snakes and at their touch he had to concentrate to keep his muscles from growing tensed. Regardless of where the snakes touched him, he would not move.

Beside him, he felt the slightest motion from Rama. Slowly Gene opened his eyes. He could see the black, beady eyes of the black snake lying on his stomach, focused on face—just staring, not offering to move as its tongue flicked in and out of its mouth. And from the corner of his eye, he could see Rama. Sweat was pouring off the frightened boy.

From above the box, he sensed someone watching them. Slowly moving his eyes upward, he saw the chief's daughter. She held a small rock in her hand. She smiled at Scott and whispered just loudly enough for him to hear.

"Give up, Scott. My brother must win. He want Susan. I want you."

Scott just stared up at her. His muscles remain still. She smiled and dropped the rock toward his hand where a brownish snake lay. The snake struck at the rock and hit Scott's hand.

From across the clearing, Susan cried out and leaped to her feet, dashing toward the box. Michael grabbed her and covered her mouth.

"Susan," he whispered harshly. "Susan, you have to calm down."

"Oh, Michael, he's been bitten! Help him, please!" She burst into tears.

"It might not have been one of the venomous ones." Michael turned to the chief with a frown. "You know what your daughter did was cheating, Takama. You need to call off this whole silly game."

A scream came from the box. It was Rama. "Let me out! I've been bitten, Father!"

Instantly the chief went to the box, with the entire village gathering around.

"Get snakes out!" Takama demanded. "Hurry!"

He looked down at Scott and his son. Rama was breathing heavily and shaking uncontrollably. Scott continued to lie quietly with his eyes shut. Looking down at him, Susan's eyes flooded with tears.

Jackie raced to Susan, throwing her arms around her. "Is he dead? Oh, Mike! Oh God! He just can't be."

"He still breathing, girls. He is just being careful not to arouse his little friends there any more than they already are." He patted Jackie's arm and turned to her. "Go find Danfield. Fast. And tell him to bring his snakebite kit. We have two serious bites to treat."

Ali, who was beside her friends, glanced about them. "Isn't the coward out here?"

"He took off when they mentioned snakes," James said with a laugh. He stopped suddenly as he gazed down at Scott. "Are you sure he's alive?"

"Oh!" Susan looked at Michael and gasped.

"I'm sure. I'm sure." He glared at James. "Do you mind guarding what you say? They're scared enough as it is."

"Sorry." He turned to Susan. "Don't worry, sweetheart. He's gonna be alright."

With their long sticks and nets, the villagers managed to get the remaining snakes out of the enclosure. Mike and James jumped in the box and untied Scott and Rama.

Scott opened his eyes and smiled at them. "Boy, I always thought you fellows weren't much to look at, but compared to them snakes, you're practically gorgeous." He stood and looked down at Rama, still lying on the ground, shaking. "Are you alright, kid?"

Rama opened his eyes slowly. "Are...are they all gone?"

Scott pulled him up to his feet.

"Every one of them. Where did they bite you?"

"My—my leg." He pointed to tiny mark on his calf.

Scott examined it closely. "You're safe. It's not a venomous bite."

Susan, who had pushed her way through the others, grabbed Scott. "Are you alright?"

"I'm fine, Susan." He laughed and hugged her. "One thing is for sure. I've got to take you home, young lady, before you get me into any more trouble."

"What about your snakebite? We have to fix it." She studied his hand. "Does it hurt?"

"Not much. It will be fine as soon as old doc fixes me up." He nodded toward Danfield, who was jogging toward them. "Hello, Danfield. What took you so long?"

"You didn't have an appointment." He chuckled anxiously, then began chattering again. "Once I saw this movie where this guy got snake bit—oh it's was so—"

"Doctor Danfield!" Fury was in Susan's voice. "Will you please shut up and fix Gene's hand?" She put her hands on her hips. "This is no time to tell us about one of your dumb movies."

Gene laughed aloud. "You heard her, Danfield. Let's get moving." He pulled Rama to him. "Let's fix this kid first."

"Oh, very well." Danfield arched his eyebrow and looked at Rama's leg. "Nothing serious, lad. We'll have you like new in no time flat."

The boy was humbled. "Rama think Scott deserve Susan. Scott best man for her."

"Oh, Rama." Susan touched his hand. "You are a very special young man too."

Scott took her arm and pulled her next to him.

"We know Rama is a very nice person Susan." He frowned. "But just to be on the safe side so I don't end up in another snake pit, why don't you let me do the telling."

"Oh." She looked down at her hands. "Anything you say, Gene darling." She gazed into his eyes. "After all, I am your woman. You won me fair and square." She glanced around at everyone watching. "And you have all these witnesses to prove it." Unconsciously her eyes drifted to his supple body."

He laughed sheepishly, glancing around at the smiling faces. "Susan, just go get ready to leave. We'll be pulling out in the morning." He looked at the rest of his party. "Well, what are you all waiting for, get moving."

Smiling, laughing, they walked toward their huts to begin packing.

Susan took Scott's good hand. "You know something, Gene Scott, I love being your woman." She looked down at the short pants he wore. "And that Tarzan outfit. You must keep it." She put her hands around his neck and locked them together. "It brings out the wild man in you."

He felt himself growing and realized how obvious it would be in this outfit. He pulled her hands free from his neck.

"Susan, please go pack." He said, his breath heavy. "Please, just go and pack."

"Alright Gene darling." She glanced down and smiled. "I see Delilah has got a lot to look forward to."

Scott noticed Danfield staring, his mouth open. He took Susan and turned her toward her hut. "Now for the last time, get going."

"I'm going." She looked him up and down and smiled. "See you in the morning."

"Yes, yes, just go and get packed." He watched her as she twisted her way toward her hut. He noticed Danfield was watching her closely too.

"What are you looking at, doc."

"Pretty nice wiggle." He chuckled. "Wouldn't mind having that swing on my back porch. In my bed for that matter."

Scott grabbed Danfield. "Look, doc," he said, glaring, "the only way you get that swing anywhere is to come through me first."

"You act as though you own her, Scott." Danfield laughed as he shook his head. "You can fool that dumb kid, but you can't fool me."

"Just try something with her, Danfield. And I'll show you I mean business." He turned abruptly and walked toward his hut.

Chapter Seventeen

Scott and his party pulled their Jeeps to a stop in front of the Taboo Hotel. They had completed their long journey back to the small village of Taboo where they would take their flight out of Africa. Scott looked back at the others.

"If you like to take a bath and get fixed up before we leave, now's the time to do it." He looked at Susan who had ridden next to him all the way back. "Better hurry along Susan and get ready to leave."

"There's not but two tubs in there. Jackie and Ali can go first. I'll help you return these things." She smiled at Jobi. "Won't we, Jobi."

He returned her smile. "Sure."

"I'm touched." He wore a skeptical grin. "How do you know there's only two tubs in the hotel?"

"Because I can read." She put her hand on his chin and turned his head so that he could see the little sign next to the door. "See, Right there it says—"

"Yes, yes, I see it now. 'Bathe in one of our two tubs.'" He turned to Jackie and Ali. "Go get in those two bathtubs. And don't spend the rest of the day there."

"How do you like this guy?" Jackie climbed out of a Jeep. "As if we spend too much time in the tub."

"Right." Michael laughed. "Just go and try to hurry. Try to make it less time than your usually fast two hours."

"Very funny, Mike." Ali followed Jackie quickly into the hotel.

The rest of the party drove the Jeeps to the supply store. Scott climbed out and stuck his head in the door.

"Hello. Is anyone here?"

The storekeeper came out of the back room. "Is anybody here? Of course somebody's here. Somebody's always here."

"We're back with your Jeeps." Scott dropped the keys onto the countertop.

"I wouldn't have believed it," the storekeeper laughed and

shook his head. "You people go to Bakuba country and come back all in one piece. Lordy mercy." He laughed again, his head tipping back. "Lordy, Lordy, Lordy."

"Well, from now on Bakuba will be a friendly place to visit." Scott walked over to the door and looked out. "Did you get the Jeep the kids rented?"

Standing beside him, the storekeeper looked out as well. "Yeh. Them really are your young-uns then." He couldn't help but chuckle. "And I thought when they told me they were your children they were just making it up."

"Oh! My kids. I see." Gene looked out at Susan. "I guess she seems to be a sweet little pretty 'innocent' girl. More innocent than she really is."

"You sure must really be a proud father. Lordy me. Letting those kids come with you on such a dangerous mission." He put his hand on Scott's shoulder. "Yes indeedy. Well, I reckon you all will get what you rightly deserve, I mean doing such good work as you do."

He nodded. "Well one thing's for sure. They will get what they deserve, believe me." He walked out to the Jeeps and took Susan's hand to help her down. "Well, my dear little children, shall we prepare to leave?"

Susan and Jobi looked at one another and tried to smile at Scott. "Sorry we made that up, Gene. We had to think of something to say to get those Jeeps and supplies."

"Yeh, and what about it being alright with your folks, hmm? What of that? Another lie I presume." Scott turned and started toward the hotel.

"We wanted to help you Reverend Scott," Jobi said excitedly. "Really!"

"And you yourself said that we were one big team, and that we should get off the bench and help one another." Susan was practically out of breath from trying to keep up with Scott's long strides.

He stopped and faced Susan, frowning. "I never meant for you kids to follow me and get yourselves into danger. And as for helping me, was putting me in a box of poisonous snakes an example of your helpfulness?"

"Gene Scott, I told you I was sorry for that. And you have to

198

admit we did help some. I mean with the children and all." Susan turned toward the hotel and her mouth flew open. "Oh, Lord!" She jumped behind Scott and pulled Jobi against her. "Oh!"

"What is it, sis?" Jobi tried to peek around Scott, only to have Susan pull his head back.

Scott followed Susan's furtive gaze toward the hotel and saw she had been looking at a tall, skinny, gray-haired man who was talking with the hotel clerk just outside the lobby.

Scott glanced back at the two behind him. "Who is he, Susan?"

"Our granddad," she said, smiling sheepishly.

"Oh. Dr. William T. Rogers, is it?" Scott chuckled and started toward the man. "Well, I need to have a little talk with Dr. Rogers."

"Please, Reverend Scott." Susan gripped his arm. "Don't tell him!"

"Don't tell him what?" Gene cradled her chin in palm. "How you came to Africa to see him? It would be nice if you did"

"But we are getting ready to leave." Susan bit her lip. "What will we tell him, 'Hello Granddad, nice to see you. So long?"

"Just leave it to me." Scott smiled slyly at the two nervous Andrews. "I'll take care of everything."

"That's what I'm afraid of," Susan mumbled to herself as she followed Gene to where her grandfather stood.

William Roger's eyes fell on the two kids standing next to the strong, good-looking stranger. His rough, old lips broke into a smile as he reached out and grabbed them.

"Bless my soul I don't believe my eyes!" He laughed aloud. "'It's really you, sure enough."

"Yes, Granddad, it's us." Susan kissed his weathered cheek.

"You're looking neat, Granddad," Jobi said with a great smile, and glanced up at Scott. "How's it going?"

"Same old Jobi, just full of questions." He chuckled and rubbed the boy's head. His gaze drifted to Scott. "Who's your friend, children?"

Susan took Gene's hand, pulling him closer to her. "Granddad, this is Reverend Gene Scott. He's been doing missionary work over here in Africa." She glanced at him with a smile and said, "We've been helping him."

"Reverend Scott, of course, been hearing about all of the great things you and your group been doing in BaKuba." He shook Scott's hand. "The world could use more like you Scott."

"Thank you, Dr. Rogers. The way I hear it from your grandchildren, the world would be better if there was a few more of you around," Gene said with a smile.

"How did the kids do? They didn't cause you any kind of trouble now did they?" Dr. Rogers hugged his granddaughter.

"They did very well, considering their age." He exchanged glances with Susan. "They did a great job working with the children. It gave me a lot more time to work on others things because of them." He nodded slowly. "I guess you could say, they were pretty valuable to have around."

"That's good to hear, "Rogers said earnestly. "It's good to know there are a few more members of the family who have a little guts."

Then you're not mad at us for going on this dangerous mission then?" Jobi asked, and immediately felt his sister nudge his arm. "I mean you don't see anything wrong with our going to help, do you, Granddad?"

"Me? Lordy no, Jobi my boy." He winked at Jobi. "But I bet your mom and dad didn't know about it, now did they?"

"Well, it was sorta a last-minute decision, Granddad. "Susan looked up at Scott for help.

"The kids were on their way over here to have a visit with you, Dr. Rogers. We met on the boat and became friends."

"Very good friends," Susan added with a smile.

"And they took to heart a sermon I preached about helping others. So they decided to come along with me to help." He forced a smile. "They followed so bravely, knowing the dangers that were lying ahead—man eating crocs, man eating natives, pit traps, lions and—oh yes—can't forget the snakes."

Susan swallowed, her eyes growing wide.

"I agree with you kids that it's best not to tell your folks about your little adventure." Rogers chuckled as he looped an arm around each of them. "Just like your granddad, both of you. Well, you kids can count on your old granddad to keep your secret. As far as I know, if they ask, you spent the whole time with me."

"Oh, Granddad, you're wonderful!" Susan hugged her grandfather's neck.

"Pretty isn't she," he said, sharing a knowing smile with Scott.

"Pretty, yes. Just like Alice in Wonderland."

"So, Susan," Dr. Rogers asked, "When will you and Jobi be heading toward your new home?"

"Very soon, Granddad. As soon as good old Reverend Scott gets our plane ready." She took her grandfather's arm "Let's go inside and talk." Glancing around at Gene, she called, "You can tell us when we have to leave."

"Yes, I will." He forced a smile and looked toward Dr. Rogers. "By the way, William, better have a talk with your little granddaughter about flirting with men. She almost got herself married off to a native boy." Gene laughed and walked passed, avoiding Susan's glare.

"Gene Scott, you beast," she muttered. Then she turned to her grandfather, standing with a broad grin on his face. "What are you smiling at?"

Dr. Rogers exchanged looks with Jobi. They laughed together.

"I do believe our little Susan has a giant size crush on the Reverend Scott."

Jobi laughed again. Susan sighed in defeat.

Reverend Scott helped Jackie with her luggage as she climbed on the private jet.

"Do you know anyone in TarSa, Reverend Scott."

"Yes, Reverend and Mrs. John W. Crain. They've been good friends of mine for years."

Scott picked Ali up and sat her on the gangway of the plane. She smiled in surprise at the strength she felt in his arms.

"My, I can't imagine what it's like having a strong man for a lover." She glanced at James. "But James is a very good lover." She giggled. "Even if he is skinny."

"Did someone mention my name?" James walked over and patted Ali's behind.

"That all depends. What did you hear?"

"The words, James, skinny and lover. "

"Then you heard your name." She kissed his cheek. "Come along, lover."

Michael walked lazily to the plane.

"I hope you fly this thing with more energy than you walk." Scott teased.

Joan Byrd

"Yeh, huh." Mike laughed "Is everyone on board?"

"No. Everyone but the Andrew kids and Danfield." Scott stared toward the gate. "Where are those two?"

"I think I saw them coming behind me. And, by the way, Danfield's not coming with us." Mike started up the steps.

"Really? Why are we so honored?" Scott chuckled.

"He's headed back to Kansas," he said. He's sailing on the ship tomorrow." He motioned toward the gate. Susan and Jobi were running through it. "Here come the kids now."

"It's about time. Thought for a minute I was going to have to rescue you again." Scott helped Susan on the steps behind Michael. "Trying to make us get a late start?"

"We're sorry, Gene." Susan climbed up the steps.

Jobi punched Scott's arm as he watched Susan from below.

"Pretty good view, huh, Scott?"

"Get up those steps, son." Scott lifted Jobi up by the arm and set him on the third step. Scott took a seat next to a window and watched as the plane left the continent of Africa.

"Goodbye snakes, mosquitos. Goodbye crocodiles and wild natives."

Ali waved from the window.

Jackie laughed. "Don't forget, goodbye heat."

"Why didn't Doctor Danfield come with us?" Susan asked, gazing out over Scott's shoulder.

"I suppose he got tired of our company." Scott chuckled and picked up a sports magazine.

"Well, he was no pleasure to be around either." Susan settled back in her seat and smiled at Jobi. "Hand me that mother's childcare book.

Scott's eyebrows arched. He pulled off his glasses and raised up in his seat to look at Susan.

"Why are you reading that?"

"Well you never know when you might need to know how to take care of a baby."

"Aren't you a little young to be thinking about having babies?" Scott took the book from her hand and looked at the cover. A blue eyed baby stared back at him.

"Isn't he darling? I hope ours looks just like you though."

She touched Scott's cheek and retrieved the book from his

hand. He stared into her eyes and, suddenly anxious, sat back down in his seat.

"Susan, you do have an imagination."

"Oh Gene, I know you love children and so do I," she giggled and winked at Jackie and Ali, who were trying to hold back their own laughter. "And I'm not too young to be a mother, as you must think. My dear grandmother had three children before she was even sixteen."

Scott stood and looked at the smiling faces surrounding him. "I think I need to be excused, if you ladies and 'children' will pardon me." He made his way quickly to the restroom.

Jackie laughed. "Oh Susan, you really had him shook up."

"Supposing he leaves TarSa soon after we arrive there. What can I do?" Susan laid her head on the back of the seat in front of her.

"We'll think of something, sis, don't worry." Jobi tried to reassure his sister.

"Jobi's right , and besides he said he had close friends living in TarSa," Jackie said with a smile.

"Friends?" Susan lifted her head. "Who? He did tell us he had some good friends there."

"Reverend and Mrs. John Crain. He preaches at the Sand Palms Methodist Church there." Ali flipped through the fashion magazine in her hand

"Have you ever been to TarSa? I mean you seem to know so much about it?" Jobi asked, tilting his head.

"Oh sure, kid." Jackie offered a stick of gum to him and Susan.

"Thanks." Jobi said.

"Yes, thank you," Susan said. "When did you go there?"

"Oh we vacationed there for about two weeks last year. Loved it. So we plan to settle down there." Jackie looked toward the front of the plane. "Michael and James got the post in Africa when we had decided to move to TarSa. So that's why we're headed there now."

"Hey, neat." Jobi laughed. "At least we have some friends on the island after all. "

Scott rejoined the group and took his seat. He picked up the sports book and began reading, pretending not to hear them.

"Well, I'm sure I will enjoy TarSa," Susan said loudly. "So

many interesting sports one could enjoy."

"Yeh!" Jobi said just as loudly. "Swimming, fishing, boating, tennis, golf, baseball, basketball, football and many, many others.

Gene smiled, shaking his head. "Well, you kids will stay so busy with all those activities and sports, you won't even miss me."

"Miss you!" Susan was practically yelling. "I mean, you don't have to leave as soon as you get there. You deserve a rest."

Jobi exchanged a worried look with his sister. "You sure do. I mean, you really put in a lot of work in Africa!"

"Well, I don't know what the bishop would say if I suggested a vacation so soon." Scott rolled his eyes and smiled.

"He wouldn't have to know you got through with your Bakuba job so soon!" Susan swallowed. "Would he?"

"Well..." Scott gazed into the pleading eyes of Susan and Jobi. "I guess a short visit with my friends wouldn't be such a bad idea."

"Great!" Susan clapped her hands and laughed and looked down quickly. "I really do think you need a rest."

"Rest? Oh yes. I am such an old man." He grinned and turned back around.

"Old." Susan got up and sat down in the seat next to Scott. "You are nothing of the kind, Gene Scott." Her voice dropped to a soft whisper. "You're a warm, gentle man who is still perfectly capable of giving a woman everything she could ever dream of wanting." She stared into his eyes. "You certainly could fulfill my desires—and needs.

His eyes refused to turn away from hers. Within his chest, his heart pounded rapidly. His hand reached out and found hers and held it firmly, gentle. Susan sighed and smiled at him tenderly.

"I want you to meet my parents, Gene."

"I would like that."

"I would like to meet your friends, John and his wife."

"Edna."

"Yes. John and Edna. Could I meet them?"

"Yes. I want you to." He bit his lip and breathed deeply."

"When, Gene?" She squeezed his hand.

"I don't know. Soon, very soon." He laid his head back on the seat, closing his eyes.

"You do care something for me, don't you, Gene?" She touched his cheek gently with the tips of her fingers.

A New Beginning

"Get some rest, Susan. We've got several more hours to go."
His eyes remained closed.

"You didn't answer my question, Gene. Do you care something for me?"

He opened his eyes slowly and turned his head to face her. For a long minute, their eyes were fixed silently upon one another.

"Yes. I do. . . . Now go to sleep." Without another word, he turned back around.

Susan gave a quiet, joyful laugh. "I will now. Just knowing you care like I care for you." She laid her head against the seat and smiled at the man she loved. "I care so very, very much for you, Gene."

Despite himself, he turned toward her again and exchange a long look. He smiled and looked away, trying to shut out what he had been afraid to admit for so long.

"God help me," he thought. "I have fallen in love with her."

"They stepped out into the bright sunshine of TarSa. Everything was green and alive. The flowers seem to be blooming everywhere and the people seemed so alive and friendly. Susan smiled at Jobi.

"Oh, it's so beautiful, simply beautiful!"

"I'll say it is!" Jobi shouted. "Wow, what a home."

"Didn't we tell you?" Jackie said, laughing.

"It sure is alive and warm," Scott said as he set out Jackie and Ali's luggage. "John wrote me all about it and it's true what he said. You can't really enjoy TarSa until you are standing on its golden sand."

"I feel like we could really be happy here." Susan smiled at Scott. "Really happy! All of us."

"Maybe." Gene gazed deeply into her eyes.

Jobi yanked at Susan's arm. "Hey sis, over there's Mom and Dad. They came to meet us. "

"I know. I called them and told them we would be arriving." She waved at her m other and father. "Mom! Dad! Over here."

Mr. and Mrs. Andrews came swiftly to greet their children.

"Oh, my babies!" Shirley Andrews grabbed Susan and Jobi. "I've missed you both so much."

"We've . . . a . . . missed you too, Mom." Jobi smiled

sheepishly, realizing he hadn't really thought much about his parents during the course his adventure.

"Your mother and I were expecting you on a commercial airline. We didn't know you were coming on a special plane." Owen grabbed the handles of their suitcases.

"Oh. Well, Michael and Jackie were good enough to let us come back with them." Susan introduced the two couples to her parents. "They're going to live here too."

"Oh!" Shirley smiled. "I want to thank you for watching my children and making sure that they returned to us safely."

"Mom, I'm not a child," Susan murmured, laughing softly.

"Oh really, Mrs. Andrews, you owe your biggest thanks to Reverend Scott. He's the one who saw to your children's safety and needs," Jackie said earnestly. "We were just glad to give them a ride home. "

"Oh yes." Michael hugged Jackie. "We really didn't mind at all. Susan and Jobi have become two of our dearest friends."

Susan and Jobi smiled and said in unison, "Thanks!"

"Reverend Scott. Oh, that must be you. You're the only one we haven't met." Owen Andrews smiled and extended his hand to Gene.

"Yes Dad," Susan said. "This is Reverend Gene Scott, my very favorite new friend." She smiled at her mother. "You know that saying, 'Save the best to last.'"

Jobi couldn't resist teasing her. "Yeh. Just like dessert—it's the best and always left until the last."

"Yeh!" Susan laughed giddily. "We want to invite Reverend Scott over to eat. Real soon."

"My, my, Reverend Scott, you have made a big impression on my children."

Owen Andrews slapped him on the back. "You must be quite a man."

"You can see that by looking." Shirley cleared her throat. "I— I mean . . . a—we would love to have you over some evening when you're free, Reverend Scott."

"I'd be glad to." He nodded to Susan. "Just let me know. I'll be staying with the Crains at Sand Palms."

"Oh, do you know them?" Shirley asked, looping her arms around Jobi.

A New Beginning

"They're some of his best friends, Mom." Susan took her father's arm. "You both seem to know them."

"Yes, oh yes, indeed." Her father squeezed her shoulders. "We have become members at his church."

"Great!" Susan said excitedly, then glanced quickly down at her feet.

"Oh my, what's with all this excitement?" Owen asked, chuckling."

Scott laughed and shrugged. Susan frowned at him.

"They're probably over excited about this beautiful new home of theirs," Gene said. He picked up his single, simple piece of luggage.

"Well, just wait until you kids see your new home." Shirley laughed gleefully. "It's bigger, much bigger than any we've had yet. The swimming pool, you'll love, not to mention all the other added attractions and surprises your father has added for you and your friends."

Susan looked at Scott. He turned and walked toward the gate. She called to him. "Reverend! Gene! See you soon."

He turned toward her momentarily and waved, then disappeared in the mass of travelers.

Chapter Eighteen

Reverend Gene Scott stared up at the steeple of Sand Palms Methodist Church. A smile came to his lips as he strolled up the sidewalk to the parsonage. The walkway was trimmed neatly in flowers and the little white fence made him feel at home. He rapped twice on the door. When it opened, he smiled into the eyes of an old friend.

"Hello, John."

"Gene, you ole rascal!" Pastor John Crain hugged Scott and pulled him inside the parsonage door." Come on in." He shook his head in astonishment. "Gene Scott! I can't believe my eyes!"

"Surprised you, huh?" Gene laughed and looked around. "Where's my favorite cook?"

"Oh Edna." He turned and yelled, "Edna, come out here quick!"

"What is it John?" Edna walked from the kitchen and stopped the instant she saw Scott. Wiping her hands on her apron, she ran to him and grabbed him. "Gene, oh Gene, it's really you!"

"My, what a welcome. I think I'll go out and come back in," he teased as he lifted Edna off the floor and twirled her around. "Been missing all that good cooking of yours, Edna."

"Oh Gene Scott!" she exclaimed with a laugh as she straightened her hair. "How long are you going to stay with us."

"How long do you want me?" He looked around the neatly kept house.

"Now that's a dumb question." Edna took his hands. "Forever, if we can keep you."

"Don't tempt me, beautiful." He grinned and walked to the hallway, gazing through the house. "Great looking parsonage you've got here."

"All thanks to Edna. She's a wonderful housekeeper as well as good cook."

"Better watch it, John. I might decide to snatch her for myself." They laughed as Scott flopped onto the sofa.

"That wouldn't be such a bad ideal," Edna said, smiling at

A New Beginning

John's sudden expression of dismay. "I mean that part about you getting married again. You're too good a husband and father to be running around loose."

"Maybe someday, Edna, when I meet the right girl." Scott picked up a magazine.

"Well, you'd be a good catch for any girl." Edna sat down next to him.

"Not just any girl Edna, the right girl." He closed his eyes and Susan's face came into view. He smiled. "Yes, her."

"Who, Gene?" Edna asked, picking up her knitting.

"Who nothing." He hopped to his feet. "Where's that rascal David?"

"He went off with a few friends swimming." Edna put her hand on Scott's. "Oh Gene, he will be so happy that you're visiting with us."

"John Crain picked up Scott's luggage "Want to see your room?"

"Oh, sure." Scott walked over and hugged Edna. "That is, if you're sure I will be no trouble staying here."

"Get up those steps, Gene Scott!" Edna gave him a push. "Trouble? You? If anything, maybe I'll get some of the odd jobs around here done."

"Let's face it, Gene," John said, nodding, "you're part of the family. And every family member does his or her job."

"I'll be only too glad to help," Gene said as they walked up the steps. He looked around the neat bedroom and smiled. "Women are so clean and neat. I'd kinda. forgotten how nice it is to have a clean house."

"Yes, I can imagine," Crain laughed, "what with you and that kid Pogo living by yourselves."

"Well, I don't intend to remain alone forever." Scott replied. He looked in the bathroom and came back out and sat down on the bed. "You know, life can get pretty lonely at times, John." He thumped the bed with his palm and lay back. "Especially at night when the rest of the world is asleep or busy with their own lives. All a lonely man has is time, time to think about what he doesn't have."

Crain nodded. "And what he needs, Gene. A man like you needs a wife. You always was a romantic devil." He joined his friend lying on the bed. "Edna and I know lots of fine Christian women who would make you a fine wife. And mother."

"Thanks, brother John, but I think I'm perfectly capable of choosing my own woman." Scott elbowed Crain, causing him to cough.

"Oh I know that, Gene. Still, I thought I could introduce you to several nice ladies in my congregation. You could do the choosing."

"Really, that won't be necessary, John. I—"

Scott stopped when he heard someone running up the steps. David Crain came flying into the room shouting.

"Gene! It's really you!"

Gene got up and grabbed the younger boy. "David, you rascal. Look how you've grown! Shit." Scott laughed and pulled David down beside him as he sat back down by John.

"You're still the same old Gene." David laughed as he stared at the man he had always admired and had set his mind to be like someday. "Where have you been?"

"I just returned from Africa." He glanced at John. "Got into the missionary field. It's really been quite an adventure."

"Wow. Sounds sharp." David shook his head in disbelief. "Gene Scott, here at our house. Darn!"

"David! Mind what you say," Edna said as she walked in the door. "I see you three fellows are taking things nice and easy." She gazed at the three on the bed. "What have you been up here gabbing about?"

"If there's gabbing going on, Edna wants to be in on it." John pulled his wife down on his knee.

"Oh shut up," she laughed pushing his head flat against the bed. "Now, tell me or no supper."

"Blackmail is it?" John said, shaking his head. "I was just telling Gene we would be glad to introduce him to some of the nicer women around here."

A smile of delight crossed her face. "Of course we will. And I know just the one—Mary Payne. She's a beautiful person Gene. She's a Sunday school teacher and she is very active in the woman's Christian society."

David popped to his feet. "And she's fat, talks all the time and is not your type at all, Gene. Mom , how could you suggest Mary

A New Beginning

Payne , of all people . Gene, I know the perfect woman for you. Her name is Katherine Royal."

"Katherine Royal, are you kidding, David? That—that book worm?"

"Mom, she is a librarian not a bookworm. She's a warm gentle person." David smiled at Scott. "I think she's your best bet."

"Really," Gene protested, "I do appreciate what you all are trying to do, but—"

John cut him off. "Kathy Royal is not the one for Gene. She's too immature and silly. She's not but about twenty-four." He looked up at Edna. "And really, dear, Mary Payne of all people? She would talk poor Gene to death."

"Well what about Pearl Leslie? Now she's a very quiet sort." Edna watched as her husband and son shook their heads. "Well, what's wrong with Pearl?"

"She's too quiet, Edna and besides, she's more interested in her dumb cat than any person." John patted his wife's arm. "I know just the match for dear old Gene. Bobbi Clarmont. Now she's perfect.?"

"Bobbi Clarmont!" David bent over his father, his hands on his hips. "Dad, are you kidding? She's as romantic as a pig."

"David's absolutely right, John, why that tomboy." Edna frowned at her husband.

"Well you know how sporty old Gene here is. At least they would have something in common."

"I don't think needing a sporting partner is Gene's trouble, Dad," David said, pacing across the room. "You see, he needs a wife, someone to bring an end to all those lonely nights in bed."

"David!" Edna gasped in surprise.

"It's true, Mom. And let's face it Bobbi Clarmont would be dead jelly in bed."

Scott burst out laughing and stood up. "I thank you very much for your interest, but you guys don't need to rack your brains any longer." He went to the window and looked out.

"We just want to help you find the right girl, Gene." Edna stood and stuck her hands in her apron pockets.

"I've already found the right girl, Edna." Scott was instantly aware of how silent the room became. "I met her on my missionary trip"

211

Joan Byrd

Edna caught her breath. "Oh Gene, that's wonderful" Her voice was full of relief. "On the mission trip? At least she's not that overly wonderful Gloria Ann Weber."

Scott turned to face his friends. He shook his head. "I would rather stay single for the rest of my life rather than marry up with that party-going brat." He laughed. "I suppose you saw the write up she put in the paper?"

"Oh yes. The Webers sent it to us when it first came out." Edna walked over to Gene and put her hand on his arm. "I called the parsonage to find out why you were going through with such a stupid thing. Pogo told us it was a pack of lies and that you had taken off on a mission trip." She laughed softly. "I could just see the expressions on the Webers' faces when you did that."

"What's so wrong with Gloria Weber?" David asked. "I always thought she was rather sexy to be the bishop's daughter."

An image of the red-haired beauty flashed through his mind. "Sexy?" Scott laughed. "She's too childish to be sexy. Why my little Su—" He turned quickly to the mirror. "You know, I'm starved. Edna, love, when do we eat around here?"

The three Crains looked at one another, puzzled. Edna went to the door.

"Real soon. I'll go set the table. Everything's ready."

"Great! Need any help?" Scott smiled broadly.

"No, dear. I can get it." She returned his smile and walked down the steps to the kitchen.

David put his arm around Scott's shoulder. "Come on, Gene. Who is this lady? You can tell us. Why is this such a big secret?"

"In time. I'll tell you when the time is right." He smiled sheepishly and went out the bedroom door.

John walked down the steps beside him with a wry grin, unwilling to let the subject drop. "Oh Gene, you can tell us. We're your friends. If it's a big secret, you know you can trust us to guard it."

"I don't doubt that, John. It's . . . the situation that you wouldn't understand." Gene flopped on the living room sofa. "To tell you the truth, I don't fully understand it myself."

"Tell us, Gene. Maybe we could help," Edna said from where she leaned against the kitchen door.

"God bless you, sweetheart. I know you mean well, all of you,

A New Beginning

but I think I have to sort this out in my own mind first. Everything's all mixed up." He shook his head, wearing an expression of confusion. "I don't know that it could ever work out between us."

"Does she know you love her?" Edna sat down next to him on the sofa.

"I've never told her I loved her. I resisted that. I wasn't sure it was the right thing to do." He dropped his head into his hands. "You can't imagine what a big mess the whole thing is."

"Oh my poor Gene. Does she love you?"

"Well, she has never said it out loud—well once, out of fear; but she had demonstrated her feelings. Clearly. Several times in many ways." He stood and brushed his fingers through his curls. "I think maybe it's best if I just move on and forget about her." He nodded. "It would probably be for the best."

"Would it?" David came to him. "It sounds as though you are madly in love with this woman. I say nothing is too big a problem when you're that much in love. I'm sure you can work it out, Gene."

"Sure you can, Gene." Edna touched his arm gently. "Love can always find a way. You have a wise head on your shoulders, Gene. I know you will come up with something."

"Oh Edna, if it was a simple as you must think. There are so many different things coming between us. "

"Still, you must have something important in common." John had listened silently as long as he could. "I know you better than to think you would fall for someone who isn't compatible, someone you couldn't possibly get along with."

"Oh we get along fine together, too good maybe." Scott went to the kitchen door. We should eat. We've talked enough about me and my problems. And when it's the right time, I'll tell you all about her."

"Alright, dear. Anything you want." Edna walked behind him into the kitchen. "Everybody grab a seat. It's time to eat."

Chapter Nineteen

Susan's hand moved her fork slowly around in the food on her plate.

She stared up at the ceiling, her mind focused on Gene Scott. "What is he doing right now?" she wondered. "Is he; thinking about me, or has he already forgotten me?"

Shirley Andrews cleared her throat and tapped her daughter's hand. "Susan, dear, stop messing in your food. Mildred fixed it especially for you and Jobi. Where is your mind, dear?"

"I'm sorry, Mom. I guess I'm not very hungry."

"That jungle food didn't turn your appetite did it, dear?" Owen Andrews asked. "I guess going away for that length of time is bound to mess up your system."

"Oh, Dad." She giggled shyly. "I ate very well, didn't I, Jobi?"

He glanced at his sister and smiled. Her hands jiggled nervously under the table.

"Sure she did. She ate just like a big old pig."

"Jobi!" His mother slapped his hand. "That's no way to talk about your sister."

"I was only fooling, Mom," he laughed. "She ate like always, I guess."

"And what about you, Jobi, dear, did you eat up everything on your plate and drink all your milk?" His mother sipped her coffee.

Susan smiled at Jobi and cleared her throat. "He was very good at eating up everything, Mom."

"Oh. Well that's wonderful then."

When Shirley stood, Susan jumped up and grabbed her arm. "Mom, when can we invite Reverend Scott over?"

"My goodness, dear! Why are you so eager to have him over?"

"Your mother is right, Susan dear. The man just got here, for heaven's sake. Give him a chance to get settled in." Owen put his arm around his daughter. "Let's spend some time together as a family before we bring strangers in."

"He is no stranger, Dad." She looked into her father's eyes. "He's the most wonderful person in the entire world."

A New Beginning

"Hey, I thought you thought your old dad was the most wonderful person in the entire world." He feigned an indignant expression. "You mean I have a rival?"

"Oh Dad." She hugged him. "You know I think you're the most wonderful dad in the world."

"But this Gene Scott ranks as the best person?" He glanced at Shirley. "We shall have to find out what is so extra special about their friend."

"When you get to know him, Dad. You'll see." Jobi ran to the front door. "How about a tour of the grounds, Dad?"

"Hey, that's not such a bad idea." He took Susan by the hand. "Will you permit the second best person in the world to show you your new home?"

She laughed. "I'd be honored to have the best dad in the world to show me our home."

He kissed her cheek and smiled at his wife. Coming, dear?"

"No, Owen dear. You show the children around. I think I'll go up and rest for a spell." She kissed Susan and Jobi and walked slowly up the steps.

Susan's eyes followed her. "I see Mom still naps after eating."

"Yes. You know your mother. She says it helps her stay awake in the late evening." He motioned toward the door. "Well, what are we waiting for?"

"Gene," Susan whispered.

"What, dear?" Owen Andrews turned to his daughter.

"I just said, that's fine." She laughed sheepishly and followed her father and brother through the door.

Reverend Scott laughed as he talked to his friend Pogo on the phone. "How's your romance with that cute little scout going?"

"Gee, Scott, you wouldn't believe it. She up and got herself a new boyfriend."

"Who could be more exciting and more romantic than you, Pogo?" Scott bit into an apple.

"What the shit was that?" Pogo laughed.

"My apple, dummy. So who is this new fellow your girlfriend is dating? A doughnut salesman?"

"Would you believe Freddie Hill? That stupid Patti prefers Freddie Hill over me."

Joan Byrd

"Freddie? The paper boy?" Scott burst into laughter. "Pogo, I think you need someone to show you the ropes of romance, kid."

"Well, I don't think the new reverend and his neat wife could help me much in that field." He grunted. "I wish I were with you, Scott."

"Well Pogo, you know I'd like nothing better than to have you come be with me, but I'm just a guest here myself."

Edna looked up from her knitting.

"Gene Scott, you're not just a dumb guest. Tell Pogo he's welcome here. He can share David's room."

"Hold on, Pogo." Scott glanced at Edna. "If he comes, he can stay in my room with me."

"Gene Scott, you are three times the size of David. There's plenty of room in his room and, besides, Pogo is closer to his age. They'll hit it off nicely."

"Don't try to argue with her, Gene. You know it's no use." John smiled, looking up from his paper. "Tell Pogo to come on."

"Thanks, to both of you." He turned back to the phone. "Pogo, when can you come to TarSa?"

"You mean I can come there? Wow, boy I don't believe it." He was practically yelling. "Wow!"

"Shit Pogo! That's my ear." Scott held the phone away from his head. "Do you have enough money saved?"

"I'm sure I have. I been saving practically every penny since Patti broke off with me." His voice grew excited again. "Oh, wow, Scott. I can't wait to get together with you."

"Well, look Pogo, this telephone call is costing me a fortune and since you're coming I think we had better say our farewells."

"Right," Pogo laughed. "You can look for me soon, very soon."

"Great, kid. Be careful and I look forward to seeing you soon." Scott hung up the phone and stretched back in his chair.

David came racing down the stairs. "Boy, you guys sure get up early around here."

"David, your breakfast is in the oven." Edna didn't look up from her knitting.

"I'm not hungry, Mom." He flopped down on ·the sofa and switched on the television.

"David, you heard your mother. Go and eat." John laid down

216

his newspaper and walked into his study.

"Really, I don't want to eat, Mom." He picked up an apple and took a bite.

Scott jerked it out of his hands. "David, if I were you, I think I would march right in that kitchen and eat my breakfast." He grinned as he tossed the apple up in the air.

David looked up at Scott standing over him and laughed lazily. "Alright. I'm going. I'm going." He jumped up and ran to the kitchen.

"Gene, I could kiss you." Edna smiled up at him.

"What's stopping you?" he teased.

The telephone rang and Edna picked up the receiver. "Oh, Gene," she said, then spoke into the phone. "Hello, parsonage."

A soft voice came from the other end. "Is Reverend Scott there?"

"Yes he is." She glanced at Scott and smiled. "Would you like to speak to him?"

Scott's eyes dropped from Edna's face to the phone. He felt himself taking a deep breath.

"Yes, please."

"Alright, one minute." She handed the receiver to him. "It's for you, Reverend Scott." She grinned coyly.

He took it slowly and held it to his ear. "Scott speaking."

"Gene . . . it's Susan."

"Hello." He swallowed. "It's good to hear your voice."

When he glanced at Edna, she looked away and returned to her knitting.

Silently Susan was asking herself, "Do you really think so?" She smiled sweetly. "Your voice has brightened up my whole morning," she said.

"Oh, come on," he laughed. "How do you like your new home?"

"It's very nice, Gene."

"And the swimming pool, is it as big as you and Jobi had hoped?"

"Bigger. Gene, Mom wanted me to call, or better, I asked if I could invite you over for dinner tonight."

"Tonight?" He gazed at the flowers on the table and saw Susan's face smiling back at him. "Are you sure that isn't too soon.

Joan Byrd

I mean I wouldn't want to come barging in on your mother after just moving into her new home and all."

"Oh, Gene. I'm glad to see you haven't changed in twenty-four hours." Susan laughed softly. "Everything is in perfect order around here. Mom hired extra help until everything was in set up. Dear Mildred takes care of the cleaning and cooking, so you are not going to be trouble whatsoever."

"Well then, I'll be glad to," he said with a lazy laugh. "Should I dress up?"

"You can wear your Tarzan outfit if you want to," she replied with a coy giggle.

"Uh, thanks, but no thanks." He glanced at Edna who sat smiling at him. "What—uh, what time?"

"Seven." She waited for him to reply. "Does that sound alright to you?"

"I'm the invited guest. I'll leave the time up to you, sweetheart." He cleared his throat when he noticed John smiling at him from the study door.

"Alright, then seven it is." Susan looked around the room to make sure she was alone. "Gene, uh . . . when can I meet the Crains? I'm looking forward to meeting your friends."

"Soon. Very soon." He turned to see that David had joined the interested group of listeners. "If we have the chance, that is. I'll talk to you more about it tonight."

"Is something wrong?" Her fingers toyed with the cord.

"Well, besides the two of us talking, I have three persons who seem to be extra interested in our call. Oh, hey! They all looked away and pretended to be busy."

She laughed girlishly. "Oh, I see. Well you can come earlier tonight if you'd like. I'm . . . I'm looking forward to tonight."

"Are you?" He couldn't hold back a smile.

"Yes, oh yes." She swallowed. "And are you?"

"Very! See you tonight." He hung up the phone and, walked to the door. "Come on, David. Get you baseball and gloves. Let's do a little pitching, buddy."

"Sure thing." He raced out to back shed to get them.

"I'll be eating out tonight, Edna," Scott said as he walked toward the front door.

She got up and followed him. "Where are you going?"

218

"The—uh—Andrews invited me over for dinner."

"The Andrews?" John joined them at the door. "You mean Owen and Shirley Andrews?"

"That's right, John. You see Jobi and Susan, their children, were on the same ship I was on going over to Africa. We played a lot of shuffleboard and they became very good friends. They want me to meet their mom and dad. So what else could I do?"

"Oh they're lovely people, Gene. I've never met their children but they told us all about them." Edna shrugged sheepishly. "I thought you were talking with the mystery woman in your life." She laughed.

"Oh Edna!" John slipped his arm around her shoulders. "There you go again. Always imagining things."

"Well you seemed to be pretty interested in my phone call too, John old boy." Gene smiled at his friend as he walked out the door.

John held the door open and called, "Come on, Gene," he said with a laugh, "It's not every day, your best friend tells you he's in love and makes such a big secret out of it."

"I told you it's a much bigger problem than any I've ever faced. You will just have to give me time."

"We will, won't we John?" Edna looked at her husband.

"All the time you need."

Scott smiled, reassured that he wouldn't be questioned again until he could put things together. He walked out on the lawn where David was waiting. Scott held out his hand.

"Let me have a glove." He put the glove on and socked it a couple times. "Alright, pal, let her fly."

Scott pull the Crain's blue Ford to a stop in front of the Andrews' large home. He got out and looked around at all the rich surroundings. He found the doorbell and rang it. The door opened, revealing a very pleasant smiling face.

"Good evening, sir. You have to be Reverend Scott."

"Yes and you must be Mildred." He returned her big smile.

"The very same. I am the maid, the cook and the nurse around this house." She laughed as she shut the door behind them. "Why shucks, the Andrews would be lost without Mildred to feed them, watch them when they're sick, and pick up after them."

"I'd say you were pretty valuable around here." His eyes took in the luxurious furniture decorating the huge room.

"Sho nuff," she laughed. "I hope you are a big eater, Reverend Scott. I love to watch someone enjoy my good cooking."

"One of the biggest, Mildred dear, one of the biggest." He noticed Susan walking quickly down the winding steps toward him. Their eyes met and their lips melted into a warm smile for one another.

"Good evening, Susan. You're looking very sweet tonight."

"Sweet?" She glanced at Mildred. "You've met Mildred, I assume."

"You assume correctly, Miss Susan. And your Mr. Scott is even better than you described him, sweetie." Mildred patted Scott on the back. "Real nice looking."

"Thank you, Mildred. You ain't such a bad looking chick yourself." He winked at her.

"Go on with you." She headed for the kitchen. "He's even a nice person besides good looking," she mumbled over her shoulder. "Most good looking men are just so skin deep, but not that man. Oh no, no sirree. He's one smart fellow, yes indeed, smart and good looking." She disappeared behind the kitchen door.

Susan and Gene looked at each other and started laughing.

"Boy, she's a cat bird." Gene smiled at Susan. "I bet she keeps things moving around here."

"Never a dull moment with Mildred around." Susan laughed and took his hand. "Mom and dad are waiting in the drawing room, come on."

"Oh boy, do we get to draw?" He widened his eyes innocently. "I want the red crayon first."

"Gene Scott!" She punched his arm and laughed. "I think you're in for a great treat tonight."

"Oh?" He smiled at her tenderly. "What sort of treat?"

"Jobi got a new train set. It takes up his entire room practically. You are going to get to see it."

"Oh, great! That sounds like fun. Can I run it too?" He smiled at Jobi who greeted him at the door to the drawing room.

"My train? Sure. We'll have a contest and see who can stay on the track the longest." Jobi gave a sly laugh. "I've beaten everyone in the house. Even dad."

"Jobi, stop telling Reverend Scott what a bad train driver I am." Owen Andrews motioned for Scott to sit down. "My son is pretty good at knocking everyone off the track."

"Oh? Is that right?" Scott rubbed the top of Jobi's head. "Too bad I'm going to ruin your record."

"Don't be so sure, Ge—Reverend Scott." Susan smiled at her hands. "I think my little brother cheats."

"That's not so, Susan! Mom, I don't cheat, do I? Susan is just jealous because she can't ever beat me."

"Jealous?" His sister burst into laughter. "That's the funniest thing I've ever heard of."

"You are jealous! Why don't you admit it?" He stood and put his hands on his hips. "Go on I dare you."

"Oh, I'm scared stiff." She covered up her face, giggling and mocking him.

"Children, please stop this constant fighting between you. Reverend Scott is going to think you're little animals." Shirley smiled at Scott. Children, always fighting over silly little things."

Scott chuckled and gazed at Susan, who glared back at him.

"Children will be children, Mrs. Andrews

"They're usually pretty good." Owen lit a cigar and offered one to Scott.

"No thanks." He stared at his hands. "Did Susan and Jobi tell you about their adventures in Africa?"

Instantly Susan and Jobi looked at each other and swallowed.

"As a matter of fact they said very little about their visit to their grandfather." Shirley glanced at Susan. "Every time Owen or I bring up the subject suddenly they've got something they have to do."

Susan shrugged. "What is there to say? We did the regular things anyone would do in Africa."

Mildred entered the room and Susan leaped up. "Oh is dinner ready, Mildred?"

"Yes, ma'am. Dinner is ready." She grinned at Scott. "And boy have I got something good for you Reverend?"

"Wonderful," he replied and stood. "What are we waiting for?"

Susan laughed at her mother's expression of consternation and took Gene's arm. "Just follow me, Reverend Scott.

Joan Byrd

His smile was conspiratorial. "Anywhere," he whispered.

The dinner was very filling. Mildred seemed pleased with herself as she watched Reverend Scott enjoying her food so obviously. Shirley smiled when he pushed his chair away from the table.

"Won't you have another piece of pie, Reverend."

"Oh no. No thank you." He nodded and closed his eyes. "Honestly I couldn't hold another bite."

Susan got to her feet. "It was extremely good tonight, Mildred."

"Thank you, Miss Susan," she said with a triumphant smile.

"Now," Susan continued, "if I could steal Reverend Scott for a while, I would like to show him the playroom. It's very appealing, especially for someone who is interested in sports."

"Sports? That sounds like my kind of place." He rose. "I hope you don't mind if Susan shows me around."

"Oh not at all, Reverend. Our home is your home." Shirley stood up. "I'll be along later. If you will excuse me."

"Of course, dear." Owen stood up. "Come on, Jobi. How about a game of chess?"

"But Dad, I'd rather go with Reverend Scott."

"Jobi, we won't be gone long," Susan said tersely. She bent to his ear and whispered impatiently, "I want to talk to Gene alone."

"Now that you mention it, Dad, a game of chess sounds pretty good."

"Great. Susan run along and show Scott the playroom."

"Thanks, Dad." She kissed his cheek and turned to Scott. "Come on. It's this way."

She led him down the steps to the playroom. He saw that it contained a bowling alley, ping pong table, separate pool table and a huge bar. Trophies lined the wall."

"My, my. Someone around here is quite the champion."

He looked closely at the trophies and saw a great variety: golf, tennis, football and swimming.

"It's mostly my dad." Susan sat down on the sofa. "He's a sports nut like you."

"You seem pretty athletic, Susan. What kind of sports are you best at?" he asked, studying the awards.

"Oh I'm pretty good at several things. Tennis, swimming and

222

kissing." She laughed quietly, softly at his surprised expression. "And I'm even better at what comes along with kissing. You are pretty sporty, I bet, when it comes to love, aren't you?"

"Well." He shrugged. "I guess I would consider myself a pretty good lover." He bit his lip and turned back toward the trophies. "Any of these yours or do all of them belong to your dad?"

"Two are mine. The two in the very corner. Four belong to Jobi."

He looked at the two in the corner. One was for swimming. The other was the championship trophy in a beauty contest.

"Well I see that our little Susan won a beauty contest."

"Yes, I won that last year. Mom and Dad were very pleased. I was up against fourteen other girls, some much older." Instantly she asked herself, "Oh Susan, why did I have to sound so proud?" She said, "I hope that didn't sound terribly vain."

"Why, winning a beauty contest at such an early age and over that many competitors, you should feel proud of yourself." He picked up a tennis trophy. "I've gotten several of these. Although most of the time I play, it's just for fun."

"What are you doing?" She tilted her head and he gazed at her, puzzled.

"Looking around. Isn't that what we're supposed to be doing down here?"

"No." She patted the sofa next to her. "Come over here and sit down."

"Susan, we're supposed to be—"

"Just come over here and sit down." She motioned him toward her with her finger. "Gene, come here."

He crossed the room slowly and sat beside her. She smiled up triumphantly.

"Now, when do I get to meet the Crains?"

"Well, I . . . Susan, do you use that bowling alley a lot?"

"Gene Scott, quit changing the subject. Answer my question."

"You can meet them tomorrow at church, if you're coming." He surveyed the room to avoid her eyes. "That's a nice bar your dad has."

She pulled his face around to hers. Gently she traced the outline of his forehead, cheeks and chin, slowly moving around to the curls on the back of his neck.

"Has anyone ever told you that you have sexy curls?"

"No. No, I can't remember anyone ever telling me that." He swallowed, aware of how rigid his body had become. Why couldn't he move away from her? Could it be, he wondered, that he didn't want to.

"And your body. You've got a very sexy body, you know." She scooted closer, so that their legs touched from hip to knee. "Kiss me, Gene."

"Susan, your father never meant for me to come down here and—"

"Will you just shut up and kiss me?" She put her arms around his neck. ". . . You know you want to. Don't you?"

His eyes melted into hers. His heart pounded in his throat. In his mind he kept saying, "Yes, yes, my darling Susan." He felt his hands moving around her waist. He could tell he was giving in to the desire to hold and kiss her, just as he had yearned for so long. And words, the words she wanted to hear, tumbled from his mouth uncontrollably.

"Yes, Susan, yes."

His mouth parted and he covered hers with a tender kiss. He pulled her closer against him and their kisses became more demanding. The desire to have more of her was tearing at his flesh. His want for her grew deeper and deeper as his breathing grew heavier. She too was breathing heavy. Her love for him ignited her body with desire for more.

"Oh Gene, Gene darling," she sighed as his tongue found her mouth and his left hand begin moving up her blouse. His finger slipped under her bra and came to rest cupped around her breast. A sigh of fulfillment escaped her lips and she whispered, "I love you."

His kisses moved down her neck and despite his ragged breathing, he moaned, "Oh Susan, my Susan." His tongue and lips moved tenderly down her neck.

There came a noise at the top of the stairs as the door opened. Owen Andrews, unable to see the sofa or the loving couple on it, called down, "Susan, how's it coming down there? Did you find anything interesting?"

Quickly they pulled away from each other's arms. Scott stood and walked behind the bar, looking at the stores of liquor. Susan sat still, trying to catch her breath.

"Yes, Dad. We were playing a game." She smiled coyly at Gene who returned it,"

"So Scott, how do you like the little play room?" Owen stepped off the stairs.

"Oh it's very interesting." He tried to hide the fact that his breathing was still a little heavy."

"Boy you too must have been really going at it, eh? You need to catch your breath?" Owen asked. "Fix yourself a drink if you like, Scott. And if you don't mind you can fix me a gin and tonic."

"Uh, glad to." Gene gazed at Susan. "Would you like a drink, Susan?"

"Yes, bartender. I'll have a small glass of sherry." Ringing her arms around her daddy's neck, she said, "We had a rousing game, Dad. Although we didn't get to finish." She suppressed a laugh when Scott nearly dropped his glass. "You see, Reverend Scott is so good at ping pong. I never could beat him on the cruise. Tonight, though, I nearly got the better of him."

"And what sort of player is Scott?" he asked with a smile as he took the drink from Scott.

Susan received her glass slowly, letting her fingers play against Gene's hand. "Reverend Scott is an excellent player, Dad, at everything. Well, at least everything I've seen him try so far."

"Yes, so I hear we must get together someday and play some tennis or a round of golf."

"Yes, I would like that very much, Owen." Scott drained his glass quickly and set it on the bar. "Well, I'll have to look at Jobi's trains and then I better be shoving off."

"So soon?" Susan took a final sip and followed Scott to the staircase.

"We've got church tomorrow, remember. And Reverend Cain has given me responsibility for the sermon."

He motioned for Susan to go in front of him. Owen follow them up the stairs. Against his will and judgment, Gene watched the rhythmic motion of Susan's legs and behind as she climbed the stairs, and he wondered if her father realized what he was doing. She stepped into the hall and smiled at Scott, seemingly aware he had been admiring her. He grinned back at her.

Jobi came running up behind him and grabbed Scott's hips. "Ready to see my train set?

"Yeh, that's the main thing I came to do." He squeezed Jobi around the shoulders. "Lead the way, Mr. Engineer."

Wearing an expression of pure delight, Jobi grabbed his hand. They filed up the winding staircase to the upstairs bedrooms. Jobi opened his door and motioned Scott in. His eyes fell on the track, which took up a good deal of the floor.

"Well? What do you think, Scott?" Jobi's eyes grow wide.

"It's something else. Every kid in the world dreams about having something like this." Gene got down on his knees. "Let's let them fly, Jobi!"

"Great!" Jobi handed Scott a red engine and handed a blue one to Susan. "Here get ready to be plastered, sis!" He laughed.

"I'll show you who gets plastered, you little smarty pants." She got down on her knees beside Scott. "Now move over, buster, and prepare yourself to get knocked off the track!"

"Now listen to her, Jobi. She thinks she's going to knock the old Red Baron off the track." Scott set his engine in its place."

"Yeh. Funny isn't she." Jobi laughed. "Especially since I'm the one who's going to knock the old Red Baron off the track."

"I got news for both of you guys." Scott clapped his hands together in anticipation. "I'm going to knock the shit out of both your engines."

Susan and Jobi laughed and set there trains down.

Owen Andrews cleared his throat and said, "I'll tell you when to begin."

"Okay, Dad. Shoot!" Jobi beamed with confidence.

"Ready? On your marks. Get set. Go!"

They mashed on their starter buttons and the trains started flying around the huge track. Scott shifted positions to get a better hold of his control. How he missed this sort of thing since his son died. His wife had often told him that, between the two of her men, she often thought Gene enjoyed playing games more than her boy.

He saw a perfect place to force Susan's train over the slope, so he put his red engine on full speed.

Jobi yelled. "Scott are you crazy? You're going to wreck yourself."

"Let me worry about that," he laughed as he bit his bottom lip in excitement.

A New Beginning

Sure enough, he managed to strike Susan's engine with just enough force to knock it over.

"Got you! He laughed and laughed again when she hit his arm.

"Oh you!" she exclaimed. "Think you're pretty tough, don't you?"

"Ha. No one messes around with daredevil Gene." He glanced at Jobi with a smile. "Alright, champ, now I'm coming to get you."

"Not if I get you first." He sat up on his knees, preparing himself for Scott's red engine. "Keep going that fast, Scott, and you will crash before you ever get to me."

"No way, kid. Scott don't give up until he creams his man!" His eyes sparkled with joy as he sent the small red engine flying around the track. Finally he had it directly behind Jobi's. "Time to move that heap of black junk out of my way."

"I got you slowed down now, huh, daredevil." Jobi gave a thrilled laugh and Susan squeezed her brother's arm.

"Smear him good, Jobi"

"Oh yeh, well here's where I switch over." Scott turned his train off on another track, curving it around so it headed right toward Jobi's.

"Good grief, Scott, you're going to smash both of us!"

"Not if I make it to the rest stop when I reach you."

His voice grew loud with excitement. Susan smiled as she watched him enjoy himself.

"Oh," Jobi said, "pretty smart. I see what you're doing now. The first train to reach the pull off will automatically win."

He set his black engine on full speed as he and Scott raced for the rest stop. Scott's train made it in two seconds before Jobi's. The little black engine went flying off the track.

"Hey!" Scott clapped his hands and a smile stretched across his face.

"Well you plastered me but good! Just like on the boat." Jobi stuck his hand out and took Scott's. "Well done, daredevil Gene."

"Well, Reverend Scott, I guess you did knock the sh—" Susan stopped when she heard her father clear his throat. "Uh—the sweet sugar out of us."

"Sweet sugar?" Scott laughed out loud and got to his feet, stretching. "Well Owen, what did you think of the race?"

"Exciting, Reverend Scott. You really kept it going."

"You have a wonderful train set, Jobi. He embraced the boy. "Well, I'd better be leaving."

"It's still early." Susan said. The reluctance in her eyes was unmistakable. "Do you have to go now?"

"I'm afraid so, Susan." He resisted the urge to trace the line of her face with his fingers. "I did have a wonderful time. Please tell Mildred again I appreciate all that wonderful food she fixed."

He made his way down the stairs steps. Susan right behind him.

Susan took hold of his hand. "Can't you stay just a little while longer?"

"Susan, Susan." Mr. Andrews put his arm around his daughter's shoulders. "I'm sure Reverend Scott will come again sometime." He smiled at Scott. "My children really think the world of you, Reverend. Will you come again soon?"

"Yes, thank you, Owen. I'd really like that."

He walked to the front door, the Andrews family close behind.

"Well I hope to see you all at church tomorrow morning."

"Oh we'll be there. I'm looking forward to hearing you preach, Scott." Owen said, pulling out his pipe and lighting it. "The children say you are very good. I believe Jobi even listened to every word of the sermon for a change."

Scott smiled at Jobi. "Yes he did seem to be paying close attention. Both of them, actually." He opened the door. "Well goodbye and thank you again for a lovely evening."

"Thank you for everything, Reverend Scott." Susan looked deeply into his eyes. "I enjoyed the ping pong game the best."

Gene wondered if he was blushing visibly at her words. He smiled sheepishly, as though he felt as if everyone knew about the game in the playroom.

"Yes, so did I Susan.' He spoke softly as his eyes took in the girl to whom he had secretly given his heart.

"Tomorrow then."

"Yes. See you." She waved as she watched him walk to the car and get in. Deep within her heart she felt a joy she had never experienced. She loved him and she believed with all her heart that he had some strong feeling of love for her as well.

Chapter Twenty

A number of people had already gathered for worship when the Andrews car pulled to the stop in front of the church. The bells chimed through the crisp morning air and Susan felt like she was floating on a cloud. She walked briskly up the steps, only to turn and see her family trailing far behind her.

"Hey, slowpokes, come on. I want to get up near the front."

"No, Susan. You know I prefer the back of the church." Shirley Andrews pulled out her green gloves.

"Why, Mom? Are you afraid they'll catch you falling asleep?" Jobi teased.

"Alright, young man. It's much too early in the morning for jokes."

Susan entered the vestibule of the church, looking about. An usher came up to her, smiling and handing her a worship bulletin. "Where would you like to sit?"

Her eyebrows arched as she smiled and said, "As close to the front as possible please."

They followed the usher to the front of the sanctuary.

Her mother whispered in her ear, "Susan why are you so determined to go up at the front?"

"I like to be able to see who's doing the talking up close. Don't you?"

The usher stopped beside the second row. Susan slid across the pew and sat beside a woman who seemed about her mother's age. A boy, about seventeen, sat beside her. He beamed joyfully when he saw Susan. She returned his smile, then looked away.

Her mother smiled and greeted the woman beside Susan. "Good morning, Edna. Lovely day isn't it?"

Susan glanced at the woman sitting beside her. She wondered if this could be Gene's friend.

"Good morning, Shirley. Yes it is a very nice day." She smiled at Susan warmly. "You must be Susan."

"Yes, I am." She returned her smile. "Are you Reverend Crain's wife?"

229

Joan Byrd

"Been his wife for 18 years." She motioned toward the young man beside her. "This is David, my son."

"Hi, Susan."

They were about the same age. He was a handsome boy, Susan thought, but next to Gene that's all he was.

She spoke softly. "Oh, I guess we will be going to college together."

"More than likely, seeing as how there's only one school here."

"It sounds like a great school, the way Mom and Dad describe it."

"It's super! There's lots of interesting extras you can take. I guessed it's about as good as school a any."

She smiled, thinking, "Gene's friends are very nice. It will be great when all of us are even closer."

The choir took their places, standing in the loft. Reverend Cain came onto the chancel, followed closely by Gene Scott. They took the two seats behind the pulpit. The choir sang the call to worship and Reverend Crain, smiling, stepped into the pulpit.

"Welcome to God's house. It's always good to see so many smiling faces. I can see a few new faces among our own and you are always welcome. Let's open the service by singing hymn number 12. It's an old favorite, so everyone sing out"

The organist began to play the hymn as the congregation rose, fumbling with their hymnals to find the right page. Susan could hear Scott singing over everyone. His voice seemed to enchant the ladies especially and it made the men try that much harder to sing out.

Shirley elbowed Owen's arm and frowned. "Not so loud, dear. I can't hear Scott's lovely voice over that croaking you're making.

Owen Andrews' face turned a slight shade of red as he hid it in his hymnal. Susan winked at her mother.

The entire congregation seemed to enjoy Reverend Scott's sermon. At least they all gathered at the door of the sanctuary and waited to shake his hand at the close of the service. He spoke with everyone as if he had known them all his life. It was obvious to Susan that the women couldn't get over how strong and good looking he was. And along with the women, the men and children like him very much.

Gene raised his eyes and found Susan near the end of the long line of worshippers. He noticed she was busy chatting with David. He felt his blood turn hot. He couldn't be getting jealous, he thought. He felt a bump on his arm. John smiled at him.

"What?" Scott looked at his friend.

Crain whispered, "Where's your mind?" He cleared his throat. "I was saying, this is Mr. and Mrs. Paul Kytal. Paul owns the hotel and the tourist restaurant."

"It's a pleasure meeting you, Reverend Scott." Mrs. Kytal smiled at him. "I truly enjoyed your sermon."

"Thank you Mrs. Kytal. Mr. Kytal, nice to meet you." He shook his hand.

"The pleasure is mine, I can assure you, Scott. Hadn't heard a sermon like that since I've been married." He laughed loudly and slapped John's back hard enough to make him cough. "Old John here does a pretty good job, but I say, Scott, you let everyone know they've got a job to do."

"Yes!" Gene raised his eyebrows and smiled. "Too bad that more don't do it rather than just listen to it."

"Yes, yes. I agree." He glanced at his wife, an expression of guilt flashing across his face. "Well, come along Natalie. We must run."

Susan finally reached Scott and he took both her hands in his. "Well, Susan Andrews. It's nice to see such a pretty face brightening up the congregation, right John?"

"Oh, certainly." He smiled at his son. "I see you agree, David?"

"Yes, sir. She's quite a dish." He smiled at Scott who was staring back seriously. David stop laughing. "Did I say something wrong?"

"Why no, David. I think that was a very sweet thing to say." Susan smiled at him, then glanced at Scott. "Don't you agree, Reverend Scott?"

"Completely." He nodded and clenched his teeth. Turning to Shirley, who was standing alongside Edna, he said, "Well good morning, Shirley. You're looking sharp today."

"Thank you, Reverend." She smiled graciously. "The sermon was excellent and I enjoyed your singing too."

"Yes, Gene. You really sounded great today." Edna took his

231

Joan Byrd

arm. "That's our Gene always outshining everyone else."

Susan bit her lip as she watched Edna holding on to Gene. She turned her head quickly to her mother.

"Well, Mom, I'll get home sometime late this evening."

"Alright, dear. Have a good time." She kissed Susan's cheek and waved to the others. "See you Edna, John and you too, Reverend Scott. Come along Owen."

"I'm coming, dear." Owen spoke to John. "We're still playing a round of golf tomorrow, aren't we?"

"Oh yes. I'll meet you on the course," John said with a laugh, "while the rest of the world works." He winked at Gene."

Owen headed toward his car. "Come along, Jobi. I'll see you in the morning, Crain."

Scott turned to Susan. "So where are you going?"

"Edna was nice enough to invite me over for lunch." She smiled at him coyly. "Wasn't it sweet of her?"

"Oh, extremely." He feigned a smile at Edna. "And what are you grinning about, David?"

The teenager took Susan's arm. "Why shouldn't I smile? I mean, with such a pretty guest eating with us, I think I have something to smile about."

Gene nodded. "Yes. Smile. By all means, smile." Scott set out toward the parsonage, Edna walking quickly beside him.

"Oh, Gene, aren't they a lovely couple?"

"What?" Scott stared straight ahead.

"David and Susan, aren't they a lovely couple?"

He slowed. "No. I don't think they go together at all." His tone was curt as he pushed his way through the parsonage door.

"Gene!" Edna's voice was full of surprise. "What's wrong with you?"

"Nothing." He stopped and gathered himself, then turned to her with a smile. He felt ashamed of how he had sounded. "Sorry I sounded like that, Edna. I must just be preoccupied. I'm going to wash my hands so I can dig into some of that tasty food of yours."

"Now that's more like the Gene I know." She patted him consolingly on the shoulder. "I fixed cherry cake for you too."

"Ha! Now that's my kind of woman," he said, twirling her around.

She laughed aloud. "Put me down. I'm too old for this kind of game."

232

"Well, Reverend Scott, still playing games, I see." Susan took his arm. "Would you show me where I could wash up please."

"What happened to your overly charming escort?" Gene studied her face with the slightest expression of anxiety.

"His father wanted him to help collect the bulletins out of the pews." She smiled. "So it looks as if you're stuck with me."

Gene tried to hide his quick smile from her. "Well come on then, beautiful. We mustn't keep Edna waiting with our lunch."

He walked up the steps, Susan right behind him.

As they sat at the table, their eyes kept meeting, all the while John busily talked about a fishing trip he had taken over the summer. And Edna, when John stopped to take a breath, spoke of the women's project they were working on. Through it all, Susan and Gene were in their own little world of thoughts.

Finally John nudged Gene's shoulder and said, "Hey, Gene. Are you hearing any of this?"

"Oh! I'm sorry, John. Did you say something to me? Scott stared down at his food to avoid the Crains' eyes.

"I asked if you have done any fishing lately?"

"No, not recently. I think probably the last fishing I've done was when I went with you." He turned to Edna. "How about some of that cake now, beautiful?"

"Oh, Gene." She shook her head in exasperation. "You may think you can get anything you want from other women by telling them they're beautiful, but you can't fool me." She set a big piece of cherry cake in front of him.

He pulled her down and kissed her. "Oh, yeah. Looks like I got what I wanted from you! Thank you, beautiful," he laughed. Then gazing at John, he said playfully, "Well I hope you burn up on that golf course tomorrow, lazy preacher."

"Yeh, well you'll be too busy with your own work to worry about me having fun." John took a big bite of the cake. "Pretty good, dear, but I still prefer chocolate."

Susan leaned across the table toward Scott. "What sort of work do you have to do tomorrow, Gene?" She pretended not to notice the surprised expressions the Crains wore in response to her sudden question.

"I'm going to be working at the home for disabled children," Gene replied. "Probably all week." They stared at each other—the moment perfect for each to fix upon the other's eyes. ". . . They say it's a wonderful hospital, set in beautiful surroundings."

"Oh it is Susan!" Edna gushed. "It's up on top of a grand hill. The lawns and gardens are breathtaking. They grow their own fruits, so the place is surrounded by beautiful trees and flowers." She sighed. "And the lake below it is as blue as the sky."

"Sounds heavenly," Susan said, her eyes still trained on Gene. "I guess with a place being so beautiful, your work won't be all that bad."

He shrugged. "Well I'll be spending most of my time with the children. Their world is braces and beds." He leaned back and glanced down at his empty plate. "They deserve more."

"Well it's good, then, that they have this beautiful place to live in." She stood with Edna and started clearing the table. Casually she asked, "Reverend Scott, could I come up for a visit with the children tomorrow. Maybe I could take them outside for some sunshine."

"That's very sweet of you, Susan," Edna interjected before Gene could answer. "I think the children would enjoy having a young face around."

"Edna's right," John added as he stood and lit his pipe. "There's something special about a young, warm, friendly face in a hospital like that. Think I'll go read the paper."

Then the third Crain spoke up. "Susan, would you like to go for a walk?" David got up and brushed off his pants."

"David stop brushing those crumbs on the floor!" Edna called in dismay. "You go ahead, Susan dear. Gene is going to help me with the dishes."

"I really don't mind helping, Edna." Susan picked up a dish towel, which Edna snatched away and handed it to Scott. "Gene will do it. Won't you, handsome?"

"Why not?" He nodded at Susan. "The youngsters can run along and play."

"Gene, you haven't told me if I can come visit the children's hospital tomorrow." Susan's look was at once casual and piercing.

For an instant he gazed back into her eyes, then replied, "I'm sure the children would enjoy it."

A bright smile spread across her face. "Then I'll come!" She laughed and turned to David, taking his arm. "Alright, we youngsters can go play now." She grinned at Scott as they walked out the door, calling over her shoulder. "Watch out that your hands don't get wrinkled there, Gene."

From the corner of his eye, Gene couldn't help but notice the odd, puzzled look Edna gave him. "Let's get this assembly line moving, beautiful," he said playfully.

Scott looked up from the hospital desk and saw Susan smiling at him.

"Well, Scott, busy as usual, I see. Have time to eat a picnic lunch with me?"

The sudden stab of joy brought a smile to his face. "You bet I do." He stood and stepped around the counter toward her. "I haven't had one break since six this morning."

"Well then, it looks as if I got here just in time before you became a madman." Susan's heart beat wildly as he grasped her hand.

"I'll call the nurse on duty and tell her I'm taking a break." He pulled the desk phone to him. Mashing a button, he said, "Nurse Clark, could you please take over at the desk while I take a lunch break."

A disembodied voice came over the intercom immediately. "Yes Reverend Scott. I'll be right down."

"Well do you know a good place where we could have our picnic?" Susan let go of Gene's hand to grip the basket of food with both hands.

"As a matter of fact, beautiful, I know the perfect spot." He glanced up as the elevator door open and a woman dressed in the prim, white outfit of a nurse stepped out. "Miss Alice Clark," he said, "let me introduce another volunteer, Miss Susan Andrews."

The nurse gave Susan a curious smile. Quickly she studied Susan and the basket and gave Scott a skeptical look.

"I'll be back in an hour or so, Miss Clark." He grinned and in a teasing voice asked, "Do you think you can handle things?"

Her eyes arched. "Yes Reverend, I'm pretty sure I can manage very well, thank you."

"Good!" He took Susan's hand and they walked out the front door. "Just follow me."

"Anywhere," she muttered.

As they walked along it came to her that Edna and Gene had

understated the magnificence of the natural beauty around the hospital. The sheer beauty of the scenery filled her heart with joy.

"Oh geez, I feel wonderful today," she said quietly. "Everything is so beautiful and I'm with you."

"Yes . . . well, what do you think about this spot?" He took the basket from her and began spreading out the picnic lunch. "Perfect isn't it? It couldn't be better if we had ordered it this way."

She sat down on the cool grass. "I hope you like what I brought."

"You know very well I'll eat practically anything. Anyway, you brought it, Susan, and that makes it perfect." He reached over and closed her eyes with his fingers. "Thank you, Father, for all our many blessings, amen."

Taking a bite of the fried chicken, he exclaimed, "Delicious! Let me guess that Mildred fixed this."

"Very funny." Susan pulled up a sandwich from the basket and took a bite. "So I helped her, though. And I made the sandwiches."

"Is a guy supposed to live off sandwiches all his life?" Their eyes met, then quickly he looked back to the food before him.

"I can learn to cook just like Mildred." Susan's heart was dancing inside as she thought. "Did he really mean something by that, or was he only joking."

They didn't speak as they ate. There were only brief seconds when their eyes met.

Susan felt as though he were trying to avoid looking at her. "He's afraid of what he must feel for me," she thought. "Probably because he thinks I'm too young for him. Oh, Gene, I will not let this opportunity pass." She stretched and began cleaning up the leftovers.

"Let's walk on up that Green Hill, shall we? You want to?" He stood up and brushed the crumbs from his pants. "Let's go."

They walked slowly up the rolling green hill. Wild flowers grew in random bunches all across the landscape.

Susan took Gene's hand and smiled at him. I think I'll lie down in the grass. "She fell to her knees and pulled Scott down beside her. "Isn't it peaceful, just lying here staring up at that blue sky?"

He stretched out on his back. "Yeh. This is the life. . . . In fact, I think I'll take a nap."

"Oh no you don't, Gene Scott." She grabbed a handful of grass and shoved it down the front of his shirt.

Gene sat up and jerked off his shirt. "Why the hell did you do that?"

"Trying to fall asleep on me, are you? Trust me, I'll never let that happen." She fell back to the ground, giggling. "Guess I showed you."

Exasperated, he shook the grass from his shirt and brushed it off his bare chest.

"Oh," he said slowly, "so you think it's funny, do you?"

Instantly he put a knee on either side of her, pinning her to the ground, and began tickling her. "I'll really give you something to laugh about young lady!" He laughed at her helpless thrashing as he continued to tickle her. He didn't stop until Susan was laughing so hard she could scarcely catch her breath.

"Gene!"

His gaze slowly shifted from playfulness to adoration and longing. Sitting beside her, he slid one arm around her waist as his smile melted into serious lips of longing. Susan sat up and silently put her arm across his bare, smooth back.

She licked her lips. "My Samson is so sexy and strong." Her fingers went up to the curls on his neck. "Kiss me, Gene."

He faced her, staring into her tempting eyes, no longer able to deny the powerful attraction she held for him. Gene pulled himself out of her embrace. He got to his feet.

"We have to go back now, Susan."

"Oh, Gene! Not now. She stood and threw her arms around him. "I don't want to go right now. I need you."

"Susan, please. Stop acting out your Delilah role. It really doesn't suit you."

She shook her head in disbelief. "Oh Gene, when will you stop resisting the obvious? You keep trying to prevent the reality of our future. I love you Gene Scott."

At first he didn't turn to her. Then, as he spoke, he gazed into her luminous, beguiling eyes. "Susan, I'm old enough to be your father."

"Yeh? Well I'm old enough to know I love you, and not as some damn father figure either." She grabbed his hand. "Do you not realize I love you as any woman has ever loved any man."

Joan Byrd

"Susan, you don't know what you're talking about." He set his jaw for a moment, then continued, "You're still a child, an Alice in Wonderland dreamer."

"I'm not a child! I'm a woman who loves a man. You! Tears filled her eyes. "And guess what, I know you have feelings for me too. . . . You just won't admit it?"

He knew he had to look away. "Susan, I told you you're young enough to be my daughter. We could never become anything." He felt as if he were betraying her, his one true love. His heart pounded as though it would explode. "Susan try to understand—"

"Understand? No, it's time for you to understand me!" Tears streamed down her face. "You call me a child? You say I'm young enough to be your daughter? Well when you were kissing me the other night, you never kissed me like a child or like you would your daughter. You kissed me like a woman—a real, grownup woman."

"I got carried away Susan. What more do you expect from a man who's been without a woman for three years." He took her hand. "Try to understand. You were there and, at that moment, I needed you."

"And now you don't need me anymore?" She jerked her hand away. "So you were only using me and I . . . I thought you cared something for me."

Susan "I do care something for you. You're a very sweet charming young lady, who's not ready to give up her fantasies."

"Oh!" She stepped away from him, tossing her head around to face him. "God help me for falling in love with Gene Scott! If I knew love was going to hurt this bad I . . ." She burst into tears and began to run down the hill.

Scott froze for an instant, thoughts whirling in his mind. "Stop her!" His heart screamed out. "You love her, you big idiot. Don't let her get away without trying at least."

He heard his voice shouting across the cool hillside: "Susan! Wait!"

Instinctively he began to run, his feet carrying him rapidly down the hill. Susan had put such a distance between them that he wasn't sure she could hear his calling, even as he continued to race after her, shouting her name. And she continued to run, as if escaping from something horrible. His heart was pierced as he

238

realized what he had done to his truest love. Instantly he stopped, drew a deep breath, put his hands on his hips and yelled as loudly as he could.

"Susan I love you! Damnit!"

Susan slowed and stopped, still facing the distant hospital. She could feel her heart pounding and rapid breathing. Had she heard him right, she wondered. She turned slowly and watched him walking towards her contritely.

She thought, "I'll wait here. I don't want to go running to him and make even more a fool of myself. If he said what I thought, then . . . " She closed her eyes. "Then I'll throw myself in his arms."

"Susan." He put his hands on her shoulders. "I do love you. I can't explain how it happened, but it did."

She squinted at him. "How exactly do you love me, Gene? Like a child? Like your daughter?"

"I wish it were like that." He bit his lip as he gazed at her, transfixed. The time had come for a confession of the full truth. "I love you, Susan, more than I've loved anyone or anything in my life. I think of nothing but you. Holding you." His eyes embraced the fullness of her as she stood still before him. "Kissing you."

Susan sighed. "Oh Gene." She put her arms around his waist and lay her head against his chest. "I wanted so long to hear you say that."

His arms encircled her tenderly as his lips found hers in a long-awaited, kiss of fulfillment.

"Oh Susan, my sweet darling Susan. I love you with all my heart."

His lips parted to cover hers and his tongue caressed hers within her mouth. His breathing grew ragged with emotion as he held her close against him in his powerful arms.

"Gene, love, what are we going to do? I need you." Her fingers slid gently across his face. "I love you so very, very much."

"We can't tell your parents. Not yet. They wouldn't understand." He gaze downward, thinking. "Oh everything is so mixed up, Susan."

"Yes I know, darling, but we love each other. That's the most important thing." She took his hand. And that's all I ever want or need—your love and you."

Joan Byrd

"Oh Susan!" He took her into his arms. "Knowing you love me as much as I love you makes up for all our big troubles."

"We could get married secretly, Gene. And when we think it's the right time, we could tell Mom and Dad." Susan closed her eyes and hugged him tightly. "Oh how I would love to be your wife."

"And I your husband." His eyes fixed upon hers intimately. "But, sweet Susan, how could it work? There's so much going against us. No one will understand our love like we do."

"Oh Gene, it will work. It has to! It must!" She shook her head in determination. "We can make it work. We have each other's love. That's all that matters."

"Yes! As God is my witness, you're right." He smiled suddenly and, laughing, grabbed her. "Why should we deprive ourselves of each other's love because the rest of the stupid world can't see it?"

"Yes! Yes! Yes!" She joined in his laughter. "I'll do anything for you, my sweet darling. You name it. I'm yours forever and ever."

"And I'm yours." He kissed her again. "I want you for all my tomorrows."

"Gladly will I be yours, yours, yours!" She twirled around, laughing joyfully. "I take back everything I said up on the hill about love. It's beautiful."

"And you are beautiful, my sweet, lovable, sexy Susan."

"Do you really think I'm sexy?" She smiled.

"Yes. That's actually why I'm taking you back now." He shook his head and chuckled as put his arm around her. He began leading her down the hill toward the hospital.

"How did you get here, hon?"

"I drove in my new car Dad got me." She squeezed his hand. "Oh geez, wait until you see it. It's beautiful. It's just the kind I wanted. A yellow Corvette!"

He shook his head. "Just what you wanted, huh?" He cast a sideways glance at her. "And I suppose you get everything you want from Daddy too?

"Gene?" She stopped and looked at him, surprised. "Of course Dad has given me lots of things I asked for, but I would give them all up for you. I love you and that's all I want or need now."

His jaw dropped. "Oh Susan, I'm sorry." He hugged her and

240

continued to walk toward the yellow Corvette. "It's that there are so many people in the world who never have much of anything. I guess I'm just a little touchy on the subject."

"I can understand that." She stopped beside the Corvette. "I guess, before, I always wanted too many things. Now all I want is you, Gene, and that's the truth. Honest."

"I believe you, Susan," he spoke softly and gently took her face in his hands and kissed her. "We'll work it out, somehow. I love you too much not to have you belong to me."

"When can we see each other again?" She held onto his waist tightly.

"Soon, very soon." He opened the car door for her and helped her in. "Call me." He bit his lip in uncertainty. "No, I'll . . . I'll call you."

"Alright. Whichever you think is best." She took his hand and kissed it. "Oh I shall be thankful for the rest of my life that I have you."

"Okay, okay. Now go along, before I decide to keep you right here." He leaned over and kissed her. "Drive carefully, Susan. I think I would die if anything were to happen to you. Think about me every once in a while."

She turned on the engine. "Only every second I breathe."

He blew her a kiss as she drove away.

Joan Byrd

To Be Continued

Book #2
In the
All My Tomorrows
Series:

Love Finds a Way

Author's Notes

After Gene and Susan profess their love to one another, they must keep it a secret until they can find a way for it to work.

Good friends become their allies and help the love-starved couple.

A secret wedding is in the near future for Gene and Susan and the night they have been holding out for.

A secret marriage means staying apart until they can find a way to break the news to Susan's parents.

Something unexpected happens and becomes the answer to their big secret coming out.